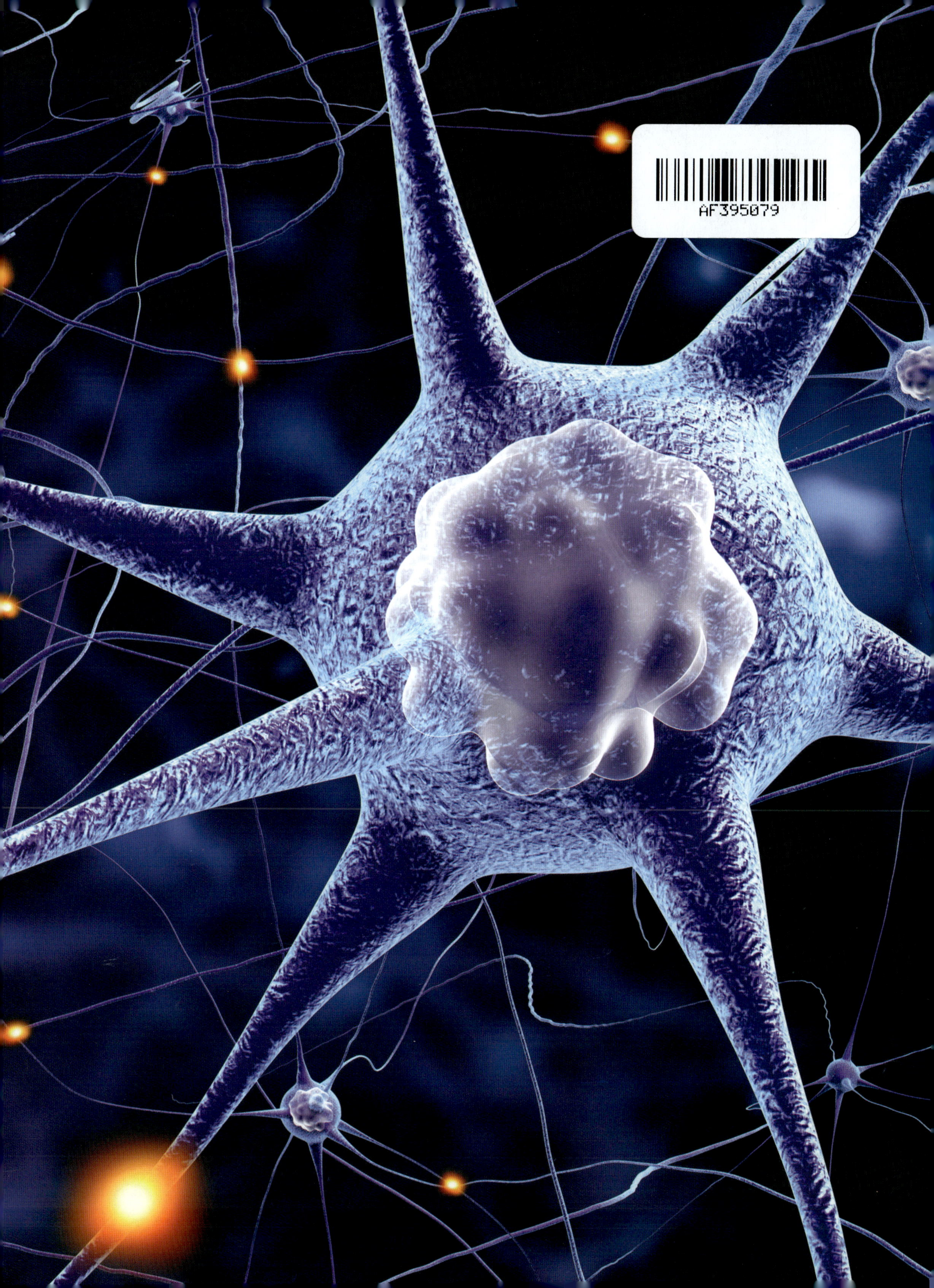

AF395079

A First Introduction to Science

ENCYCLOPEDIA of LEARNING

DISCOVER

BIOLOGY
CHEMISTRY
& PHYSICS

Predominant artwork & imagery source:
Shutterstock.com

Copyright: North Parade Publishing Ltd.

4 North Parade,

Bath,

BA1 1LF, UK

First Published: 2019

Printed in China.

BIOLOGY
Contents

CHEMISTRY
Contents

PHYSICS
Contents

A First Introduction to Science

ENCYCLOPEDIA of LEARNING

DISCOVER
BIOLOGY

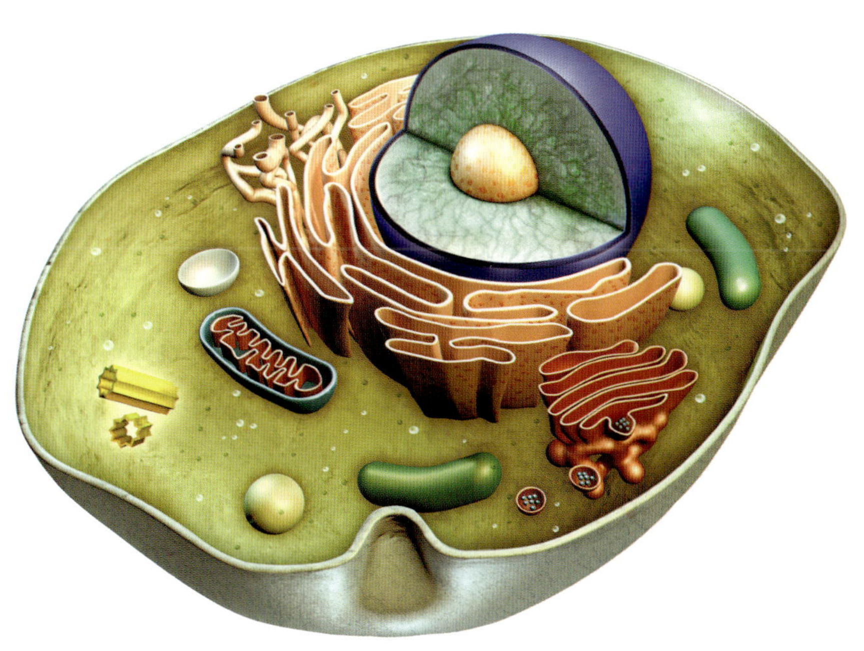

Introduction to Cells

All living things are made of cells. A cell is the most basic structural and functional unit of a living being. Some organisms (for example, bacteria) are single cells. Others, like plants and animals, are made up of billions of cells.

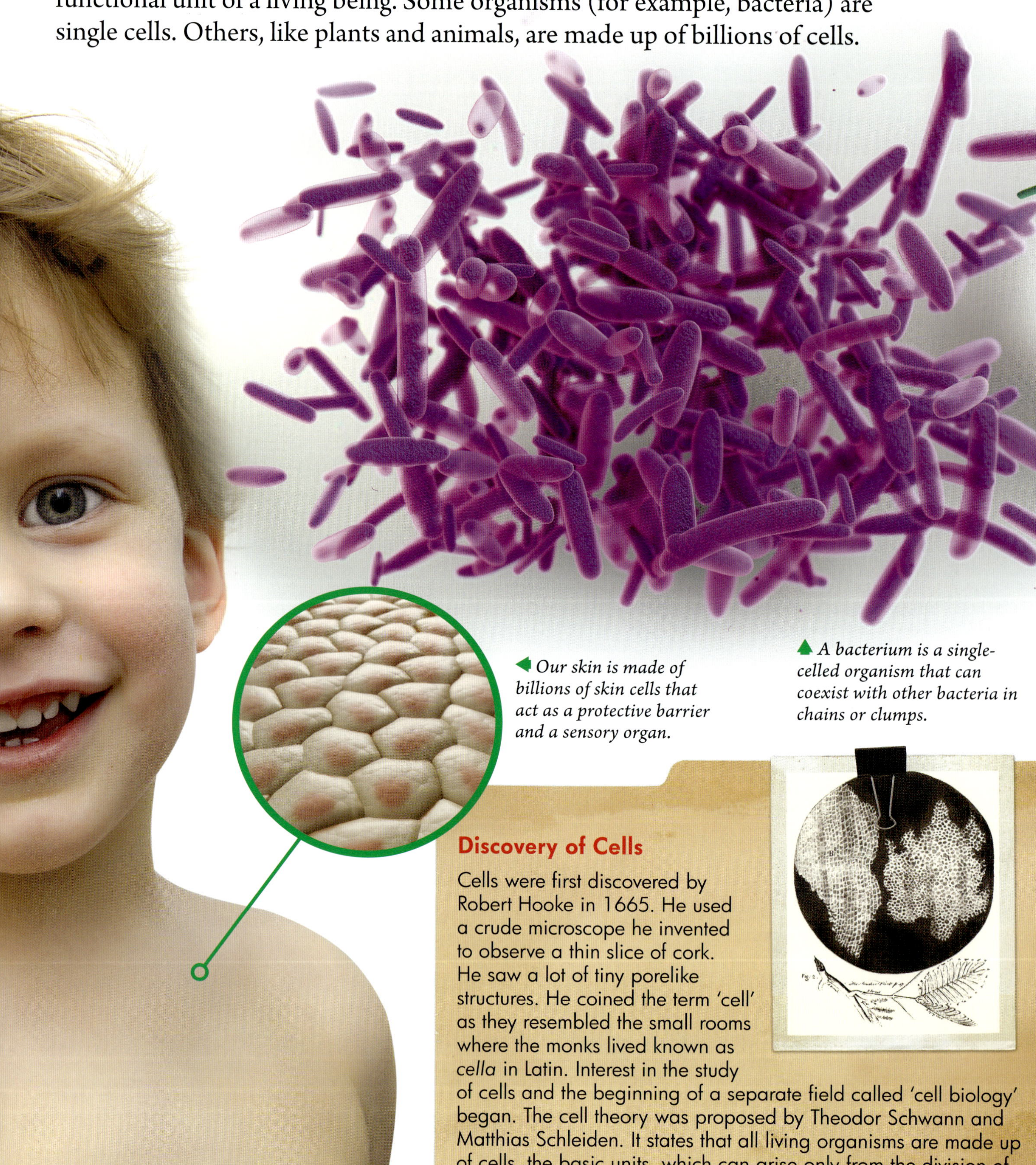

Our skin is made of billions of skin cells that act as a protective barrier and a sensory organ.

A bacterium is a single-celled organism that can coexist with other bacteria in chains or clumps.

Discovery of Cells

Cells were first discovered by Robert Hooke in 1665. He used a crude microscope he invented to observe a thin slice of cork. He saw a lot of tiny porelike structures. He coined the term 'cell' as they resembled the small rooms where the monks lived known as *cella* in Latin. Interest in the study of cells and the beginning of a separate field called 'cell biology' began. The cell theory was proposed by Theodor Schwann and Matthias Schleiden. It states that all living organisms are made up of cells, the basic units, which can arise only from the division of other cells.

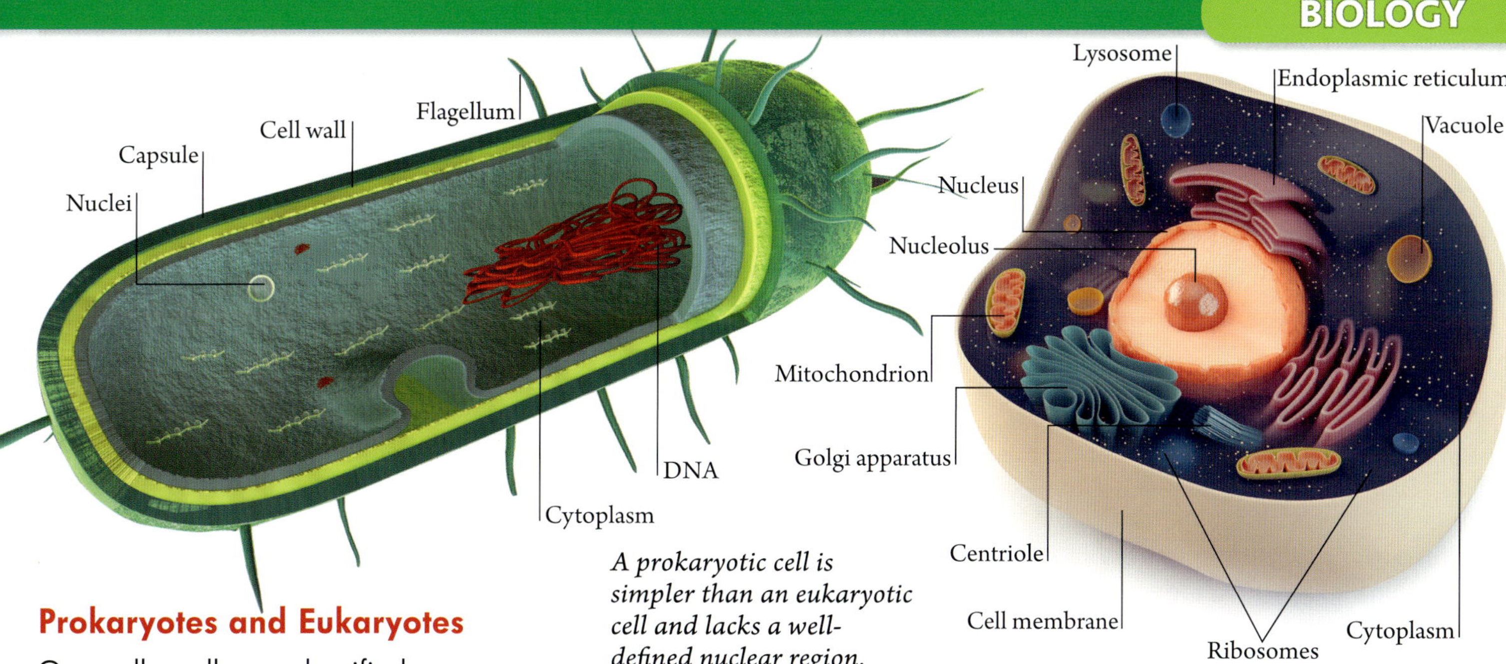

A prokaryotic cell is simpler than an eukaryotic cell and lacks a well-defined nuclear region.

Prokaryotes and Eukaryotes

Generally, cells are classified as prokaryotes or eukaryotes.

Prokaryotes: (*Pro* = primitive, *karyote* = nucleus). As the name suggests, prokaryotes have primitive nuclear material. There is no well-defined nucleus and the genetic material (DNA) is not arranged in the form of chromosomes. Instead, it is found as a single, compact loop that contains all the information to code for proteins needed for the cell to survive and reproduce. Prokaryotes were the only life-forms on Earth for millions of years until more complex eukaryotes evolved.

Eukaryotes: (*Eu* = True, *karyote* = nucleus). The defining feature of a eukaryotic cell is the presence of a well-defined region where the genetic material is concentrated. This region is called the nucleus. The nucleus is covered by a nuclear membrane.

Prokaryotes

1. Contain genetic material as a single circular loop

2. Do not have a well-defined nucleus or specialised site for DNA

3. The genome is very compact and contains only regions that code for proteins

4. No well-defined membrane-bound organelles present

5. Possess complex cell walls that vary from one organism to another

6. Usually unicellular

Eukaryotes

1. Contain genetic material as linear chromosomes

2. Have a well-defined nucleus with nuclear envelope and nucleolus

3. The genome has large chunks of repetitive DNA that does not code for any proteins

4. Well-defined membrane-bound organelles present

5. Cell walls are absent except in plants and algae

6. Usually multicellular

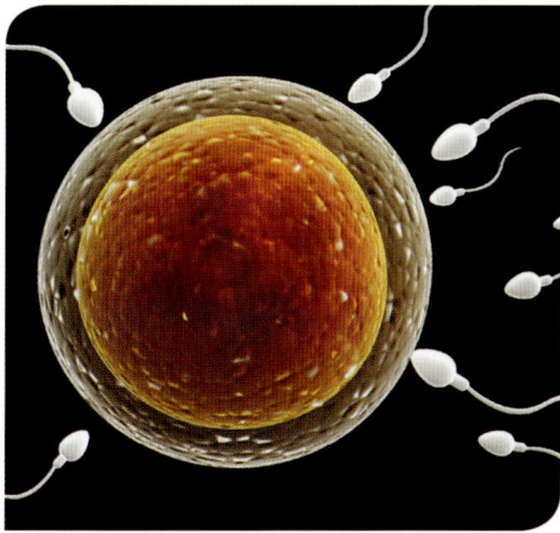

▲ *The egg cell (ovum) is among the largest cells in the human body and can measure up to 0.1 mm.*

Size of Cells

Individual cells are microscopic; this means they can only be viewed under the magnification of a microscope. The size of cells varies greatly. An amoeba is about 0.1 millimetre in size (one-tenth of a millimetre) and can be viewed with the naked eye under the right conditions. Similarly, a human egg cell is comparatively large in size. On the other hand, red blood cells are among the smallest cells in the human body.

Fact File

The average size of prokaryotes is 1 to 10 micrometres. (One micrometre is one thousandth of a millimetre). Eukaryotic cells range in size from 10 to 100 micrometres.

Animal and Plant Cells

Animal cells possess a well-defined plasma membrane as well as membrane bound organelles. Plant cells have a prominent cell wall that is absent in animal cells. While plant cells can produce their own food from sunlight, animal cells are capable of locomotion, enabled by the lack of cell walls.

Organelles are components of animal cells that are involved in specific functions. They include:

Plasma membrane: A protective membrane that protects the cell and contains all the organelles.

Nucleus: It is the most important part of the cell and contains all the DNA (genetic information) needed for the growth, activities and reproduction of the cell.

Mitochondria: Called the 'powerhouse of the cell,' they convert oxygen and nutrients into energy.

Endoplasmic reticulum (ER): A network of sacs that manufactures, processes, and transports chemical compounds.

Golgi apparatus: It helps in distributing the chemical compounds produced in ER outside the cell.

Ribosomes: Tiny organelles made up of RNA (ribonucleic acid) and proteins, which help with protein synthesis.

Lysosomes: Double membrane organelles containing enzymes that assist in digestion.

Centrioles: Made of nine bundles of microtubules, they assist in cell division.

Flagella/Cilia: Extensions that help in locomotion.

Microfilaments, microtubules and intermediate filaments: Provide structural support to the cell.

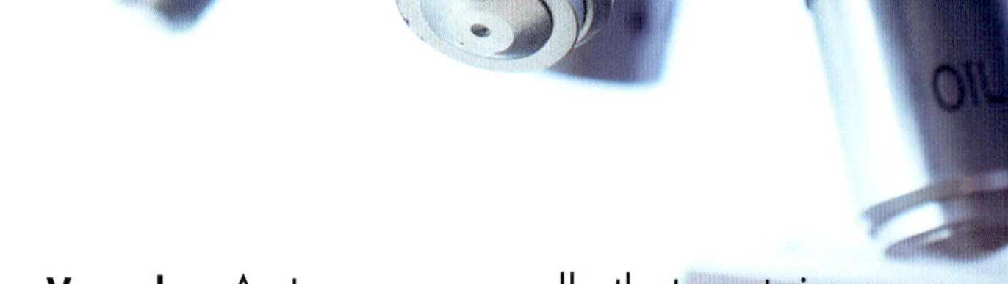

Vacuoles: A storage organelle that contains essential chemical compounds and assists growth.

Plant and algal cells also have these components:

Cell wall: A protective layer that provides support and structure to the cell.

Chloroplasts: These organelles are involved in photosynthesis, a process by which plants make their own food from sunlight.

▼ *A plant cell varies from an animal cell as it possesses a well-defined cell wall.*

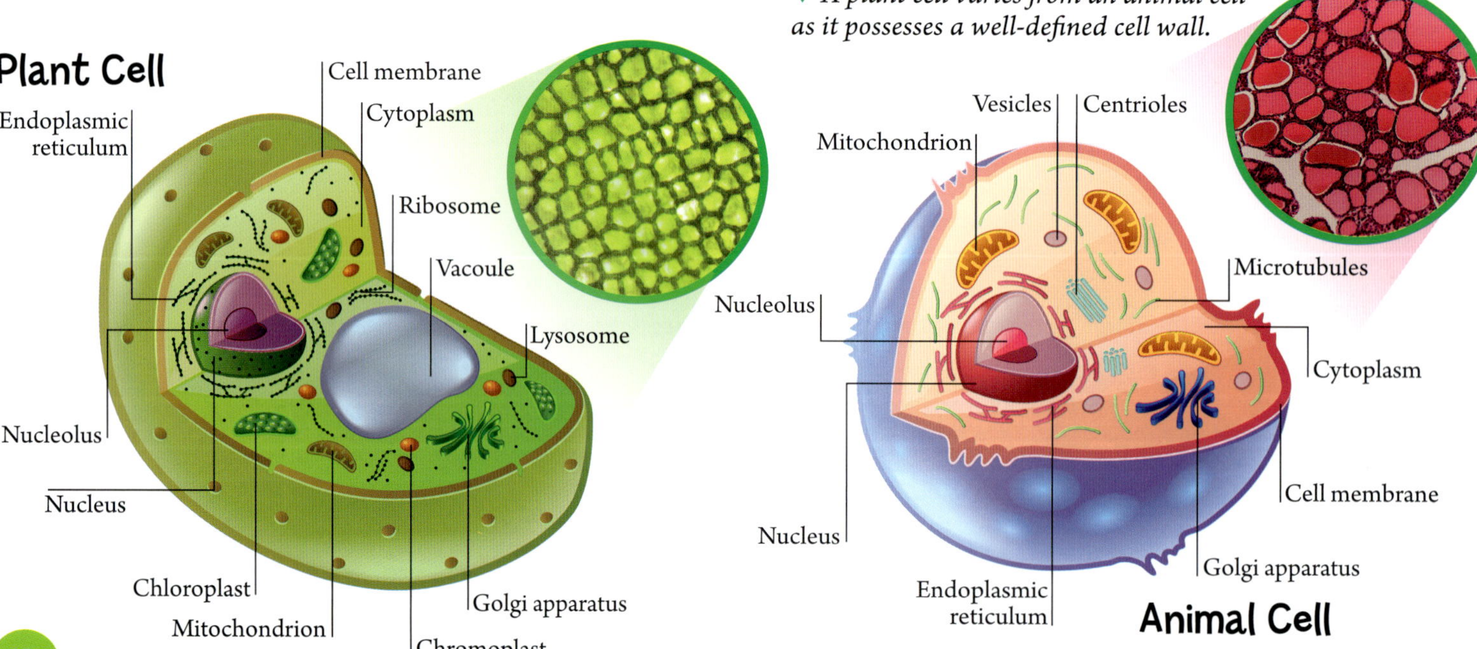

Cell Differentiation

The process by which a young, immature cell develops into a specialised cell capable of a specific function is called cell differentiation. Any cell that is capable of this process of evolving into another cell is said to be 'totipotent.' Some cells, like the stem cells in animals and the meristematic cells in higher plants, can differentiate into different types of cells. Such cells are 'pluripotent.'

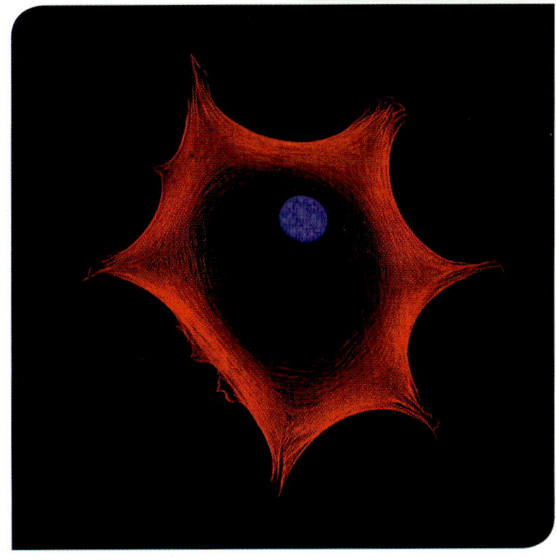

▲ *A pluripotent cell can differentiate into any type of cell.*

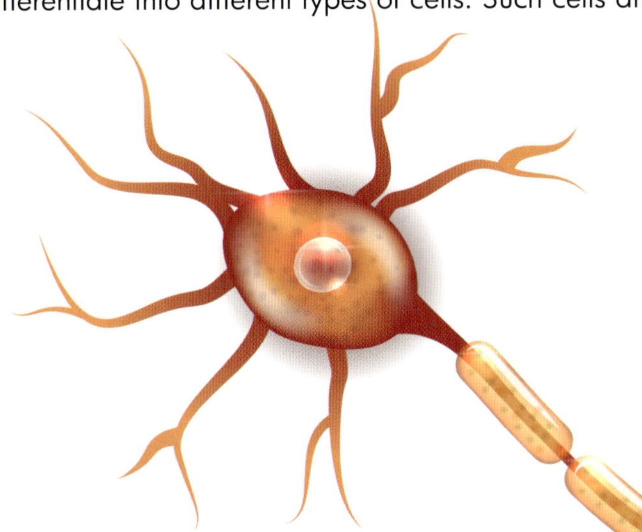

◀ *A neuron is a specialised cell that communicates through electrical signals.*

Cell Specialisation

In single-celled organisms, all the functions for survival and reproduction are present in the cell. Multicellular organisms are more complex. Certain cell groups are assigned a specific function and such cells are called 'specialised cells.' Depending on their purpose and function, cell groups may have different sizes, shapes and cellular makeup. The difference in structure and function of the cells happens at the genetic level—that is, certain genes are activated to make a cell specialised in its particular function.

Let us look at some examples of specialised cells:

Neuron: Also called a nerve cell, it can grow to be about a metre in length. Nerve cells transmit signals from different parts of the body to the brain.

Red blood cell: This is a button-shaped cell that contains the pigment hemoglobin. Red blood cells carry oxygen from the lungs to different parts of the body and bring carbon dioxide from the body to the lungs.

Root hair cell: It is a specialised cell that is present in the root. These cells have hair-like projections to absorb nutrients and water.

Guard cell: Present on leaves and stems, guard cells open, close, and control the stomata through which plants exchange water and carbon dioxide.

Fact File

An adult human has more than 200 specialised cells in their body to perform different functions.

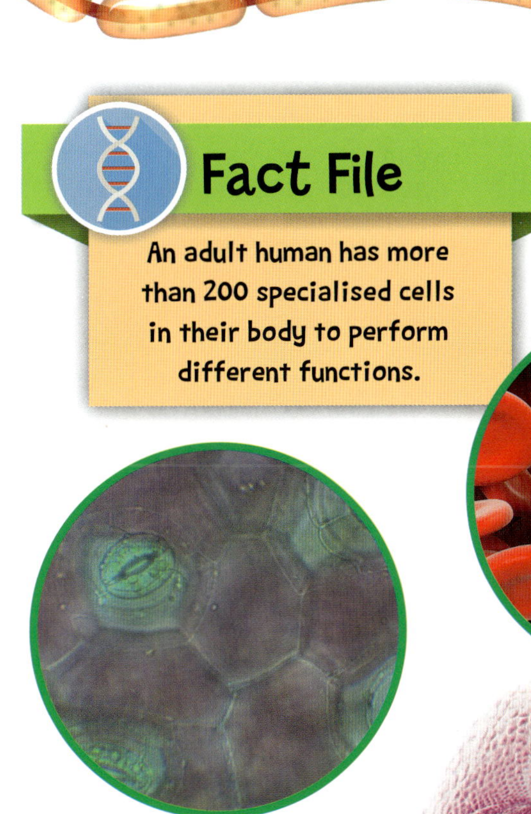

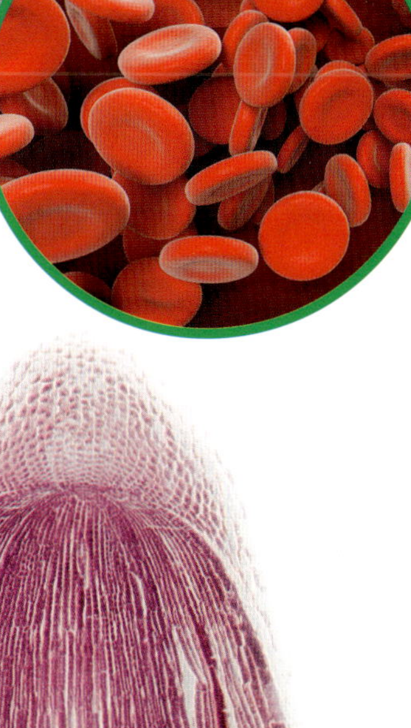

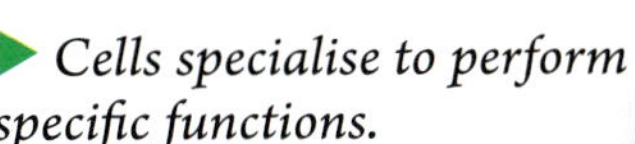

▶ *Cells specialise to perform specific functions.*

Cell Division

The cells in our body divide all the time and make new cells. Old cells are replaced by newer cells. A single cell divides into two, and these two cells can produce four cells and so on. This process is called 'cell division.' We began life as a single cell and by the time we become adults, there are trillions of cells in our bodies.

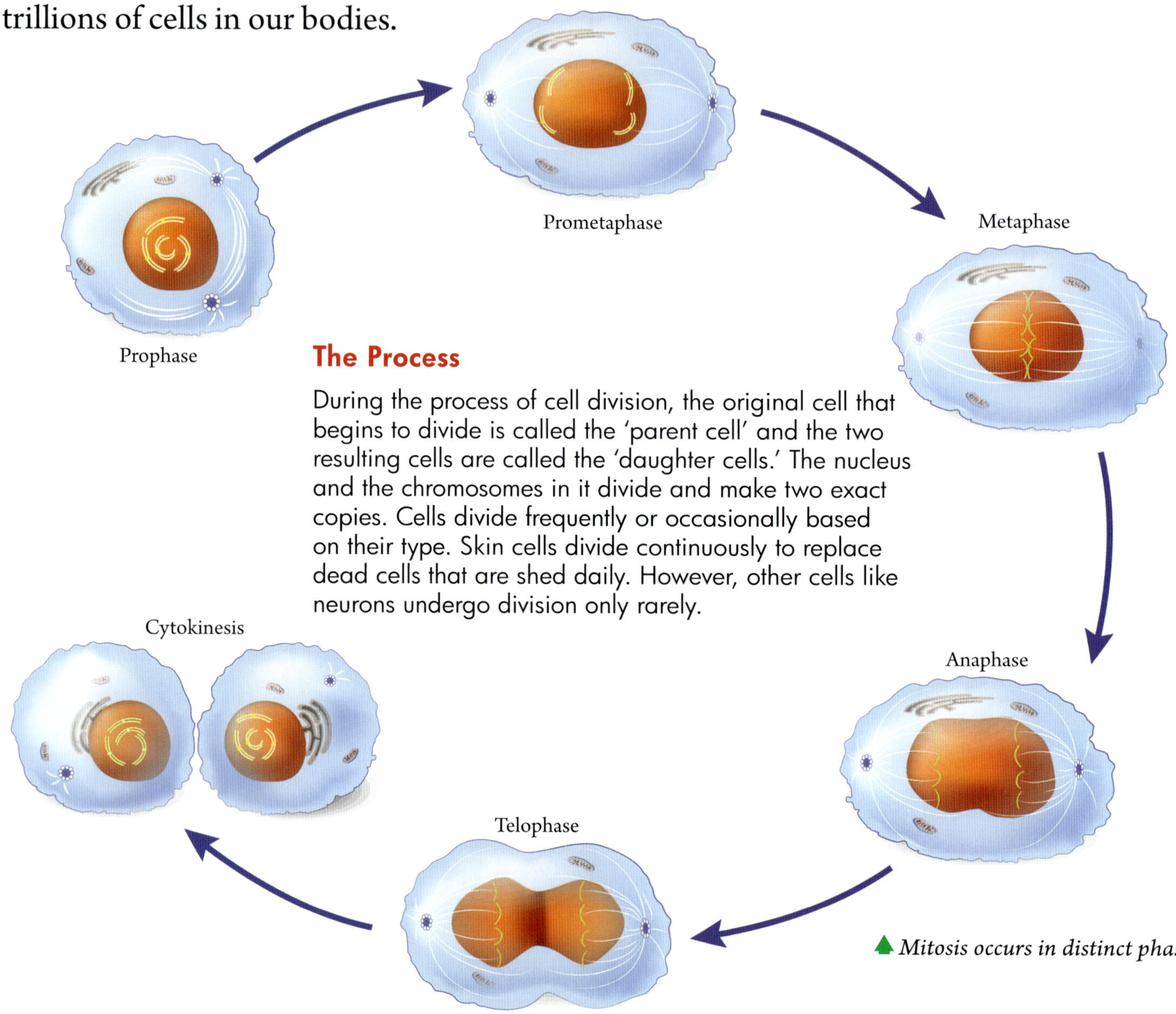

Prophase
Prometaphase
Metaphase
Anaphase
Telophase
Cytokinesis

▲ *Mitosis occurs in distinct phases*

The Process

During the process of cell division, the original cell that begins to divide is called the 'parent cell' and the two resulting cells are called the 'daughter cells.' The nucleus and the chromosomes in it divide and make two exact copies. Cells divide frequently or occasionally based on their type. Skin cells divide continuously to replace dead cells that are shed daily. However, other cells like neurons undergo division only rarely.

Mitosis

The process by which nonreproductive, regular cells undergo cell division is called mitosis. When the parent cell divides into two daughter cells, the newly formed cells have the same number of chromosomes as the parent.

Meiosis

Meiosis is the process by which a parent cell divides twice to form four daughter cells, each having only half the number of chromosomes as the parent. Meiosis is responsible for the production of sperm in males and eggs in females. Since a sperm and an egg have only half the set of chromosomes, the new cell will have the complete set of chromosomes from both the parent cells when they fuse.

Fact File

We lose about 50 million skin cells every day, and they are replaced through skin cell division.

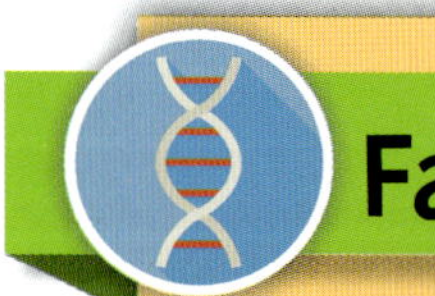

Cell Cycle

Cells that are actively dividing go through several stages collectively known as the cell cycle. The stages are:

Gap 1 Phase: The cell prepares for division by undergoing certain metabolic changes.

Synthesis Phase: DNA synthesis occurs and the genetic material in the nucleus undergoes replication.

Gap 2 Phase: Metabolic changes occur to produce more cytoplasm as the cell prepares for division.

Mitosis Phase: Division of the nucleus (called nucleokinesis) and the division of the entire cell (called cytokinesis) occur in this phase.

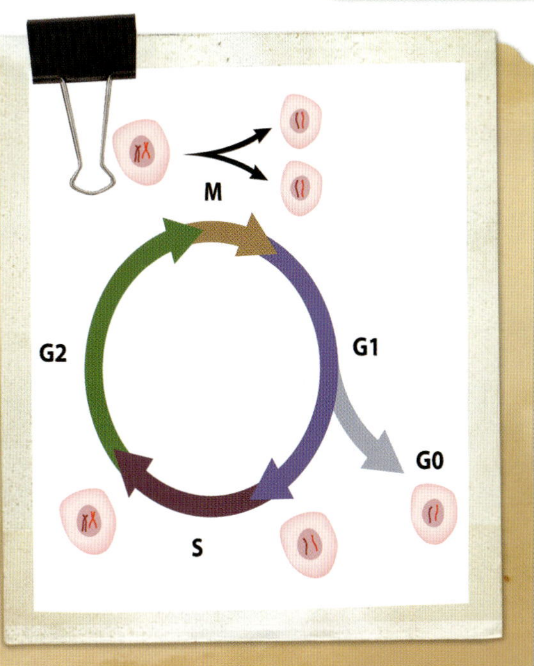

Stem Cells

Stem cells are remarkable in that they have the ability to differentiate into a range of different specialised cells such as bone, skin, blood and many others. Stem cells remain dormant for years and then can be activated to replace cells that are lost or damaged.

The two main types of stem cells are:

1. Embryonic Stem Cells: These stem cells provide all the different types of cells that a developing embryo needs as it grows into a baby. They are pluripotent and capable of developing into any type of cell.

2. Adult Stem Cells: Found in the bone marrow, they can replace damaged cells in a full-grown adult. They are multipotent, that is, they can differentiate into certain types of cells, but not all.

Scientists have identified many useful purposes for stem cells. In the laboratory, stem cells can be induced to produce entire organs such as skin and heart. They can also be used for producing blood cells in patients who have lost their blood cells due to cancer or another disease.

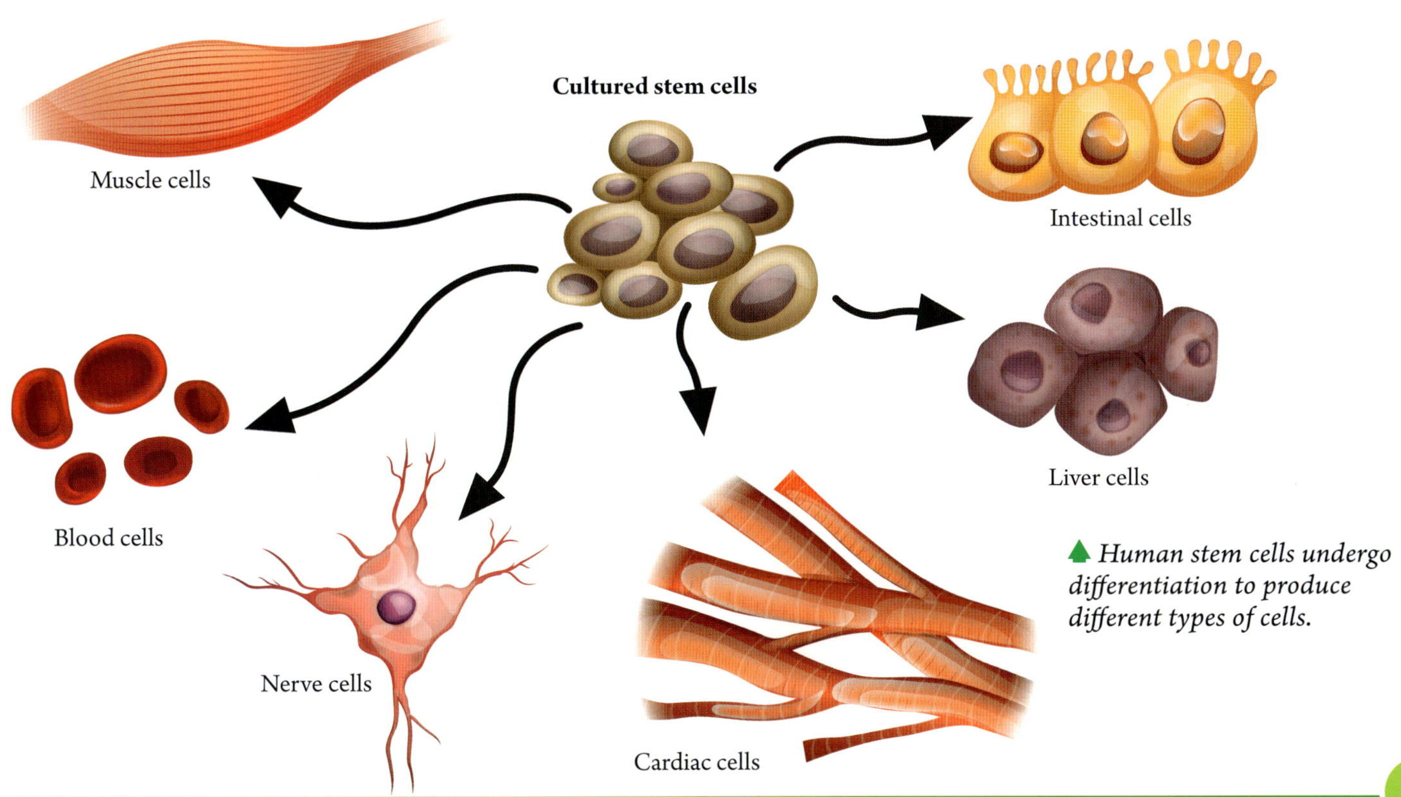

▲ *Human stem cells undergo differentiation to produce different types of cells.*

Cell Transport

Movement of materials and water in and out of the cell occur due to the semi-permeable nature of the membrane. This is known as cell transport. Cell transport can be active or passive: active transport requires energy, passive transport does not.

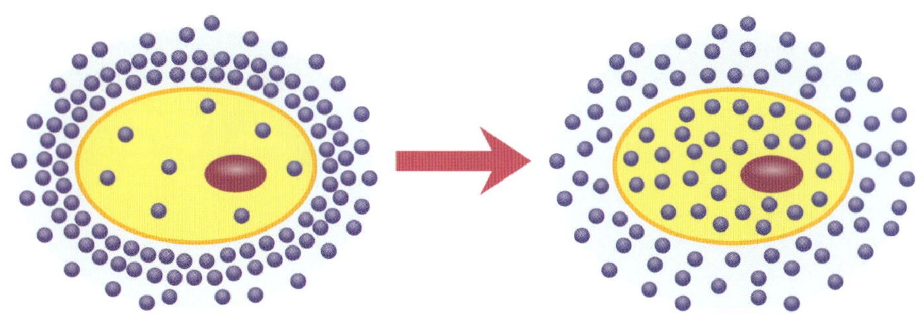

▲ *The semipermeable membrane allows movement of molecules.*

Gap junction is a type of passive transport mechanism that enables the heart muscles to contract in a coordinated, smooth manner.

Passive Transport

1. Simple Diffusion: Diffusion is a process by which molecules move from a region of higher concentration to a region of lower concentration. The difference in concentration between the two regions is called a 'concentration gradient.' Diffusion usually continues until the concentration is uniform on both sides. Some of the factors that affect diffusion are:

1. Surface area of the membrane

2. Temperature

3. Concentration gradient

2. Facilitated Diffusion: When diffusion occurs with the help of a carrier protein, it is known as facilitated diffusion. Each carrier protein is of a specific shape and only allows specific molecules to pass through.

3. Osmosis: Osmosis is a type of diffusion that occurs in the presence of a semipermeable membrane. Here, water travels from a less concentrated region to a more concentrated region. Roots absorb water from the soil through osmosis.

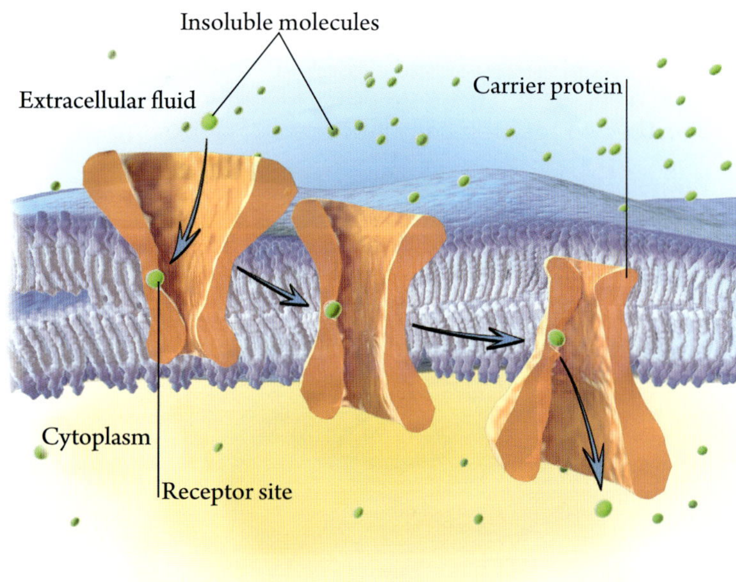

▲ *Carrier proteins are important in facilitated passive transport.*

Active Transport

The movement of molecules from a region of lower concentration to a region of higher concentration is called active transport. Active transport requires energy, which is usually supplied by the mitochondria in the cells in the form of ATP (adenosine triphosphate). This method is used for bringing in glucose, ions and amino acids that the cell needs.

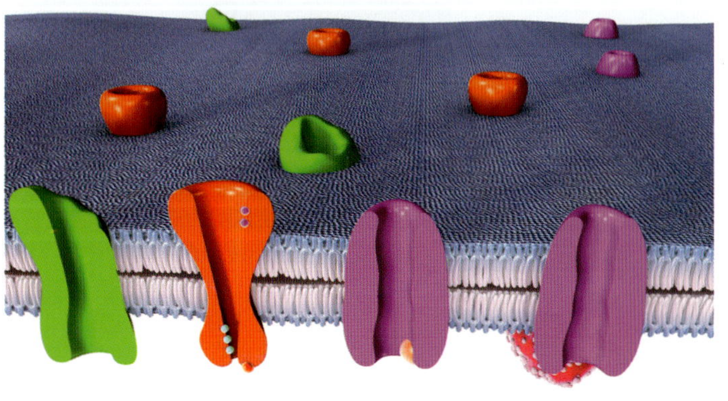

◄ *Active transport utilises energy in the form of ATP molecules.*

Cell and Tissue Organisation

In a simple one-celled organism, such as an amoeba living in a pond, nutrients are absorbed directly from the environment and the wastes excreted out. In complex multicellular organisms, specialised systems are needed to carry out different functions. In general, cells that perform a similar function organise into a group to form a tissue. In turn, one or more tissues that perform a specific set of functions organise into organs.

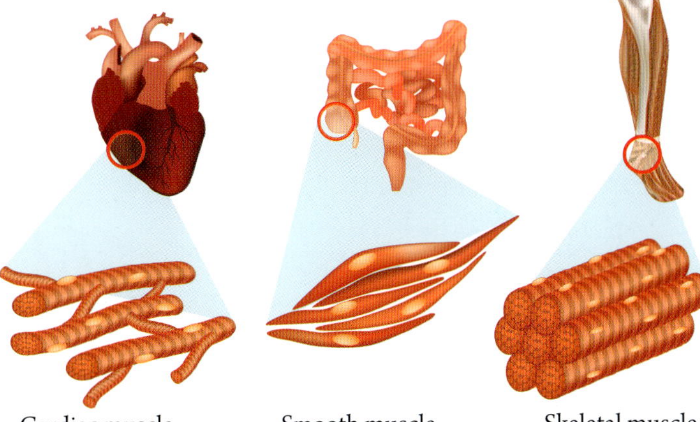

▶ Epithelial cells form the outermost protective layer of the skin.

Organ Systems

One or more organs can also be grouped into an organ system that is involved in one function, such as digestion or respiration. It must be noted that at every level (tissue, organ, organ system), the structure is related to the function performed.

In humans, some of the major tissue types include:

Epithelial tissue: Forms the outer layer (skin) of the body

Connective tissue: Forms a support network for the organs and blood vessels

Muscle tissue: Forms the muscles capable of movement

Nervous tissue: Forms the brain and spinal cord that process information and transmit signals

▼ Different types of muscle tissue are found in different organs.

Cardiac muscle   Smooth muscle   Skeletal muscle

Skeletal System   Respiratory System   Muscular System   Circulatory System   Digestive System   Nervous System

▲ Organ systems consist of organs that perform certain functions.

Organs

Organs such as the heart, lungs, kidneys, liver, and pancreas are made up of tissues involved in the same function. Almost all organs contain epithelial, connective, muscular, and nervous tissues. In an organ system such as the circulatory system, the heart and the blood vessels work together to pump blood to all parts of the body.

Fact File

Epithelial cells come in different shapes and are classified as cuboidal, ciliated, columnar and squamous.

Chromosomes and Genes

DNA forms the basic hereditary unit of a cell. It possesses all the information needed for the complete body to function. Genes code for essential proteins and are present along with noncoding segments of DNA in chromosomes.

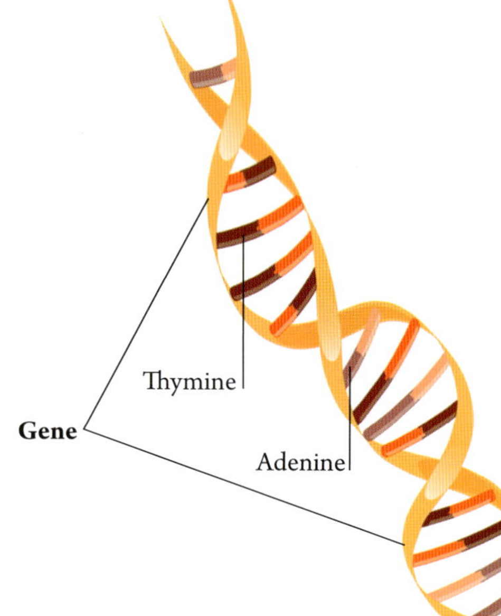

DNA

All the information necessary for the functioning of our cells is stored in the chemical macromolecule called deoxyribonucleic acid or DNA. DNA is a double helix structure made up of repeating units of four nucleotides—adenine, guanine, cytosine, and thymine. Each nucleotide is in turn made up of a sugar molecule, a nitrogenous base, and a phosphate molecule.

All functions of the DNA, such as making copies of itself through replication and forming RNA through transcription, are dependent on interaction with different proteins.

▲ *Chromosomes are made up of DNA tightly wound into a compact structure.*

Genes

A gene is defined as the functional and physical unit of heredity. A gene, made up of a specific DNA sequence, acts as the instruction blueprint for making a protein. A person gets two copies of the same gene from their parents. A typical human has 20,000 to 25,000 genes coding for different proteins and which are responsible for various functions necessary for survival and reproduction.

Different forms of the same gene are called 'alleles.' A person inherits an allele from each parent and the combination of the alleles results in a particular feature. For instance, a person's eye colour depends on the combined effect of the two alleles inherited from the parents.

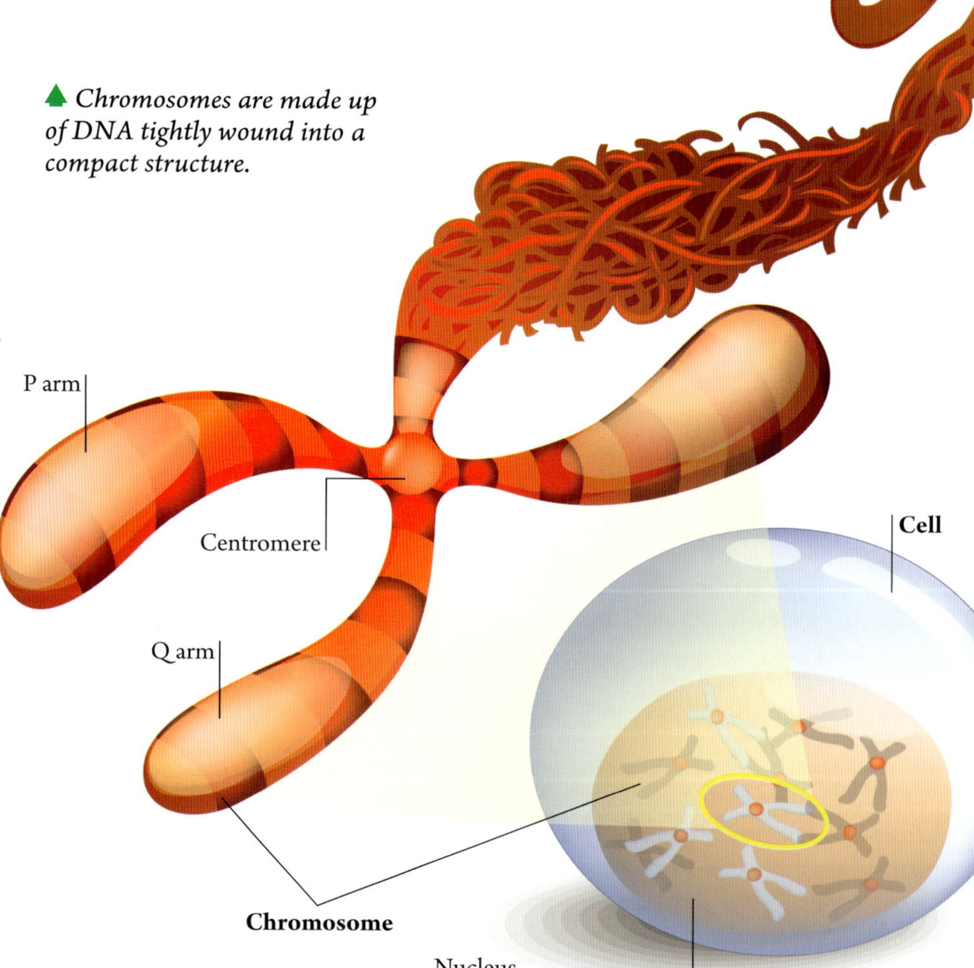

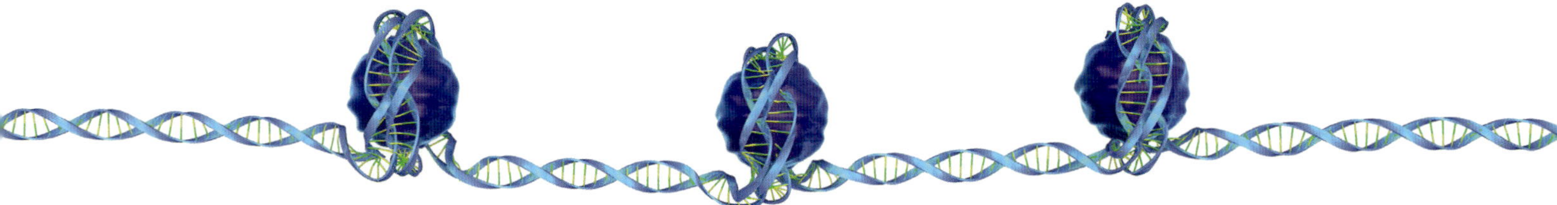

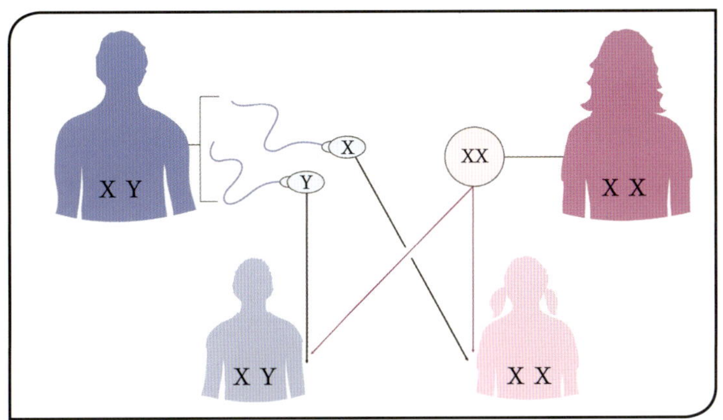

▲ *A segment of DNA wrapped around eight histone proteins makes up a nucleosome.*

Chromosomes

The DNA present in a single cell stretches out to about 2 metres. The only way to fit the DNA into the tiny nucleus within a cell is to pack the DNA into compact structures called chromosomes by binding with proteins called histones. Chromosomes are usually not visible under a microscope, unless a cell is undergoing cell division.

It is during this time that the chromosomes are tightly packed and visible. A chromosome has a short 'p' arm and a long 'q' arm. The presence of a centromere in the center of the chromosome gives it its characteristic 'X' shape.

▲ *In humans, the XX-XY chromosome determines sex.*

Genetic Disorders

Diseases and disorders can occur due to many reasons, but genetic disorders are caused by one or more faulty genes in a person's cells. Some disorders are caused by recessive alleles. This means that a person will get the disease only if they inherit faulty copies of the genes from both parents. Cystic fibrosis is an example of a recessive genetic disorder.

X-linked disorders are those associated with genes in the X chromosome. Since females have two copies of X chromosomes, two faulty copies from both parents is needed to cause the disease. On the other hand, a male will get the disease even if one X chromosome has a faulty gene, as there isn't an equivalent gene in the Y chromosome to compensate for it. Red-green colour blindness and hemophilia are examples of X-linked genetic disorders.

Sex Determination

Sex determination can vary across the plant and animal kingdom, as does the number of chromosomes. In humans, the chromosomes determine the sex of the person. The body cells have 23 pairs of chromosomes each. Of the 46 chromosomes, males have one X and one Y chromosome, whereas females have two X chromosomes.

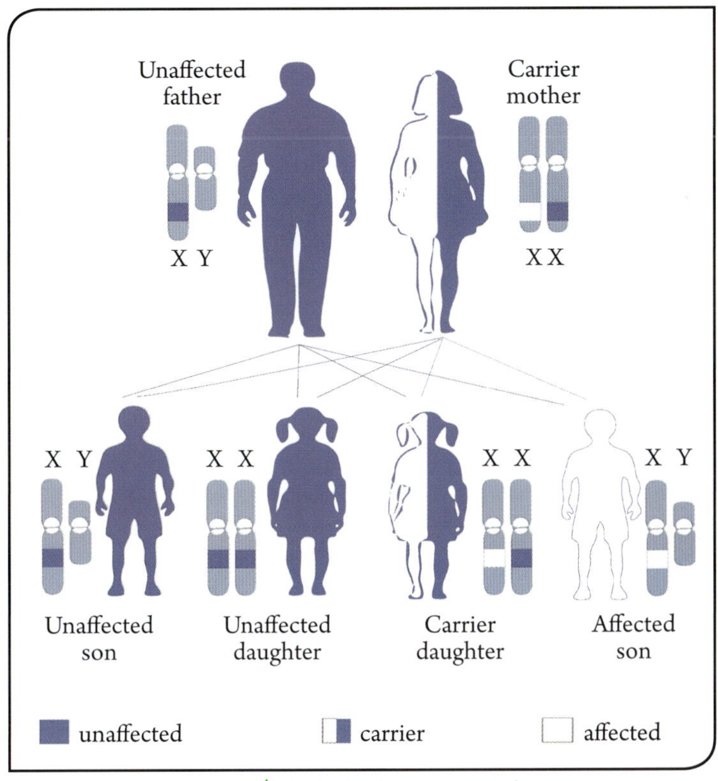

▲ *X-linked recessive inheritance disorders affect males more than females.*

Fact File

If it were possible to remove the DNA present in all the cells of an adult human and place it end to end, it would stretch to at least 6 billion miles!

Genetic Engineering

Scientists can now isolate genes from one species and insert them into the genome of another species by a process called genetic engineering. This technique has immense potential to address many of our needs but, considering the fact that genetic engineering is equivalent to meddling with nature, it is also controversial.

By definition, the introduction of foreign genes in an organism's genome or altering specific genes through certain techniques is called genetic engineering.

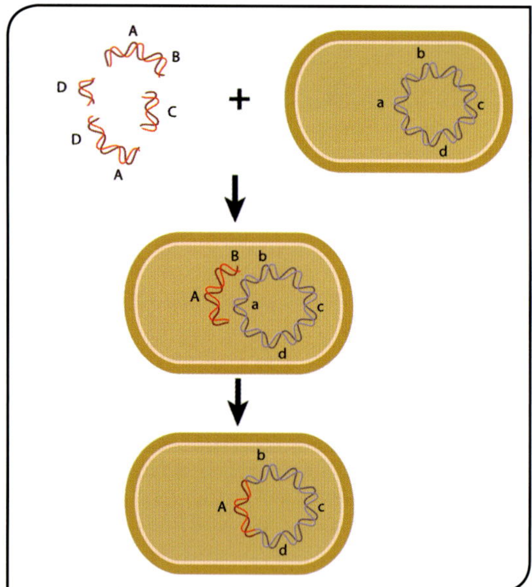

▲ *Bacterial cells accept foreign DNA through a process called 'transformation'*

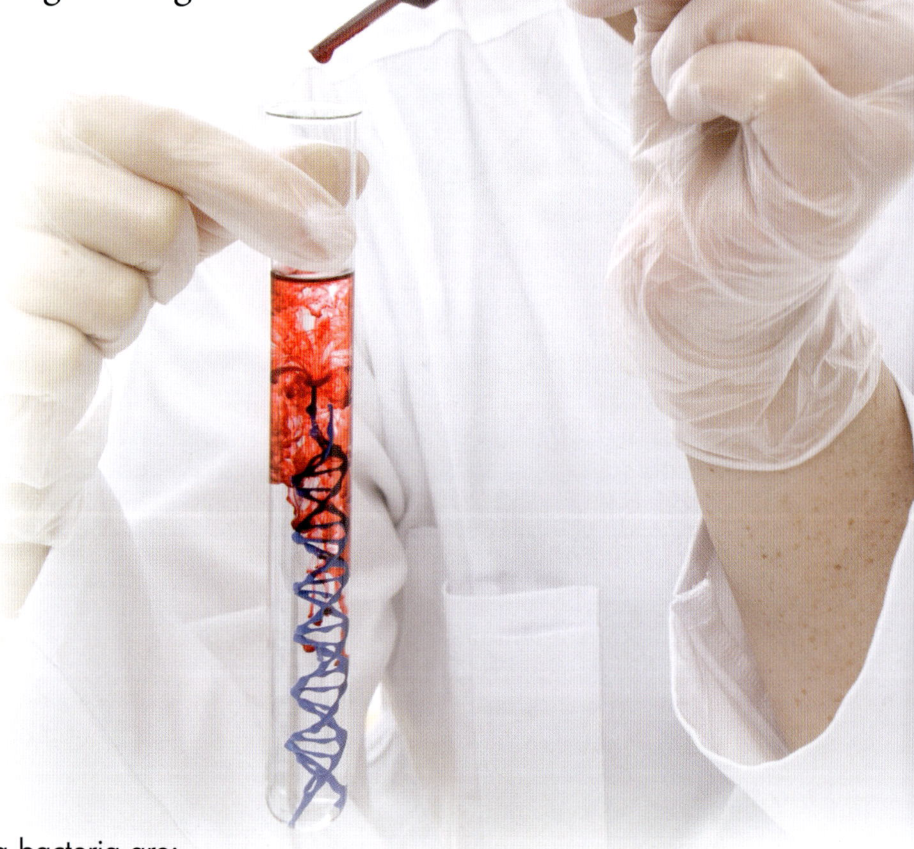

Steps in Genetic Engineering

The major steps in genetic engineering using bacteria are:

Cutting out desired gene/DNA: Specific enzymes called 'restriction' enzymes, found in bacteria, are used in genetic engineering for cutting out specific DNA sequences of interest.

Insertion in vector: The isolated DNA segment is introduced into bacteria that are referred to as 'vectors.' The desired DNA is usually inserted into a plasmid, which is the bacteria's extra-chromosomal DNA. The plasmids readily accept DNA inserts and replicate inside the host bacteria and transfer the new genes across generations when the bacterium divides.

Gene replication: When the host bacteria reproduce, the plasmids also replicate and make multiple copies of the inserted segment.

Recovery: Bacterial cells that contain the plasmid with the desired DNA segment are selectively isolated from the culture.

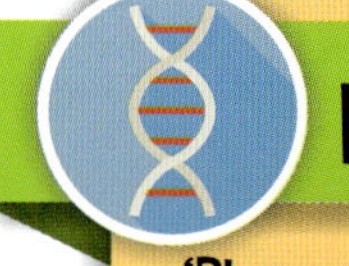

Fact File

'Pharming' is a gene-altering technology that uses plants and animals to produce useful proteins and drugs.

Applications of Genetic Engineering

Some of the products/applications are:

• Many drugs and compounds have been mass-produced, such as insulin, growth hormones, albumin, vaccines, monoclonal antibodies, and anti-hemophilic factors

• Genetically engineered animal models are used for research on human diseases including arthritis, diabetes, Parkinson's disease and heart disease.

• Gene therapy is a process of inserting genes into a patient to compensate for the faulty or missing genes that cause a disease. Already, trials have been carried out for certain diseases, and it shows great promise for curing many others.

Flavr Savr tomatoes remain firm for a longer duration.

• Genetic engineering is used on an industrial scale for mass production of food supplements and biofuels.

• Production of genetically modified organisms and plants is possible through genetic engineering. Some examples of genetically modified crops (GMOs) include Flavr Savr tomatoes that remain firm for a long time, golden rice that is enriched with vitamin A, and Bt Cotton that is resistant to a bacterial pest.

• Genetically engineered farm animals can increase yields; for example, cows can produce more proteins in their milk for increased cheese production.

Genetically engineered animals help in studying different diseases.

Concerns of Genetic Engineering

• Genetically modified crop plants that have resistance to pesticides and herbicides can affect the natural ecological balance.

• Despite precautions, there is the danger of genetically engineered organisms spreading to the wild. Once it occurs, it is impossible to repair the damage.

• On moral grounds, many people argue that humans should not meddle with nature and do not have the right to alter or introduce traits in organisms.

• It is possible to create potentially harmful organisms through recombinant DNA technology; they could cause serious epidemics if released into the environment.

• Due to commercial interests, many products are not labeled 'genetically modified food.' Even if they are labeled, the ingredients are not revealed to the general public.

• There is also opposition on patents on animals, plants and organisms on the grounds that life-forms are not commodities.

A researcher examines a genetically modified crop for desired features.

Cloning

Cloning is the process by which one living organism can make an exact copy of itself. The offspring is not only physically identical to the parent, but has an identical genome as well. Interestingly, the word 'clone' is borrowed from the Greek word *klon* which means 'twig' to refer to the process of a new plant arising from a twig.

Cloning in Plants

Cloning occurs naturally in plants in different ways through asexual reproduction:

• Potato plants produce tubers, which can grow roots and shoots and develop into new plants.

• Spider plants have tiny plantlets growing on their stems

• Strawberry plants have stems that creep on the ground, called runners, that have plantlets on them.

There are also artificial means through which plants can be cloned:

Cuttings: A branch from a parent plant is cut off and, after the lower leaves are removed, it is planted in moist compost in a warm environment. In a few weeks' time, roots develop and a new plant grows.

Tissue Culture: A piece of a plant's tissue or a seed can be grown in the laboratory under artificial light and heat conditions in a 'nutrient gel' called a 'medium' that is designed to be similar to soil. This method is known as tissue culture. Usually, plant hormones are used to encourage the cells to divide and differentiate into roots and shoots.

▲ *Plant tissue culture is relatively easier to grow than animal culture in lab conditions.*

Advantages

• Cloning provides a way to produce plants in bulk quantities otherwise difficult to grow only with seeds.

• Since all plants grown through cloning are identical, the grower can choose plants with the best qualities for cloning.

Disadvantages

• Since all plants thus grown are identical, there is no diversity. As a result, if a disease affects one plant, it is likely to affect all other plants.

• High levels of training and expensive lab equipment are required for successful plant tissue culture.

Cloning in Animals

Embryo Transplants: In this technique, a developing embryo is removed from the uterus of an animal at the initial stage when the embryo has not yet specialised. The cells of the embryo are separated and grown in the laboratory and then transferred to hosts.

Assisted Nuclear Transfer: An adult cell can be cloned through the nuclear transfer method. A special tool is used in the laboratory to suck out the nucleus of the egg cell. Then the nucleus of another cell is transferred into the egg. An electric shock is given to induce division. The dividing embryo is then implanted in the uterus. The developed embryo will then be a clone, or exact copy, of the parent whose nucleus was transferred.

▲ *The assisted nuclear transfer is done under a powerful microscope and special equipment.*

▲ *The creation of Dolly through cloning created a revolution in genetic engineering.*

Dolly

In 1996, Dolly the sheep became the first mammal to be born through cloning from an adult cell. Dolly was created through the nuclear transfer technique at the Roslin Institute, at the University of Edinburgh.

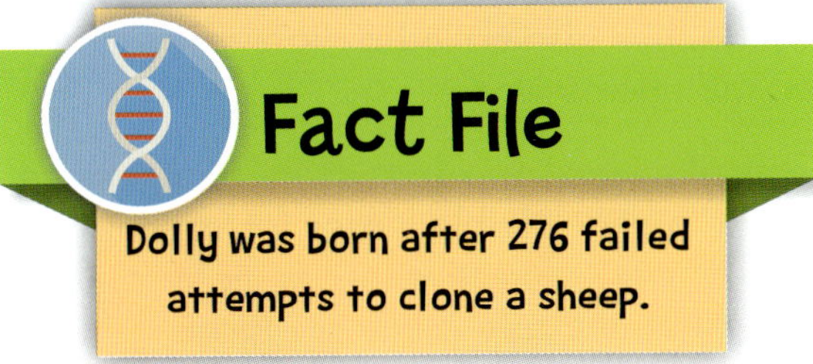

Advantages

• It is possible to mass-produce animals with desirable characteristics, such as cows with high milk production capacity.

• Cloning can produce genetically engineered animals that can provide useful products.

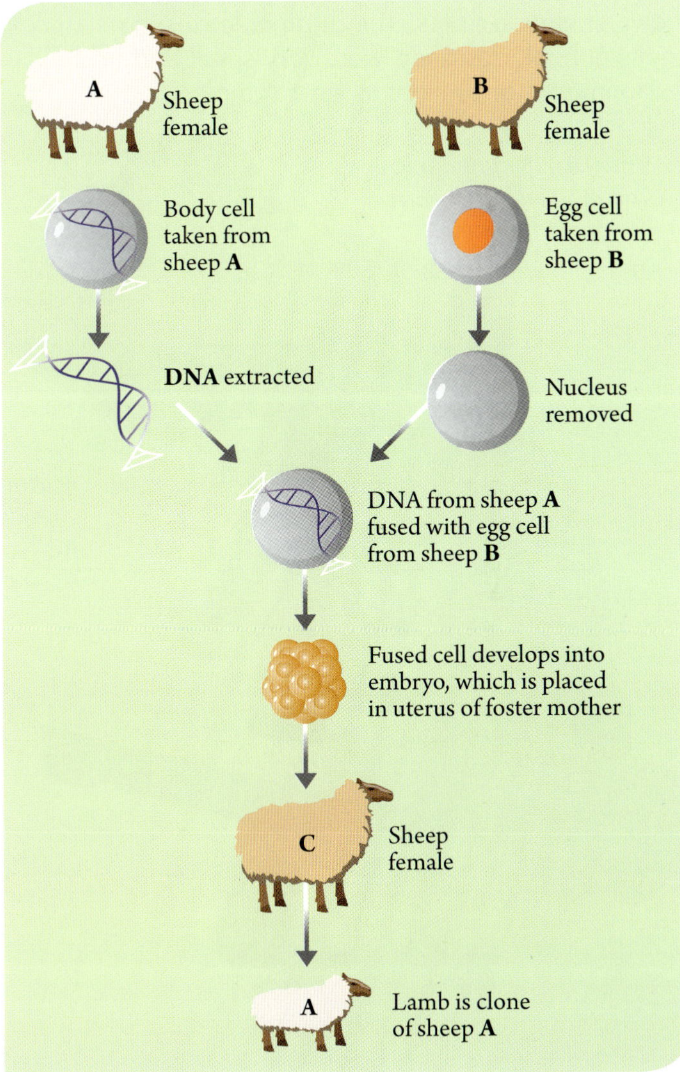

▲ *A cloned sheep resembles the parent that donates the DNA.*

Disadvantages

• The major challenges for cloning are the moral and ethical issues relating to how much humans should interfere in the production of life.

Microscopy

Microscopy is the field of science that deals with the use of instruments called microscopes to magnify objects and microbes that are not normally visible to the naked eye. The optical microscope is one of the most basic devices used for observing microbes, while electron microscopes provide very high magnification.

Origin of Microscopy

Anton van Leeuwenhoek, a Dutch businessman and scientist, is often considered as the 'Father of Microbiology.' He created more than 500 different optical lenses, extensively studied different samples, and meticulously noted the bacteria, cell vacuole, sperm cell, and close-up views of muscle fibres. The original lenses that Leeuwenhoek designed were very small and had to be in front of sunlight to view samples.

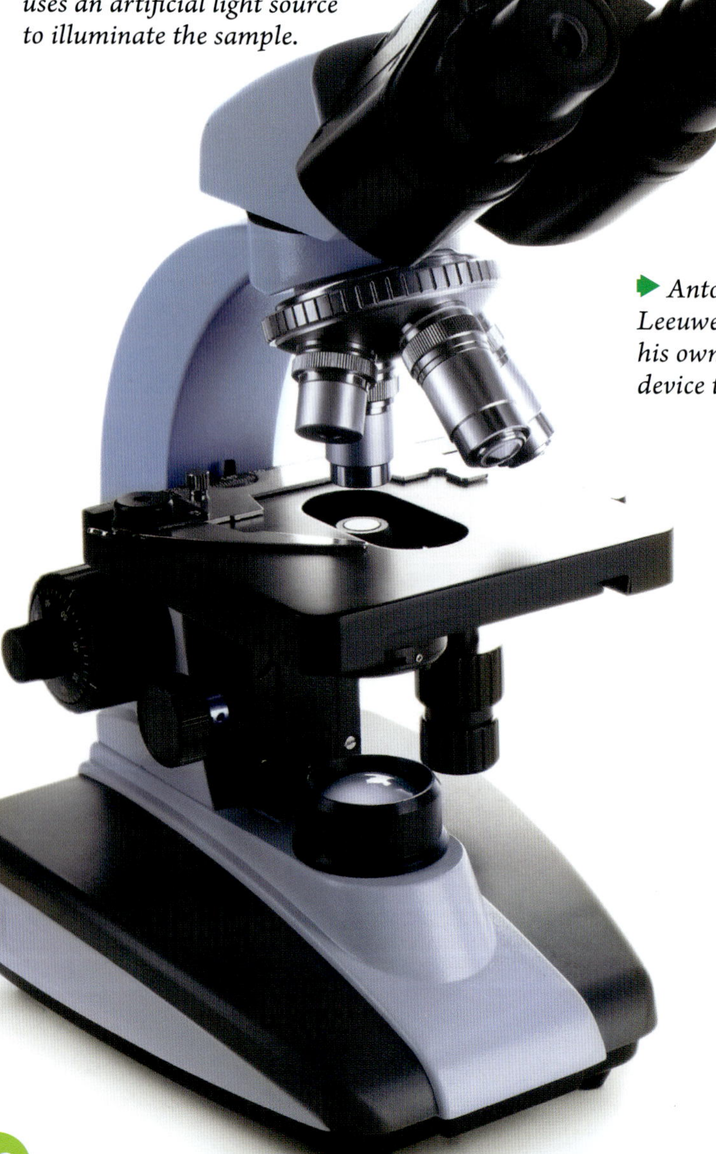

▶ *A modern light microscope uses an artificial light source to illuminate the sample.*

▶ *Anton van Leeuwenhoek invented his own magnifying device to view microbes.*

Optical Microscope

Like Leeuwenhoek's magnifying device, an optical microscope employs lenses and requires sunlight or a light source to illuminate the sample that is loaded on a glass slide. It is also called a 'light microscope' or a 'compound microscope.'

A typical optical microscope consists of an eyepiece, a nose piece with changeable lenses (of varying magnification power), objective lenses, light source, and a stage (where the glass slide is placed for observation). The magnification power of a microscope is the combination of the magnification of the eyepiece and objective lenses.

The sample is loaded on a slide with suitable dyes to increase visibility. Modern optical microscopes are equipped with photographic plates to capture the images viewed.

Magnification and Resolution

Magnification of a device is its ability to make things appear larger. The total magnification achieved through a microscope is calculated using the following formula:

$$\text{Magnification} = \frac{\text{Size of magnified image}}{\text{Actual size of object}}$$

If you are viewing a microbe whose actual size is 1 micron (1×10^{-6} metre) and under a microscope it measures 1 millimetre (1×10^{-3} metre), then the magnification is 1,000X.

At a magnification of 400X, you will be able to clearly view many species of bacteria, blood cells and protozoa. At a higher magnification, say 1,000X, you'll be able to see them in much better detail. For instance, you will be able to distinguish the organelles in protozoa and see the flagella of bacteria.

A microscope's resolution is the shortest distance between two points on a specimen that can be easily distinguished as separate objects by the viewer.

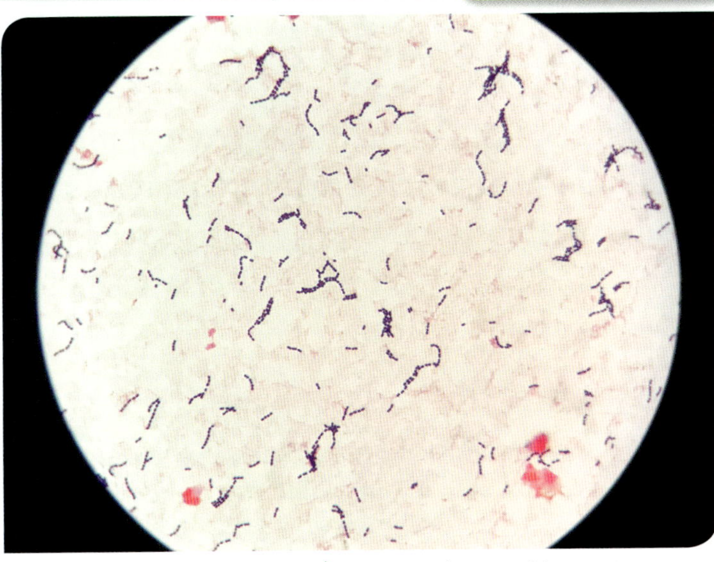

▲ *A view of stained bacteria seen under a light microscope.*

Fact File

On average, an optical microscope can offer magnification ranging from 5X to 100X the object's original size.

▲ *Cellulose fibers of plant seen through a powerful scanning electron microscope.*

◄ *An electron microscope is large, powerful, and expensive.*

Electron Microscope

An electron microscope, as the name suggests, uses a stream of electrons instead of visible light to provide the magnification. As a result, very high magnification, in the range of 100,000X to 200,000X is possible with this microscope. Unlike light microscopes, live samples cannot be used directly. The samples are processed to remove water, embedded in a resin, cut into thin slices, and stained suitably for viewing in an electron microscope. With an electron microscope, it is possible to view cell organelles, viruses that are extremely small, in the range of nanometres (1 nanometre = 1×10^{-9} metre) and even individual atoms. Electron microscopes are expensive to construct and maintain. Those who operate them need special training to handle them with care.

Other Microscopes

There are many other advanced microscopes in use. This includes the scanning tunneling microscope, phase contrast microscope, fluorescence microscope, and atomic force microscope, which has helped view microbes and cellular features in better detail.

Growing Microbes in the Lab

Different species of microbes grow on different substrates. To study and understand microorganisms, scientists grow them under the right conditions in the laboratory using specially designed artificial substrate called 'medium.' Bacteria are the easiest and most common microbes to be artificially grown.

Reproduction

Bacteria grow rapidly through a method of asexual reproduction called 'binary fission.' In binary fission, the duplication of the genetic material of a bacterial cell is followed by cell elongation and division to form two separate cells. This method of reproduction is very simple compared to that of cell division in eukaryotes.

Bacteria reproduce through binary fission.

Growing Bacterial Culture

In the laboratory, bacteria are grown in a specific chemical medium to produce 'colonies.' It was biologist Robert Koch who first grew bacteria in a specially designed petri dish, a technique that is still followed today. Koch had grown bacteria that caused tuberculosis and cholera. Today, many different bacteria can be cultivated and investigated in the lab.

Even though the requirements vary for different species, the common nutrient medium is a jelly-like substance called agar, derived from a type of red algae. Agar provides the ideal surface for the bacteria to grow and produce colonies. The agar is enriched with nutrients like beef or yeast extract to provide amino acids and nitrogen needed for the growth of bacteria.

Bacteria are grown in special liquid growth medium in the lab.

A laminar air flow cabinet offers the ideal environment for safely working with microbes.

Requirements for Growing Bacteria

In order to encourage the growth of bacteria in a laboratory, the whole process of transferring bacterial culture from a solution to the petri dish is done under sterile conditions, typically in a laminar air flow cabin, with the work area swabbed with alcohol. The nutrient agar is allowed to solidify in a sterilised petri dish. Samples are collected from soil, air, surfaces, or body fluids and diluted in water.

An inoculation loop is used for transferring bacteria from a solution to the agar. It is sterilised by exposure to flame before use. The loop, dipped in bacterial solution, is then gently rubbed over the agar quickly and sealed with tape.

Incubation

The process by which bacteria inoculated in the petri dishes are stored under suitable conditions is called 'incubation.' Since bacteria reproduce quickly in warm conditions, they are stored at an optimum temperature of 25°C.

A sterilised inoculation loop is used for transferring microbes to a petri dish.

Bacterial Colonies

Different species of bacteria produce different colonies varying in colour, shape and texture. If the same petri dish has two different colonies, studying the morphology of the colonies helps identify the bacteria species.

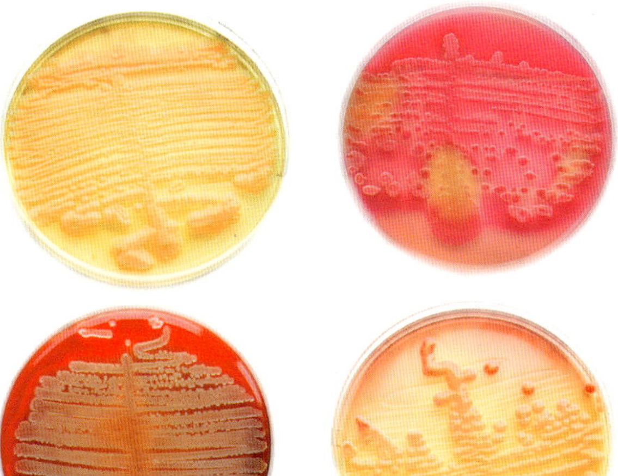

Different bacterial species form different colonies.

Fact File

Petri dishes are generally never incubated at room temperature (22°C) as many harmful bacteria that can cause diseases grow and flourish in this temperature range.

Disposal

Petri dishes with bacterial culture must be disposed of carefully to avoid contamination. Gloves are worn when handling petri dishes with bacterial colonies, and bleach is poured over the agar to destroy the bacterial growth before disposal.

Testing for Antibiotics and Disinfectants

One of the useful functions of culturing microorganisms is to identify the efficiency of an antibiotic, disinfectant, or any antibacterial substance. For this, the bacteria are inoculated evenly across the entire petri dish with a swab or inoculation loop. Then a drop of the antibacterial substance or an antibiotic disc is placed in the centre of the dish and incubated. The presence of a 'halo' surrounding the antibacterial substance shows a region of no growth of bacteria around it. The diameter of the halo also indicates the efficiency of the antibiotic/antibacterial agent.

Diseases

Health is the state of well-being, whereas a disease or disorder is an affliction that affects one or more parts of the body. Diseases can be of different types and can be caused by infection, poor lifestyle, genetic predisposition, deficiency, or other factors. The most common classification of diseases is communicable or noncommunicable.

Noncommunicable Diseases

Diseases that cannot be spread from one person to another through physical contact or exposure are known as noncommunicable diseases. Some of the common examples of noncommunicable diseases are:

Diabetes: It is caused by high blood sugar levels or deficiency of insulin.

Cancer: It is a result of abnormal growth and division of cells.

Cardiac arrest: Blockages in the heart's blood vessels cause a heart attack

Stroke: Changes in the blood supply to the brain can result in a stroke.

Asthma: A disease that affects the lungs and causes difficulty breathing.

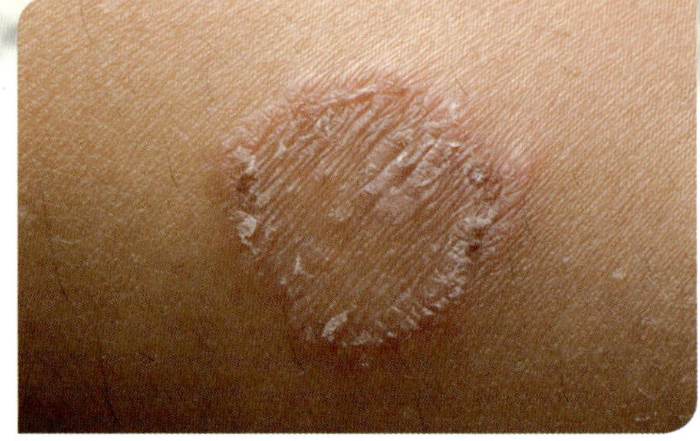

▲ *Ringworm is a skin infection caused by a fungal species.*

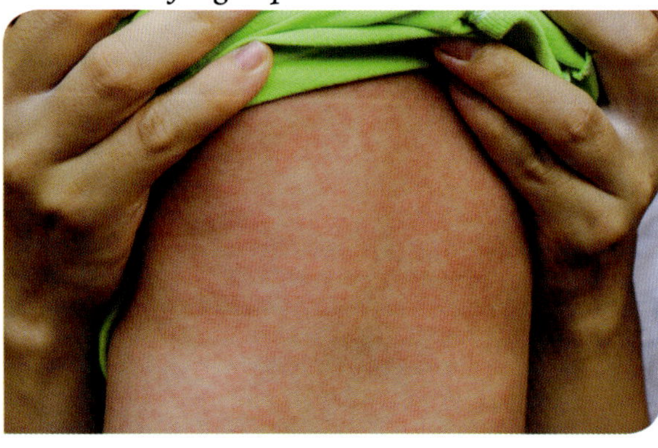

▲ *Measles is a viral infection that affects children.*

Communicable Diseases

Diseases that can spread from one person to another through different means are termed as communicable diseases. The mode of spreading varies from one disease to another, as does the severity. The common cold is a relatively mild condition caused by bacteria or viruses, whereas smallpox is a severe and sometimes deadly disease caused by a virus.

The disease spreads from one person to another through air, water, soil, animals, birds, insects, or body fluids.

- Diseases caused by bacteria: sore throat, tuberculosis, gonorrhea, pneumonia

- Diseases caused by protists: sleeping sickness, Chagas disease, malaria

- Diseases caused by fungi: ringworm, psoriasis, yeast infections

- Diseases caused by viruses: chicken pox, polio, measles, hepatitis, influenza

Risk Factors

Both communicable and noncommunicable diseases are caused by certain aspects and lifestyle choices that may increase the chances of the person acquiring the disease. They are known as 'risk factors.' Some risk factors associated with both types of diseases include:

- Poor hygiene
- Lack of exercise
- Unhealthy diet
- Deficiency of vitamins or minerals
- Excessive consumption of alcohol
- Smoking cigarettes
- Obesity
- Exposure to harmful chemicals, radiation, or cancer-causing agents (carcinogens)
- Genetic factors, as in the case of inherited diseases
- Lack of, or poor functioning of, one or more components

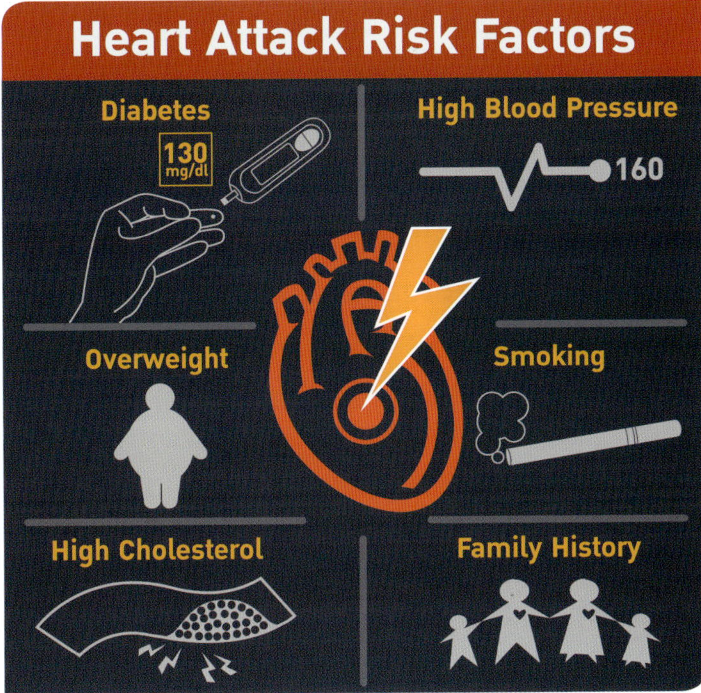

▲ *Citrus canker in leaves of lemon tree exhibit brown, raised spots.*

Diseases in Plants

Diseases can affect plants too. These diseases are caused by microbes like fungi, bacteria, viruses, and also insects. Plants exhibit different symptoms corresponding to the disease as spots, stunted growth, decay, cankers, malformed leaves or stems, and discolouration.

◀ *Some stems have thorns to protect against animals.*

Defense Mechanisms

Plants have different defense mechanisms to protect against herbivores and diseases. They are:

- Thick cell walls
- Waxy and tough cuticle on leaves
- Dead cells around stems in the form of bark
- Secretion of chemical compounds
- Secretion of poisonous substances
- Thorns and hairs
- Mimicry
- Leaves that curl or droop when touched

Fact File

Communicable diseases are caused by infection of microbes such as bacteria, fungi, protists, and viruses that are referred to as 'pathogens.'

Classification of Organisms

There are millions of organisms that exist on our planet. Classification is a method devised by scientists to place organisms in specific groups based on physical and biological similarities.

Though certain organisms might seem different from others, if they have enough similarities, they can be grouped into one category. This systematic method of classifying organisms is called taxonomy. Carl Linnaeus, a Swedish botanist, was responsible for classifying organisms on the basis of physical appearance and characteristics and giving a scientific name (also called binomial nomenclature) for every species.

Divisions

In taxonomic classification, organisms are sorted in a hierarchical system on the basis of these ranks, or taxa:

Domain > Kingdom > Phylum > Class > Order > Family > Genus > Species

The five-kingdom system of classification was proposed by R.H. Whittaker in 1969. Many countries follow this system of classification. The classification is based on many factors like type of nutrition, cell structure, and type of reproduction.

▶ *R.H. Whittaker proposed the five-kingdom classification system.*

Five-Kingdom Classification

The known organisms are classified into any of the five kingdoms:

Kingdom	Characteristic Features	Examples		
Animalia	Multicellular No cell walls No pigments for photosynthesis	Chamaeleon	Sea turtle	Chimpanzee
Plantae	Multicellular Cell walls present Photosynthetic pigments present Manufactures own food from sunlight	Ferns	Apple tree	Green algae

Fungi	Unicellular or multicellular Cell walls present No pigments for photosynthesis	Mushrooms · Yeast · Moulds
Protists	Unicellular Well-defined nucleus May possess pigments for photosynthesis	Green euglena · Amoeba · Paramecium
Prokaryotes	Unicellular Cell walls present Primitive/not-well-defined nucleus May have extra-chromosomal DNA called 'plasmids'	Bacteria · Archaebacteria · Cyanobacteria

An example of how humans would be classified in this system:

Classification	Name	Reason
Domain	Eukaryotes	Possesses well-defined nucleus
Kingdom	Animalia	Multicellular, capable of ingesting food, no cell walls
Phylum	Chordata	Presence of backbone
Class	Mammalia	Give birth to live young, nurse offspring with milk
Order	Primates	High level of intelligence; apelike
Family	Hominidae	Capable of walking upright
Genus	Homo	Human
Species	sapiens	Modern-day human

The classification system is an indication of the evolutionary relationship between organisms. All living beings classified under a phylum, for example Chordata, are assumed to have evolved from a common ancestor.

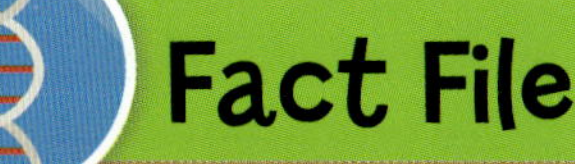

Fact File

No classification system includes viruses in any group because they are not considered to be true living organisms.

▶ *Human species are thought to have evolved from a common ape ancestor.*

Bioenergetics: Photosynthesis

Plants, algae and certain species of bacteria can directly use sunlight to make their own food in the form of simple sugars. This process is known as photosynthesis, where *photo* means 'light' and *synthesis* means 'putting together.' Photosynthesis requires special cell organelles and pigments.

Photosynthesis Process

Plants can perform photosynthesis to make their own food by using sunlight, water and carbon dioxide. Sunlight is absorbed by a type of green pigment in the cells called chlorophyll. Water is absorbed from the soil and air through the roots and leaves. Carbon dioxide is taken in through small pores on leaves called stomata.

▲ *Green leaves have chloroplasts that perform photosynthesis.*

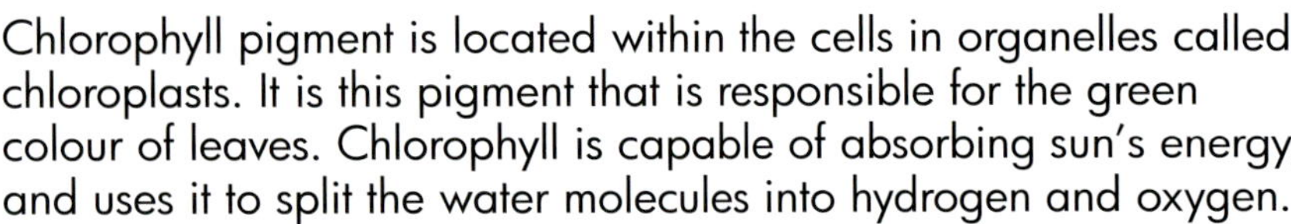

▲ *Sunlight, water and air are essential for plants to survive and make their food.*

Chlorophyll pigment is located within the cells in organelles called chloroplasts. It is this pigment that is responsible for the green colour of leaves. Chlorophyll is capable of absorbing sun's energy, and uses it to split the water molecules into hydrogen and oxygen.

Even leaves of other colours perform photosynthesis. Leaves can be red or yellow in colour due to the presence of different pigments like anthocyanin, carotene or xanthophyll. Even coloured leaves possess chlorophyll to perform photosynthesis.

While oxygen is released into the atmosphere as a byproduct, hydrogen then combines with carbon dioxide to produce a simple sugar called glucose. Glucose molecules are used for providing energy for the growth and development of the plants. The rest of it is stored in the leaves, roots and fruits.

The chemical reaction can be written as:

Carbon dioxide + Water $\xrightarrow{\text{Sunlight}}$ Glucose + Oxygen

$$CO_2 + H_2O \xrightarrow{\text{Sunlight}} C_6H_{12}O_6 + O_2$$

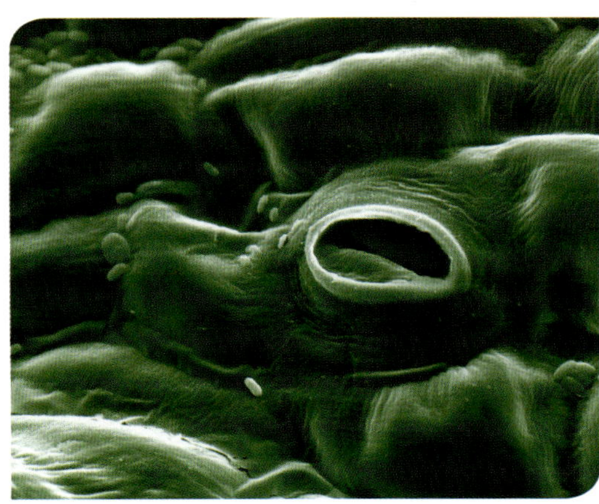

▲ *Carbon dioxide is taken into plant cells through a stomata opening.*

Light Reaction: This reaction occurs in the thylakoid membrane of chloroplasts and requires sunlight. This is the process by which light energy is converted into chemical energy. The water molecule is broken down into ions (H+ and OH-). These ions help form the molecules - ATP (adenosine triphosphate) and NADPH2 (nicotinamide adenine dinucleotide Phosphate). These two molecules are used in the next stage.

Dark Reaction: In the second step, no light is required. This is a slower reaction that uses enzymes to synthesise sugars from carbon dioxide and water with the help of the energy molecules ATP and NADPH2. This stage is also known as 'carbon fixation,' or the Calvin cycle.

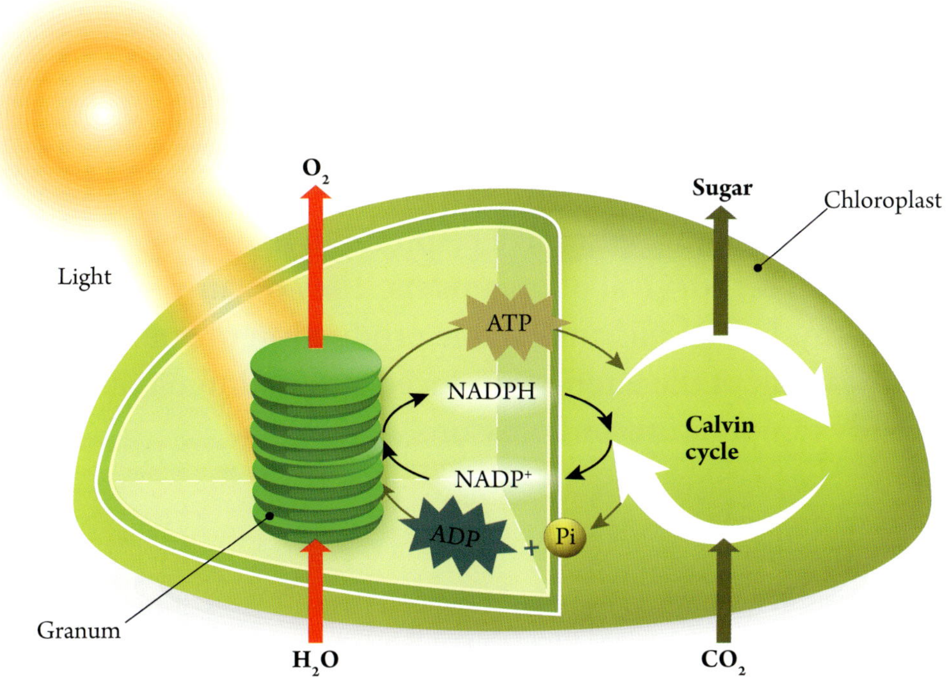

▲ *The light reaction occurs through a series of steps.*

Importance of Photosynthesis

Photosynthesis sustains life on Earth. Plants use the glucose created for growth and energy. Animals then consume plants for energy needs and survival. The animals that feed on plants are known as primary consumers or herbivores. Photosynthesis facilitates respiration for animals because the oxygen produced by the plants is used for respiration. Photosynthesis is therefore directly related to the life and survival of all living creatures on earth.

Coal and natural gas are products of dead and buried plant material from millions of years ago. We use these fossil fuels for generating electricity.

Fact File

Photosynthesis is essential for balancing the levels of carbon dioxide and oxygen on the planet.

▲ *Coal is formed from dead remains of plants that died millions of years ago.*

▶ *Fossil fuels form under the surface from buried parts of plants and animals.*

Bioenergetics: Respiration, Metabolism and Homeostasis

Biochemical processes like respiration, metabolism and homeostasis are vital for survival of organisms. They occur continuously in healthy, living cells and enable production of energy, effective utilisation of the energy produced and maintenance of constant body temperature and pressure.

Metabolism

The cells in the body convert fuel obtained from the food that is consumed and convert it into energy required for performing all functions. This process is known as metabolism. In a human body, different proteins control the chemical reactions of metabolism in a coordinated manner. At any given time, thousands of metabolic reactions are occurring inside the body.

The sugars produced by plants through photosynthesis are consumed by animals. These sugars are broken down into important cell-building chemical components. Metabolism has two functions:

1) It helps build up body tissues and energy reserves.

2) It breaks down energy stores and body tissues to generate fuel for functioning.

Metabolism is of two types:

Anabolism: Also called constructive metabolism, it is involved in building and strengthening. Anabolism is involved in cell division, growth, maintenance of body tissues, and storing energy. Small molecules are converted into complex carbohydrates, proteins and fats. Bone mineralisation and increase in muscle mass occur due to anabolism.

Catabolism: Also known as destructive metabolism, it is a process that generates energy for cellular activities in the cells. Cells break down complex carbohydrates and fats to release energy. This release of energy is followed by an increase in body heat and muscular movement. The waste products of catabolism are removed through the kidneys, skin, intestines or lungs.

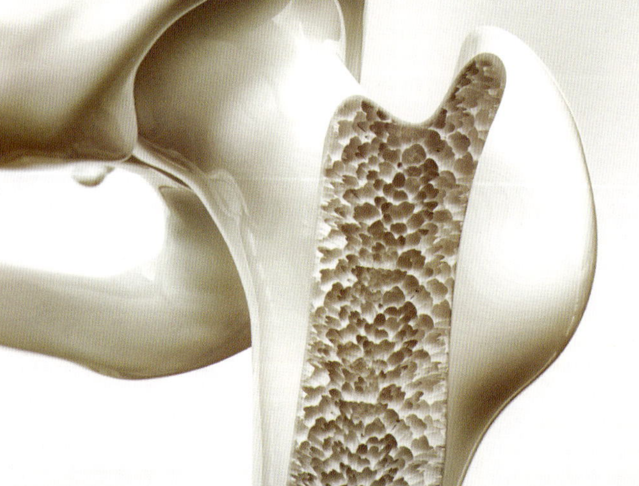

▲ Bone mineralisation occurs through anabolism.

Respiration

Cellular respiration is a process that breaks up sugar into energy molecules. Respiration can be either aerobic (when it uses oxygen) or anaerobic (when oxygen is not required). Anaerobic respiration is not as efficient as aerobic respiration and also produces carbon dioxide as a byproduct, which then gains entry into the circulatory system. Mitochondria are organelles in the cell that facilitate respiration.

Respiration consists of four stages:

- Glycolysis
- Link reaction
- Krebs cycle
- Electron transport chain

Aerobic respiration can be represented by the formula:

Glucose + Oxygen $\longrightarrow$ Carbon dioxide + Water + Energy

$$C_6H_{12}O_6 + 6O_2 \longrightarrow 6CO_2 + 6H_2O + ATP$$

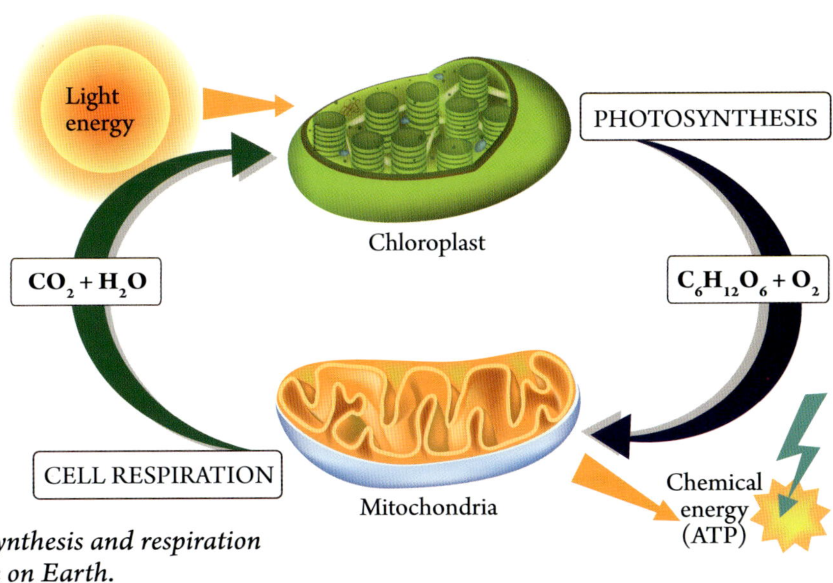

▶ *Photosynthesis and respiration enable life on Earth.*

Fact File

Approximately 30 ATP molecules are produced through oxidation of one glucose molecule. The theoretical estimate is 38 ATPs.

Homeostasis

Homeostasis refers to the body processes involved in maintaining the optimal conditions in the body for the cells to function effectively. It includes keeping the body temperature, blood glucose and water at the right levels.

To achieve the optimal conditions, the control systems involve nervous and chemical responses such as cell receptors that detect stimuli, coordination centers like the brain and spinal cord that can process information, and effectors that elicit the response such as muscles and glands.

There are different ways by which the human body maintains homeostasis. Body temperature is one of the most important factors that is regulated for optimal functioning of the body. When the body temperature rises in response to hot weather, the body reacts by sweating to cool down. The internal organs like the lungs, pancreas and kidneys help maintain ideal levels of oxygen, blood sugar, and ions. The endocrine system secretes different hormones that maintain homeostasis in the body.

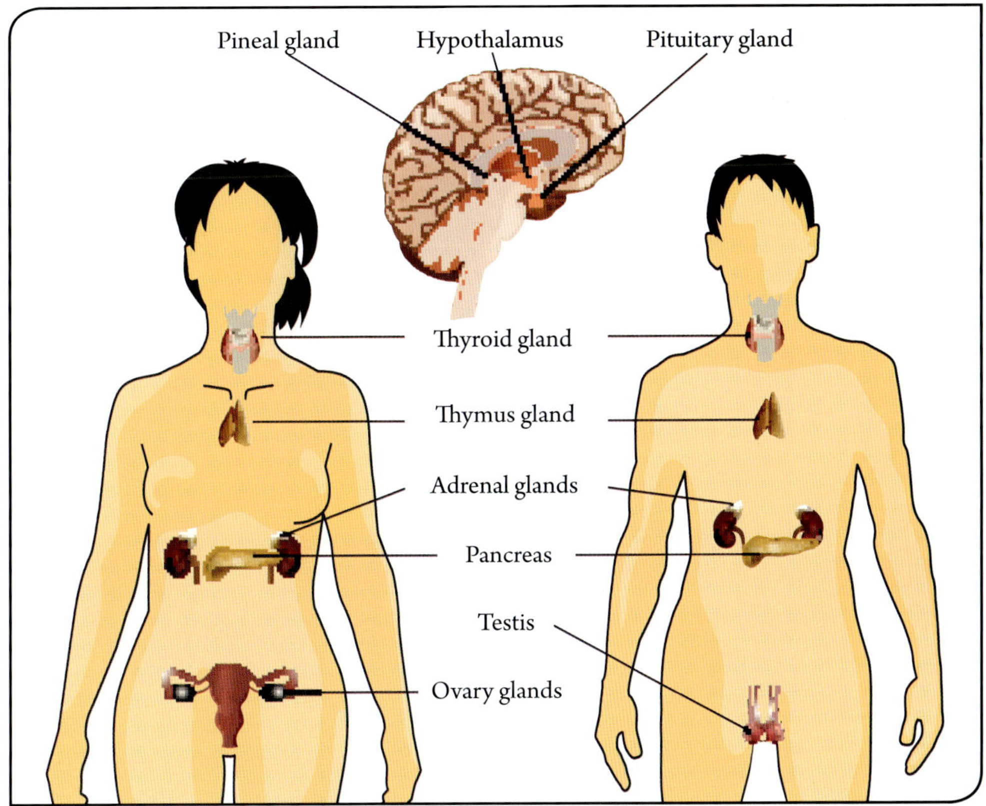

▲ *The endocrine system maintains homeostasis in the body.*

Human Systems

The human body is complex and involves seamless coordination of tissues and organ systems to ensure that all activities from movement, respiration, circulation, coordination, digestion, and excretion are carried out efficiently.

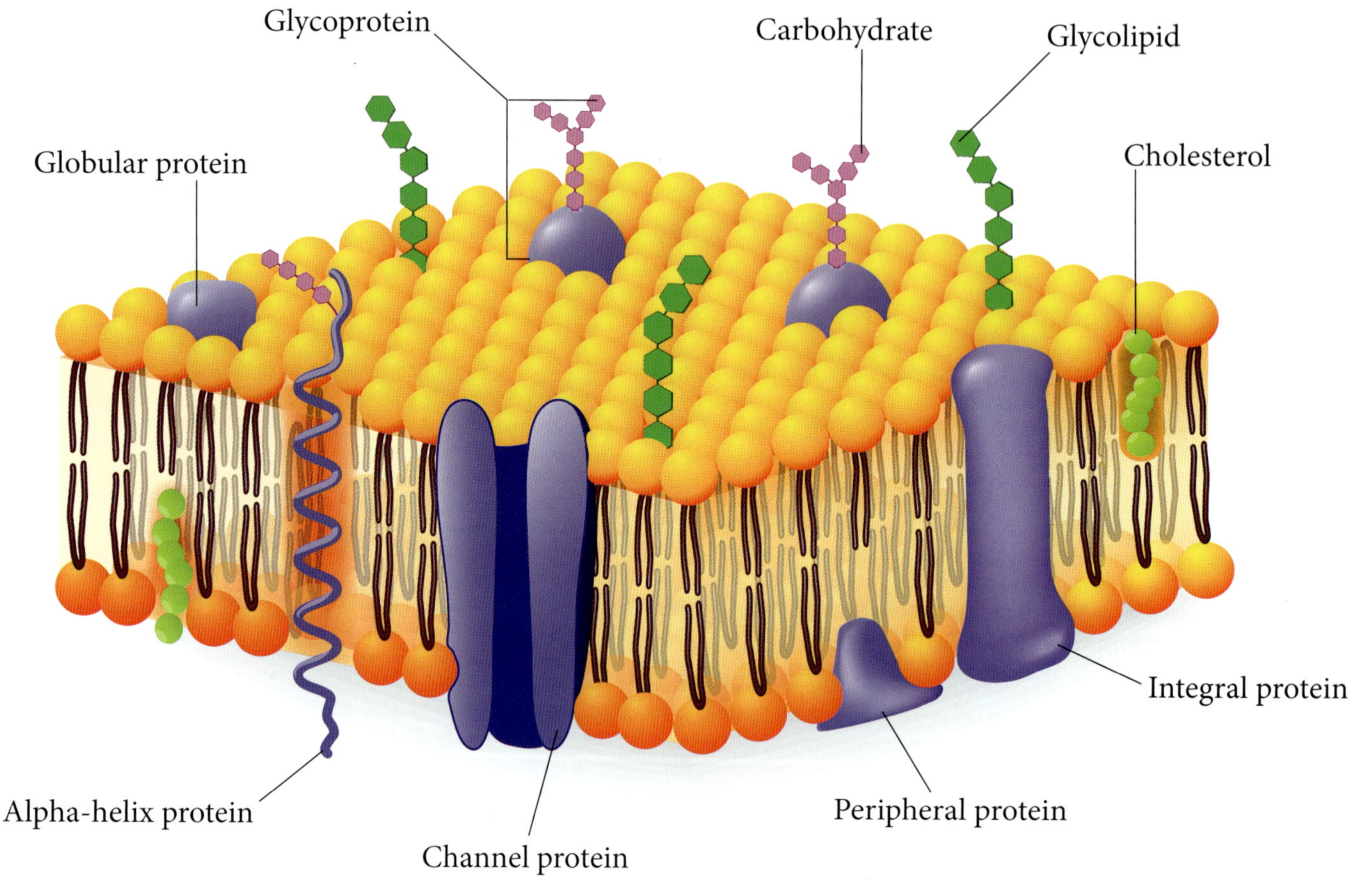

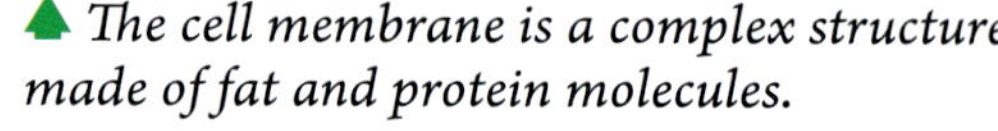

▲ *The cell membrane is a complex structure made of fat and protein molecules.*

Chemical Composition

The cells of the human body are made up of carbohydrates, proteins, lipids (fats), nucleic acids, organic compounds, minerals and water. Water is a major constituent in extracellular fluids such as blood, plasma, and lymph and is also found within the cells. By weight, water makes up 60 percent of the human body.

Lipids, especially the phospholipids and cholesterol, form the structural component of the cells in the body, act as energy reserves, and provide insulation and shock absorption. Proteins also form the structural framework of cell membranes, and enzymes are proteins that are crucial for many functions.

Carbohydrates, in the form of sugars, mainly serve as a source of fuel. Nucleic acids are the genetic material of the body that carries all the information needed for survival and reproduction. The minerals and other organic compounds play different important roles within the body.

Fact File

The larynx, or voice box, consists of a flap of elastic cartilage called epiglottis that makes sure that food and air go to the right destinations.

The Different Systems

Systems are the highest and most complex working units of the human body. The major systems of the human body are: nervous, skeletal and muscular, cardiovascular, lymphatic, respiratory, digestive, reproductive and excretory.

Skeletal and Muscular System

The skeleton and the different groups of muscles form the structural framework of the body and enable movement. Cartilage and bones are the structural components of the skeletal system. The bones, apart from providing a structural framework, also store minerals such as calcium and phosphate. The bone marrow is the site for production of red blood cells. The human skeletal system has a total of 206 bones.

The muscular system is the largest system in the body and is located throughout all regions from head to toe. The three types of muscles are: cardiac, skeletal and smooth.

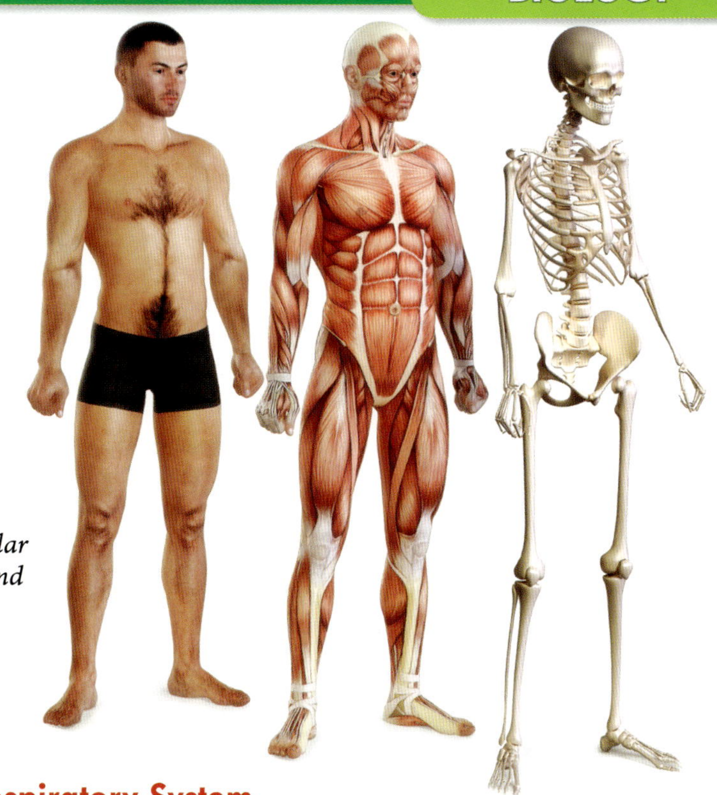

▶ *The skeletal and muscular system provides support and enables movement.*

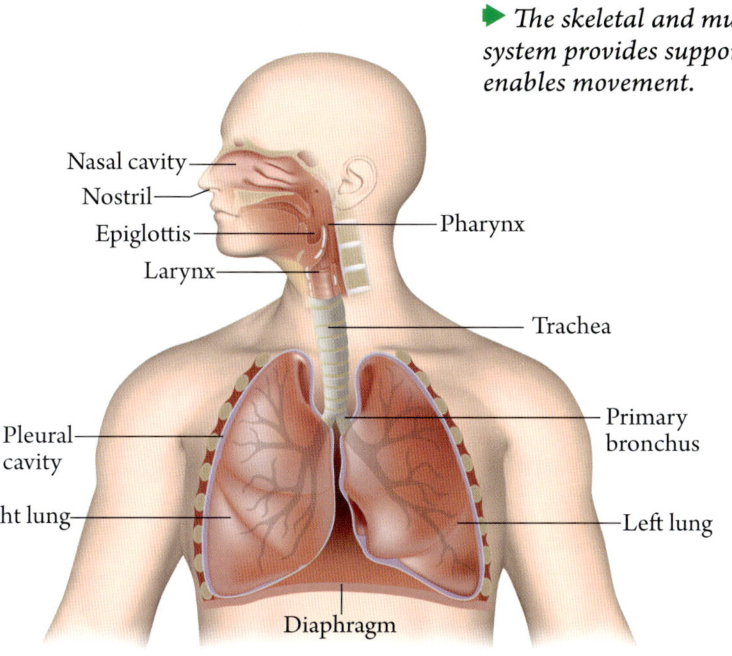

▲ *The lungs are the main organs of respiration.*

Respiratory System

The respiratory system—which comprises the nose, mouth, pharynx, larynx, lungs, trachea and alveoli—is responsible for supplying the body with oxygen and removing carbon dioxide produced in the body. The nose or the nasal cavity breathes in air that is taken to the lungs. The pharynx, also referred to as the throat, is a muscular pathway that transports food and air to the larynx. From the larynx, air moves into the trachea or windpipe. The trachea branches into bronchial tubes and bronchioles that lead into the lung chambers. The lungs have alveoli that take up oxygen and expel carbon dioxide.

Reproductive System

The male and female reproductive systems are distinct. The male reproductive system is responsible for the production of the sperm cells that are delivered into the female's reproductive tract. The sperm is produced in the testes and travel through the penis. The eggs are produced in the ovaries in a female and travel down the Fallopian tubes. When a sperm fuses with an egg cell, it gets embedded in the uterus to divide and develop into a fetus.

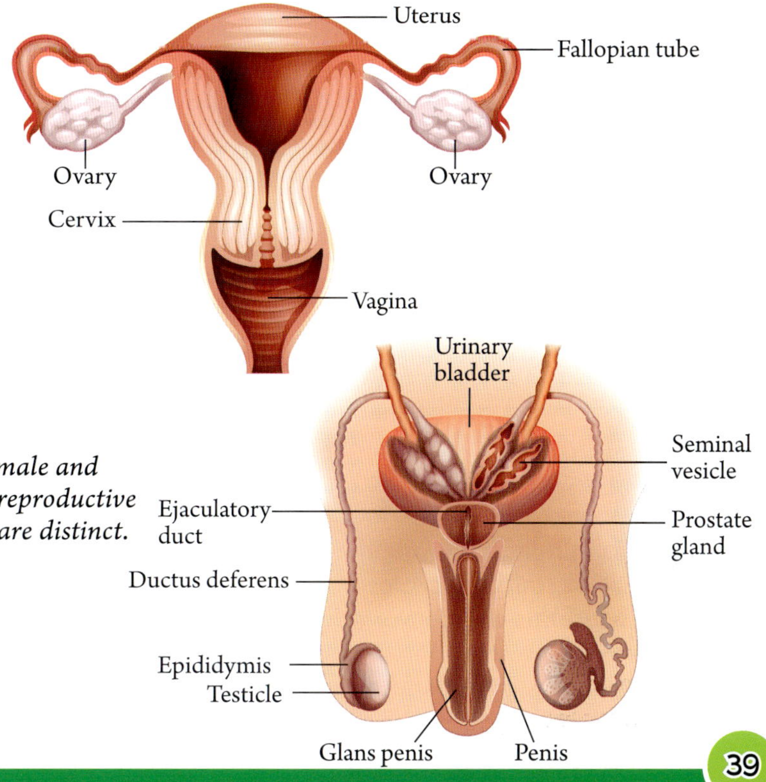

▶ *The male and female reproductive system are distinct.*

Integumentary System

It is commonly known as the skin and covers the entire body and offers protection and temperature regulation. The skin also hosts millions of nerves that respond to external stimuli like pressure, pain, touch and temperature.

Nervous System

Considered to be the main controlling and communicating system in the body, the nervous system controls all our actions, thoughts and emotions. Even though it is a single system, it is divided into the central nervous system, comprising of the brain and spinal cord—as well as the peripheral nervous system, which includes the nerves that extend from the brain and spinal cord—the cranial and spinal nerves, respectively. The brain is enclosed in a protective covering called the cranium or brain box.

Immune System

The skin forms the first line of defense, acting as a physical barrier against pathogens and harmful substances. The lymphatic system is responsible for fighting bacteria and fungi. Inside the body, the lymphatic system consists of the T-cells, B-cells, antibodies, and platelets that tackle wound sites. While platelets repair the wound, the B-cells produce antibodies that bind to pathogens and enable the T-cells to attack them.

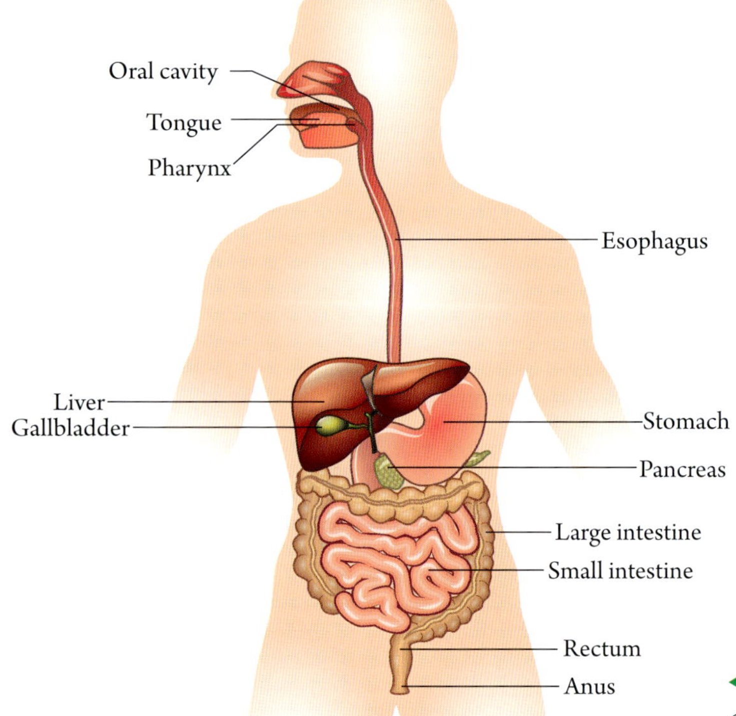

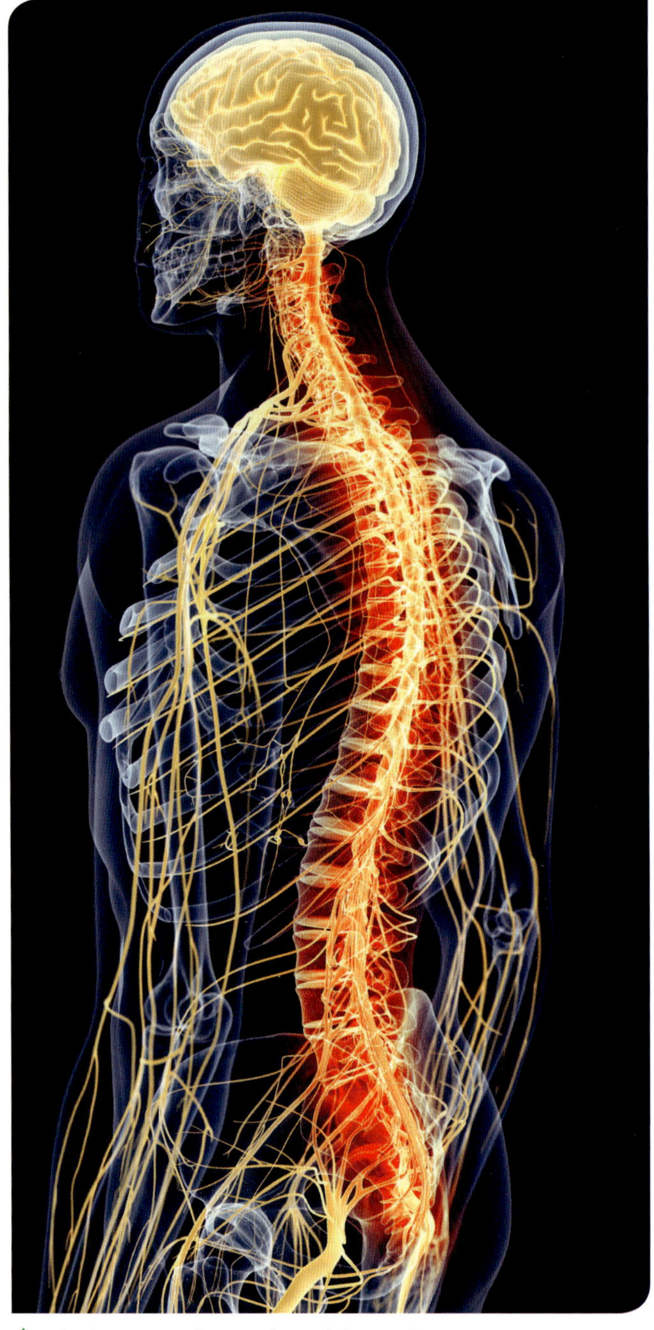

▲ *The brain and spinal cord form the nervous system.*

◀ *The digestive system begins in the mouth and ends at the anus.*

Digestive System

Digestion starts in the mouth and ends at the anus. The food we eat through the mouth is mixed with saliva, broken down into pieces, and passed through the alimentary canal, all the way to the stomach where many enzymes are present. The food is then broken down into simpler nutrients—proteins are broken down into amino acids, carbohydrates are converted into simple sugars, and fats are converted into fatty acids. Digestion continues in the small intestine and the large intestine, where nutrients are absorbed and the waste products are eliminated through the anus as feces.

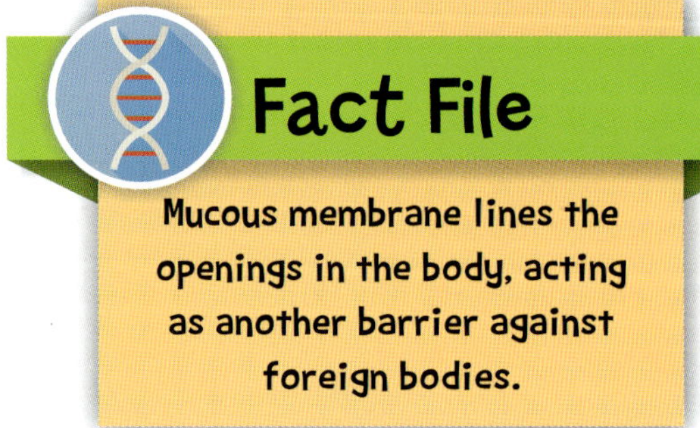

Fact File

Mucous membrane lines the openings in the body, acting as another barrier against foreign bodies.

Excretory System

The waste products produced in our body after digestion are expelled as urine. The kidneys are the major organs involved in excreting wastes and purifying blood. The urinary bladder, ureters, and urethra form the urinary system that expels the urine produced in the kidneys. The bladder is a hollow, muscular sac that can hold urine. The kidneys are bean-shaped organs enclosed by transparent and fibrous renal capsules.

Endocrine System

The endocrine system regulates different metabolic functions in the body through hormones. The hormones are chemical compounds released into the bloodstream, and tissues respond to the hormones in specific ways. The organs of the endocrine system are small. They include the pituitary gland, the thyroid and parathyroid glands, adrenal gland, pineal gland, and the thymus. Hormones are of two types: steroids and amino acid–based compounds.

Circulatory System

The heart is the organ that pumps oxygen-rich blood to all parts of the body. The heart has four chambers and is made up of cardiac tissue that helps the organ pump blood. The arteries carry oxygenated blood from the heart to the other parts of the body while the veins bring deoxygenated blood from across the body back to the heart in a continuous circulatory network.

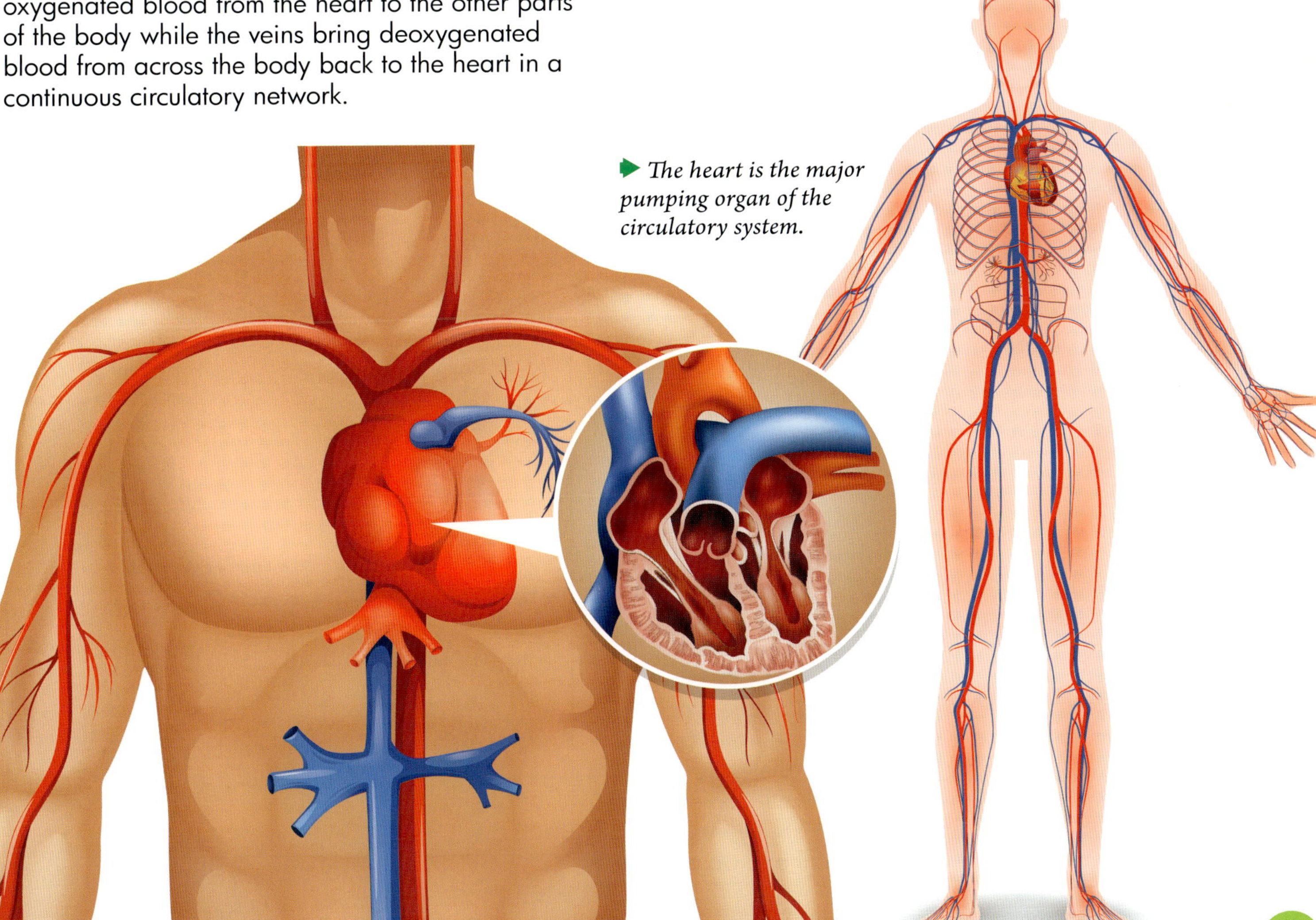

▶ *Kidneys dispose waste as urine and purify blood.*

▶ *The heart is the major pumping organ of the circulatory system.*

Genetics

For centuries, people have observed genetic inheritance (where offspring inherit the characteristics of their parents). This knowledge has gradually been used for improving animals and crops with favorable characteristics, but it wasn't until the 19th century that scientists discovered the depths of modern genetics that we are familiar with today.

History of Genetics

Imre Festetics de Tona was a pioneer of experimental genetics. He did extensive studies on sheep and was the first to propose a set of rules of heredity. He was the first to use the term 'genetic' when he wrote about the genetic laws of nature in 1819.

Gregor Mendel, an Austrian priest, is known as the 'Father of Modern Genetics.' He gained inspiration from his mentors and colleagues to study variations in plants. He chose the pea plant to conduct his experiments on. For eight years, starting from 1856, Mendel grew pea plants in a garden plot in the monastery and studied different traits like size and shape of seed, pod shape, flower colour, plant height, and a few other factors and noted his observations.

Fact File

The Human Genome Project enabled the sequencing of the entire human genome in 2003.

Inheritance

The property by which organisms pass on heritable units called genes from one parent to offspring is known as inheritance. Gregor Mendel was the first to discover this while studying heritable traits in pea plants. One particular observation he made was how pea plants possessed either purple or white flowers but never an intermediate colour. The components that give rise to these two different colours are different versions of the same gene, called alleles. An organism with two copies of the same allele is called homozygous, while those having two different copies of the alleles are called hetrozygous. The set of alleles make up the organism's genotype, and the physical and observable character they result in is the phenotype.

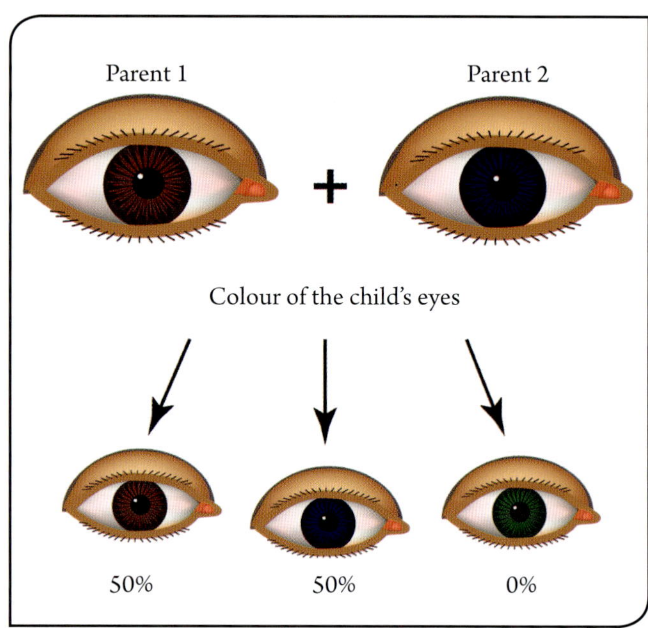

▲ *The eye colour is determined by alleles inherited from parents.*

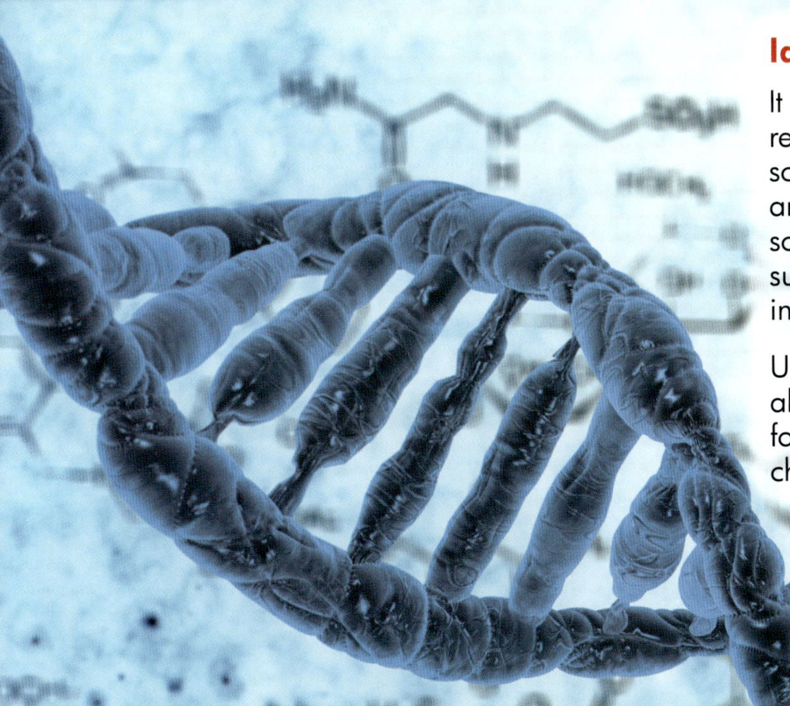

Identification of the Heritable Molecule

It wasn't until 1900 that Mendel's work gained recognition when Hugo de Vries and a few other scientists understood the significance of his experiments and research. In 1905, William Bateson, another scientist who was a strong proponent of Mendel's work, suggested the name 'genetics' to describe the study of inheritance in organisms.

Up until the early 20th century, nobody was sure about what molecules in organisms were responsible for inheritance. Thomas Morgan Hunt identified that chromosomes were responsible for it in 1911.

However, scientists found that chromosomes were made up of proteins and DNA, and nobody was sure which of the two components aided inheritance.

Experiments conducted from 1928 to 1952 conclusively identified DNA as the genetic material.

Structure of DNA

Two scientists, James Watson and Francis Crick, with the help of X-ray crystallography pictures from Rosalind Franklin and Maurice Wilkins, successfully determined the structure of DNA in 1953. DNA is a double helix, shaped like a corkscrew, with two strands of nucleotides bonded in a 'twisted ladder' fashion.

The four nucleotides in the DNA—adenine, guanine, cytosine, and thymine—formed complementary bonds. Adenine bonded with thymine and guanine with cytosine. RNA also has four nucleotides, but with one difference—instead of thymine, RNA has uracil.

The process of replication occurs when the two strands of DNA are unwound and partner strands are generated by adding complementary nucleotides to both the strands, thus forming two strands of which each has the original parent strand. The elucidation of the structure of DNA was followed by other discoveries, giving a clear picture of the inner molecular events.

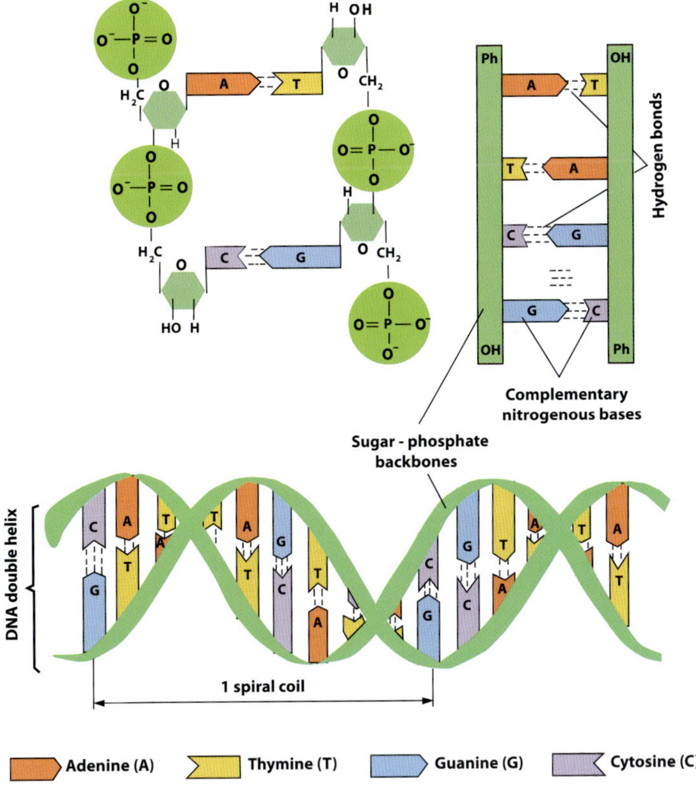

▲ *DNA is made up of molecules that form a double-helix structure.*

Evolution

The organisms that exist on the planet are complex, each with its own distinct features and genetic makeup. The complexity and organisation are due to millions of years of evolution and the selection of the fittest for survival and propagation.

Theory of Evolution

Charles Darwin, an English naturalist, went on a five-year voyage around the world, studying variations in plants and animals. He proposed the theory of evolution, and other ideas, in his work *On the Origin of Species,* published in 1859. The idea behind the theory of evolution is that all the different species evolved from simple, single-celled life-forms. These simple organisms are believed to have first developed 3 billion years ago.

Even though Darwin's theory is more popular and widely accepted among evolutionists, he was not the only person to propose an evolution theory. A French scientist, Jean-Baptiste Lamarck, developed an alternative theory in the early 19th century. His theory suggested that an organism's characteristics that are used more often become bigger and stronger.

Evolutionists have noted that Lamarck's theory of evolution did not hold true for many observations. According to his theory, all organisms would evolve and become more complex over time. It did not account for the presence of simple microorganisms that have remained that way for billions of years.

▲ *Charles Darwin is known for his theory of evolution of species.*

▲ *Quails and other animals are selectively bred for their best features.*

Natural Selection and Selective Breeding

Natural selection is a key feature of Darwin's theory of evolution. Quite simply, it means that individual species show variation, caused by differences in one or more genes. Individuals with characteristics best suited for survival are more likely to survive, reproduce, and pass on the genes responsible for the beneficial characteristics.

Selective breeding is an artificial process by which humans choose desirable characteristics in animals and birds and mate them with others in their species with the same or a different beneficial characteristic. As a result, the offspring will be robust and possess ideal characteristics inherited from the parents.

The Quagga and the dodo are two species that became extinct just a few centuries ago.

Mutation and Speciation

Mutations are changes that occur in genes that can be beneficial or harmful. These changes are also random and often caused by background radiation, chemicals and other factors. If mutations occur in the reproductive cells, they get transferred to the offspring. If the mutation is beneficial and not harmful, it will continue getting transferred across generations through natural selection.

The combined effect of mutations, environmental changes, and natural selection can produce enough changes in an organism to become so different that it results in the formation of a new species. This process is known as 'speciation.' The new species that has thus evolved is no longer capable of breeding and producing fertile offspring with the original species.

▲ *White tigers are a variation of the Bengal tiger, with different pigmentation genes.*

Evidence of Evolution

Fossils: Most of the evidence for evolution came from fossils (preserved remains unearthed from Earth layers) of organisms that lived during different periods of time.

Peppered Moths: Before the Industrial Revolution in Britain, only the pale variety of peppered moths was common. The mutant moths with black colouring were at a disadvantage as they were easily spotted and eaten by birds. With an increase in pollution, the black variety of moths became better camouflaged compared to their paler counterparts.

Antibiotic Resistance in Microbes: Bacteria and viruses can rapidly evolve and change their outer coats that are targeted by antibiotics, thus gaining antibiotic resistance. This happens due to beneficial mutations that offer an advantage to the mutated species which, in turn, reproduce and make more copies.

▲ *Fossils provide important evidence for evolution.*

▶ *The black variation of peppered moths became common after Industrial Revolution.*

◀ *The quagga is an extinct species resembling a zebra.*

Extinction and Factors

Organisms become extinct due to rapid changes in the climate or environment, excessive predation, new and deadly diseases, and new competitors or loss of habitat. In the present, many species have become extinct, and more are critically endangered due to human activity.

Ecosystems

Ecology is a branch of science that studies the interaction between organisms and their environments. Human beings have not only played a role in threatening biodiversity, but also in taking measures to limit activities that endanger the environment and protect other species.

Ecosystems

The Sun is the source of energy for virtually all organisms and is responsible for sustaining life on the planet. The energy from the sun is harvested by trees, plants, and organisms that are capable of photosynthesis. This energy is passed on to other organisms and cycled continuously.

A community of organisms that live in a certain space and interact with other living organisms as well as the environment is known as an ecosystem. These organisms are usually dependent on one another for food and survival.

Plants compete with other plants for space, water and nutrients. Animals compete for territory, shelter, food and mates. In an ecosystem, where every organism depends on another for pollination, seed dispersal, and food, the removal of even one species will affect the others. This is known as interdependence.

The ideal ecosystem is one in which all the species and environmental factors are in balance and the population size of the species is more or less constant.

▲ *The Sun provides energy for almost all organisms on Earth to survive.*

Biotic and Abiotic Factors

Organisms in any ecosystem depend on biotic (living) and abiotic (non-living) factors.

Biotic factors affecting organisms include:

- Food (as plants or other animals)
- Microbes capable of causing diseases
- Other species that compete for the same food or space
- Predators

Abiotic factors that affect a community are:

- Light
- Temperature
- Moisture
- Soil
- Wind
- Carbon dioxide and oxygen levels

Levels of Organisation

A food chain is described as a linear link of organisms, starting from producers and ending in decomposers. It represents the feeding relationship within a community.

The producers are usually green plants, trees, algae, or phytoplankton species capable of producing glucose from sunlight through photosynthesis. The producers are eaten by primary consumers, the herbivores. The herbivores are in turn eaten by the secondary consumers, the carnivores and omnivores. The secondary consumers are also known as predators and the organisms that they hunt are known as prey. Tertiary consumers are carnivores at the topmost level in a food chain that feed on other carnivores. Decomposers act on the dead matter of living organisms and play a crucial role as scavengers.

In a stable ecosystem, the number of prey and predators rise and fall in cycles.

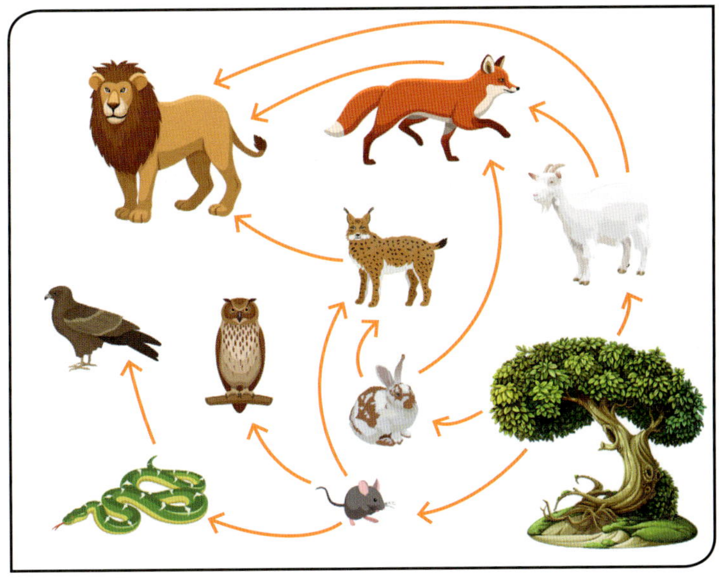

▲ *A food web displays the predators and prey in an environment.*

Fact File

Only about 10 percent of biomass is transferred from one trophic level to another. Respiration and excretion causes loss in biomass.

Trophic Levels

The different levels of feeding habits of organisms in a food chain are the trophic levels. They are represented by numbers, starting at level 1, which consists of the producers and then level 2 with herbivores, and further levels with predators. The apex, or the topmost level, is occupied by one or more carnivore species that have no predators.

Biomass pyramids are useful for representing the amount of biomass at each trophic level.

◀ *Trophic levels represent the producers and consumers.*

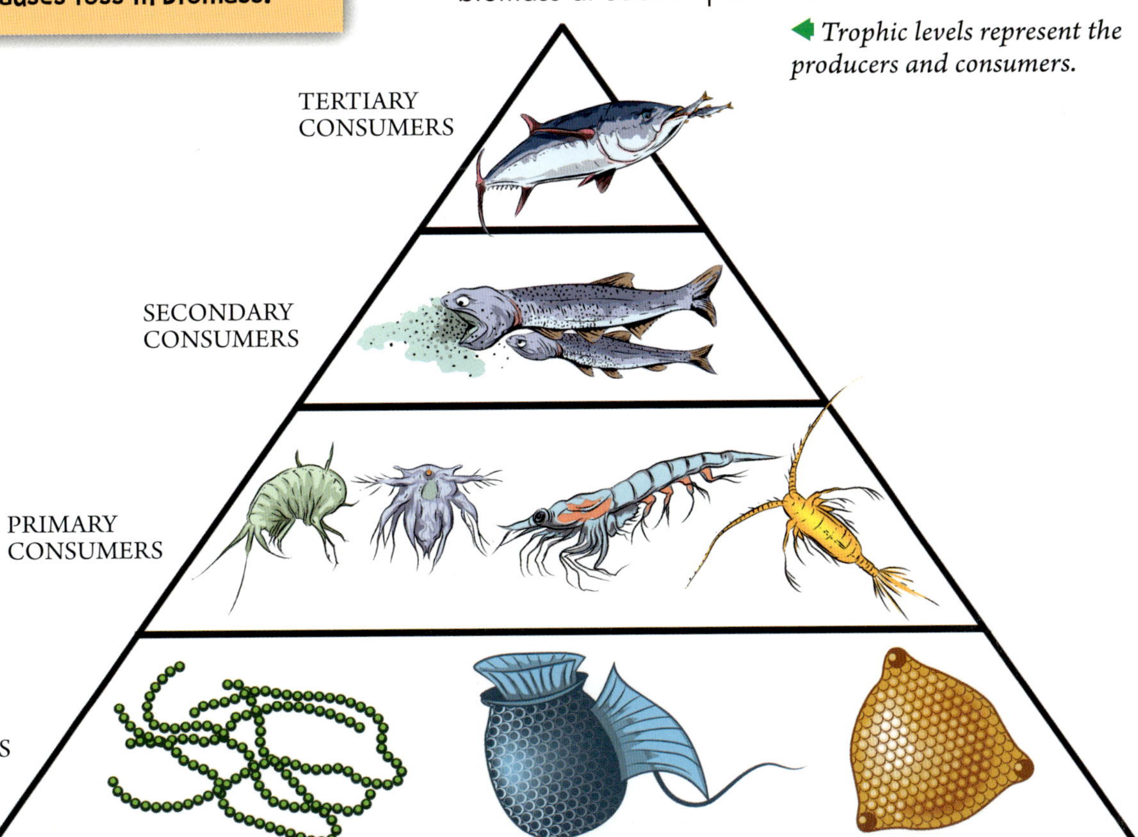

A First Introduction to Science

ENCYCLOPEDIA of LEARNING

DISCOVER
CHEMISTRY

Atomic Structure

All the matter in the universe is made up of atoms. An atom is the smallest and most fundamental part of an element. An atom is made up of protons and neutrons in the nucleus and electrons spinning around it.

▲ *A gold nugget is a pure substance made up only of gold atoms.*

Elements, Compounds and Mixtures

An element is a substance made up of identical atoms. All the atoms in an element have the same atomic number (the number of protons in the nucleus). An element is represented by a chemical symbol. There are more than a hundred known elements discovered so far.

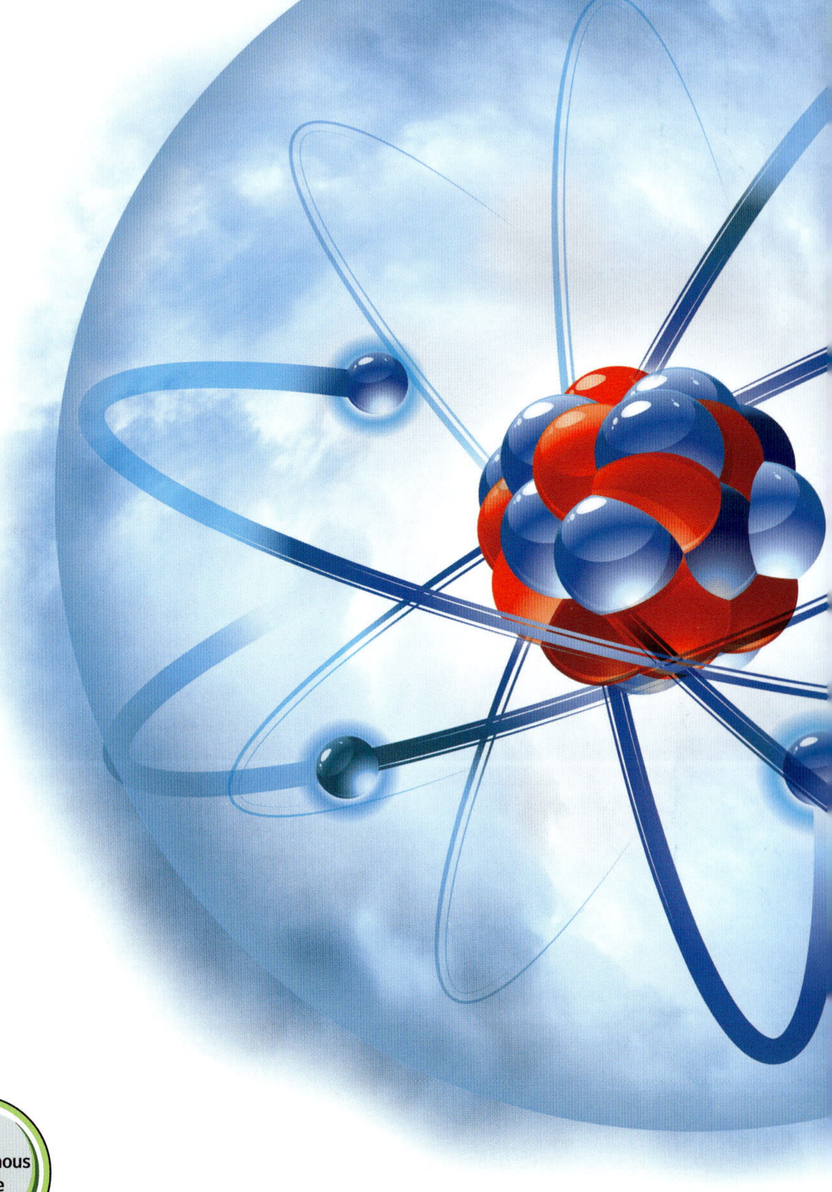

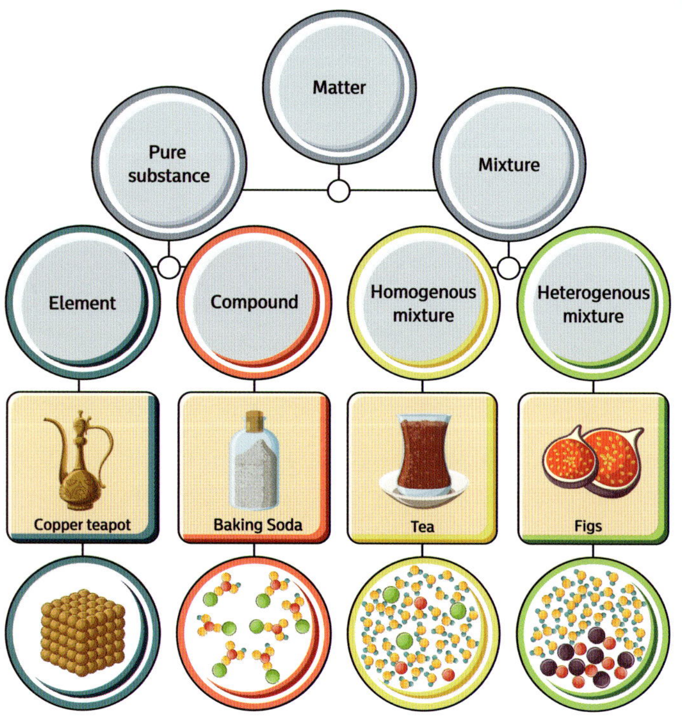

▲ *Matter exists in the form of elements, compounds and mixtures.*

Compounds are formed through the reaction of elements and are made up of two or more elements chemically combined in specific proportions. Once formed, a compound can be separated into its individual elements only through chemical reaction under specific conditions.

A mixture comprises of two or more elements and compounds that are not chemically combined in specific proportions. The chemical properties of each individual component remain unchanged in a mixture. The components of a mixture can be separated through many techniques.

Atom Models

Even after atoms were discovered as the simplest unit of matter, their exact structure was not known. They were thought to be spheres that could not be subdivided. One of the earliest models of an atom was the 'plum pudding' model proposed by J.J. Thomson. According to this proposal, the atom was considered to be a ball of positive charge with negatively charged electrons embedded in it.

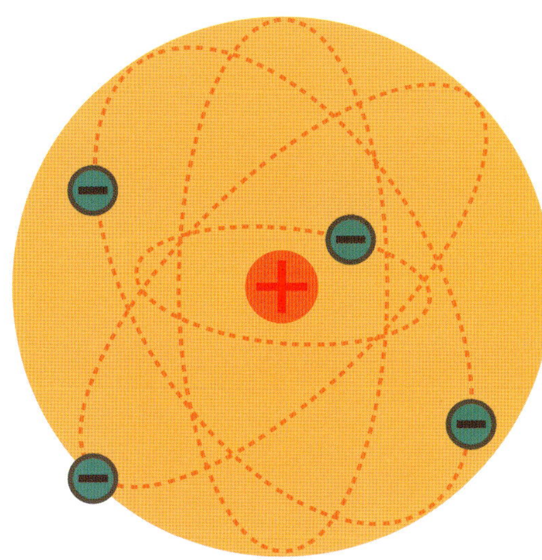

▶ *The plum pudding model described the atom as a sphere of positive charge embedded with negative charges.*

The alpha particle scattering experiment was important in giving a better idea about the nature of atoms. It helped the scientists identify that an atom's positive charge was concentrated in its center. This center was referred to as the nucleus. The nuclear model replaced the plum pudding model.

It was the scientist Niels Bohr who produced a clearer picture of the atom by adopting the nuclear model and adding that the electrons orbited around the nucleus at specific distances.

Much later, further experiments showed that the nucleus consists of smaller particles—the positively charged protons and the neutrally charged neutrons. It was James Chadwick who provided experimental evidence to prove the existence of neutrons apart from protons in the nucleus.

Nature of Atomic Particles

In any atom, the number of electrons is equal to the number of protons in the nucleus. Atoms are minuscule and typically have a radius of about 0.1 nanometre (1 nanometre is equal to 1×10^{-9} metre).

The sum of protons and neutrons is an element's atomic mass, or mass number. The sum of protons or electrons is the atomic number. The electrons revolve around the nucleus in certain energy levels known as shells.

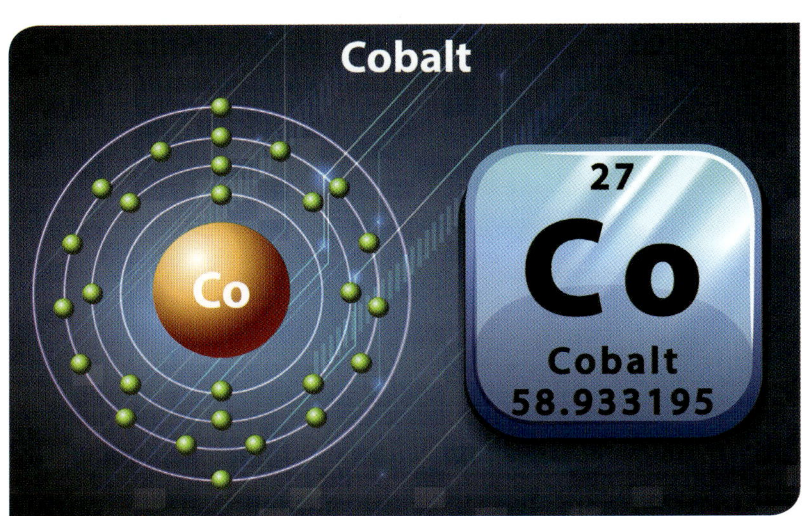

▲ *Cobalt has an atomic number of 27 and mass number of 58.93.*

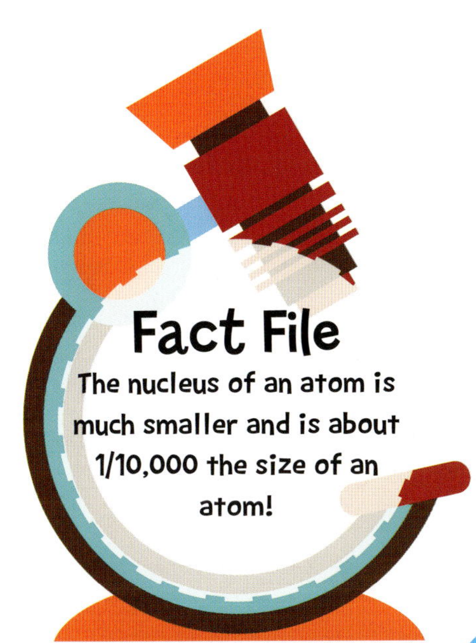

The Periodic Table

The periodic table is a systematic arrangement of the elements known to us. The elements are organised in a way that shows a trend in their physical and chemical properties. A periodic table is so called because similar properties of elements are observed at regular intervals.

History of the Periodic Table

Even though many elements such as gold, platinum, silver and tin were known since ancient times, it is only in the last century that scientists attempted to devise a system to classify the known elements in a useful way. In a way, the discovery of new elements also paved the way for the invention of the periodic table.

Antoine-Laurent de Lavoisier was a French chemist who defined elements as simple substances that cannot be broken down any further. His list included hydrogen, oxygen, nitrogen, phosphorus, mercury, zinc and sulphur. It formed the basis of a modern list of elements.

Another chemist, Johann Wolfgang Döbereiner, listed elements in groups of three based on similarity in physical properties. He called these groups 'triads.' Chlorine, bromine and iodine are an example of a triad. In 1864 an English chemist, John Newlands, classified the 64 known elements at that time into groups of eight that he called 'octaves.'

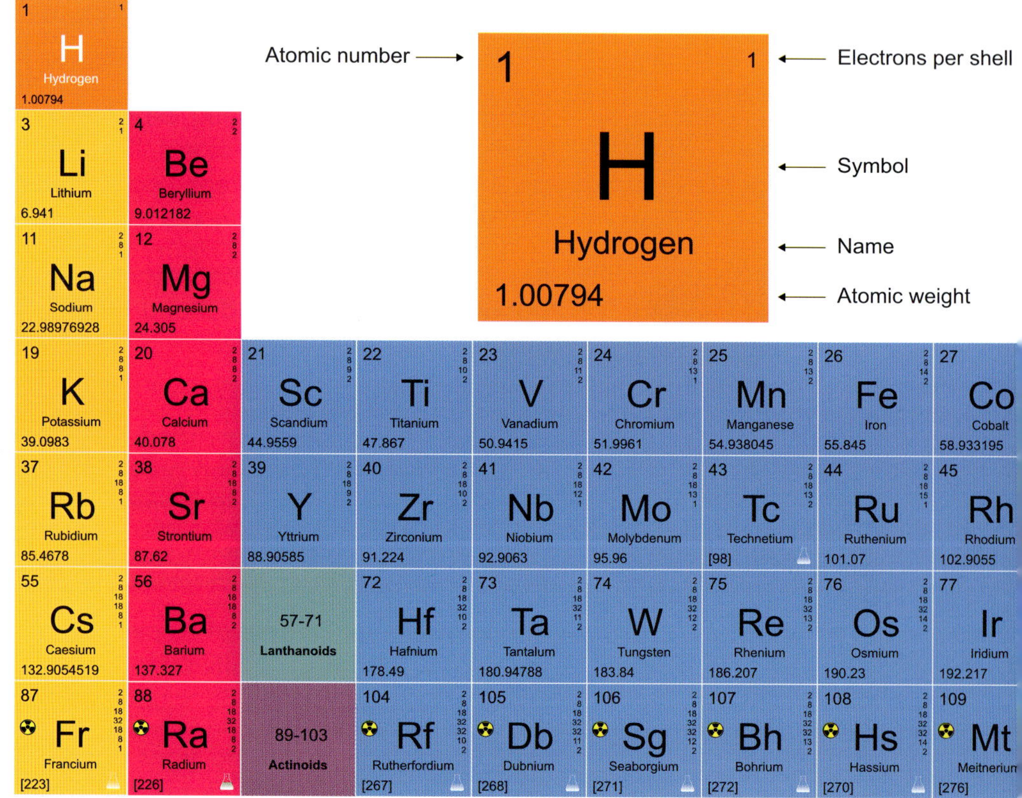

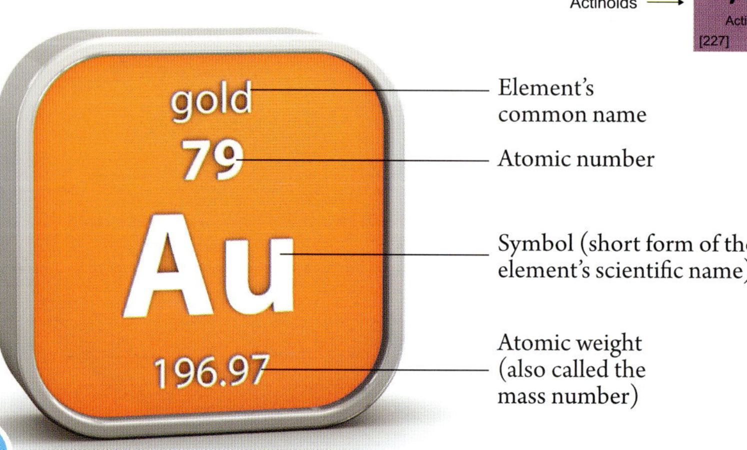

Mendeleev's Classification

It was the Russian chemist Dmitri Mendeleev who first developed a periodic table similar to the modern version we use. Mendeleev arranged the elements in the order of their atomic mass. When arranged in this manner, the elements exhibited a periodicity, or trend in their properties. He discovered that elements with similar chemical properties often had atomic weights that were also similar or in increasing magnitude.

▲ *Dmitri Mendeleev is considered the 'Father of the Periodic Table.'*

Mendeleev was able to predict the properties of a few elements which were yet to be discovered at that time. He left gaps in the table corresponding to the undiscovered elements, which were filled up later. True to his prediction, germanium, gallium, and scandium were discovered and included in the table. Mendeleev's periodic table was published in the year 1869.

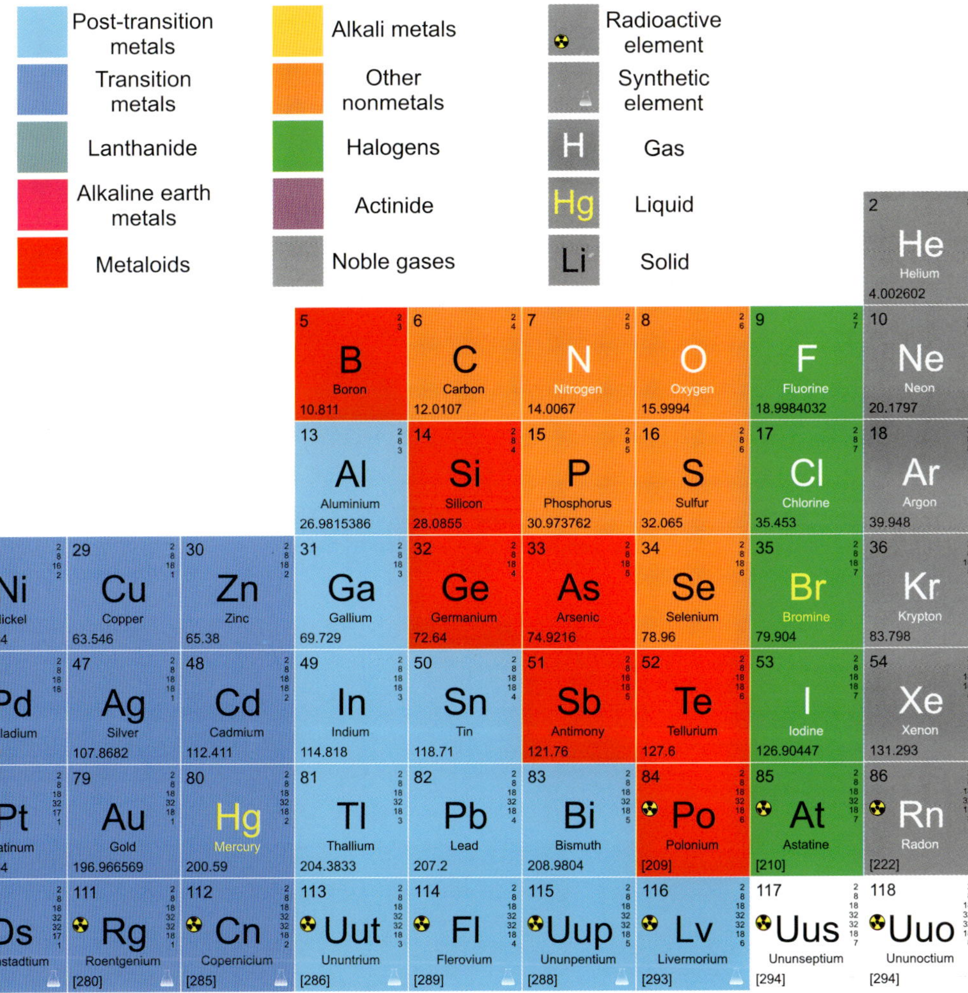

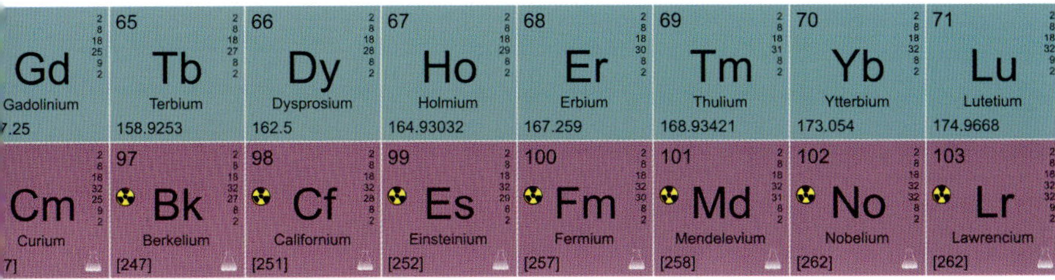

◄ *The element germanium was predicted even before it was discovered.*

Fact File

Hennig Brand, a German merchant, was the first person to discover an element when he produced phosphorus from distilled urine.

Elements of the Periodic Table

In the periodic table, elements with similar chemical properties are placed under a group. Currently, the periodic table has 118 known elements, of which 94 occur naturally while the remaining elements are synthesised only in the laboratory.

Alkali Metals

The alkali metals make up Group 1 of the table. They are some of the most reactive elements because they have large atomic radii and contain a single electron in their outermost shell that is readily donated. Lithium, sodium, potassium, rubidium, caesium, and francium make up the alkali metals found on the left side of the table.

Metals and Nonmetals

Elements that are capable of forming positive ions are referred to as metals, and those that do not form ions are nonmetals. Many of the elements in the periodic table are metals. They are mostly found at the left and toward the bottom of the periodic table. Nonmetals occur on the right and top portion of the table.

Alkaline Earth Metals

There are six elements in the alkaline earth metals group—beryllium, magnesium, calcium, strontium, barium, and radium. Like the alkali metals, they are highly reactive. Among these, radium is radioactive, that is, it has an unstable nucleus that decays and emits radiation.

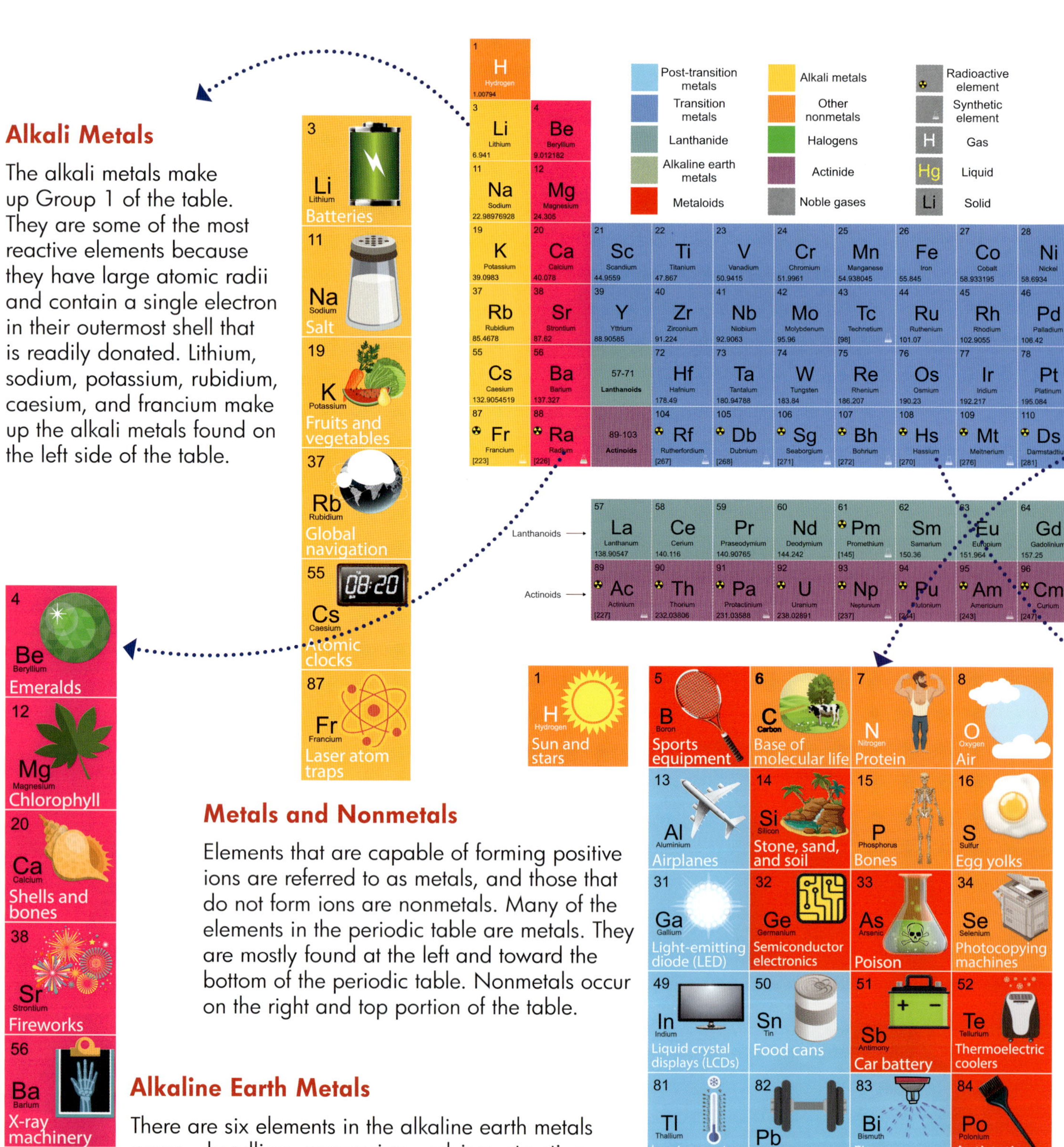

Inert Gases

Group 0 of the periodic table contains the noble gases, also known by the names 'inert gases' or 'rare gases.' The members of this group have eight electrons in their outermost shell (the exception being helium, which has two electrons), which gives these elements their stability and non-reactive nature. Helium, neon, argon, krypton, xenon, and radon make up this group.

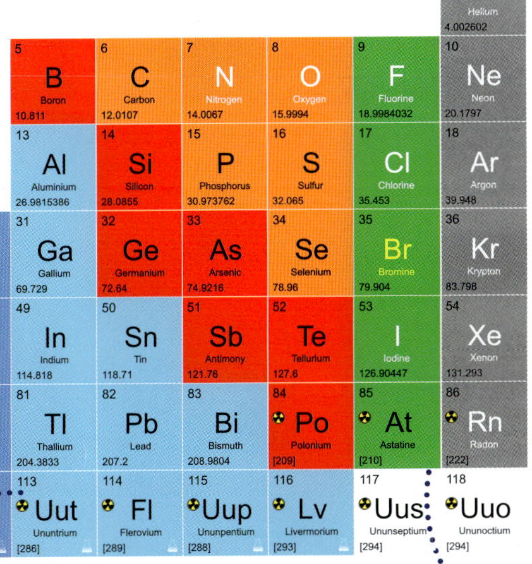

Halogens

The elements in Group 7 of the periodic table are known as the halogens. The halogens contain seven electrons in their outermost shell. Fluorine, chlorine, bromine, iodine, and astatine are the halogens. All halogens exist as a molecule (a pair of atoms). When a halogen combines with another element, the product is known as a halide. Sodium chloride, or common salt, is a halide. Halogen lamps typically contain a tungsten filament within a glass container, with inert gas and a small quantity of halogen like bromine or iodine.

Lanthanides and Actinides

The lanthanides and actinides are a set of elements that are located separately below the main table. Consisting of 30 elements, the group includes many that are rarely found on Earth.

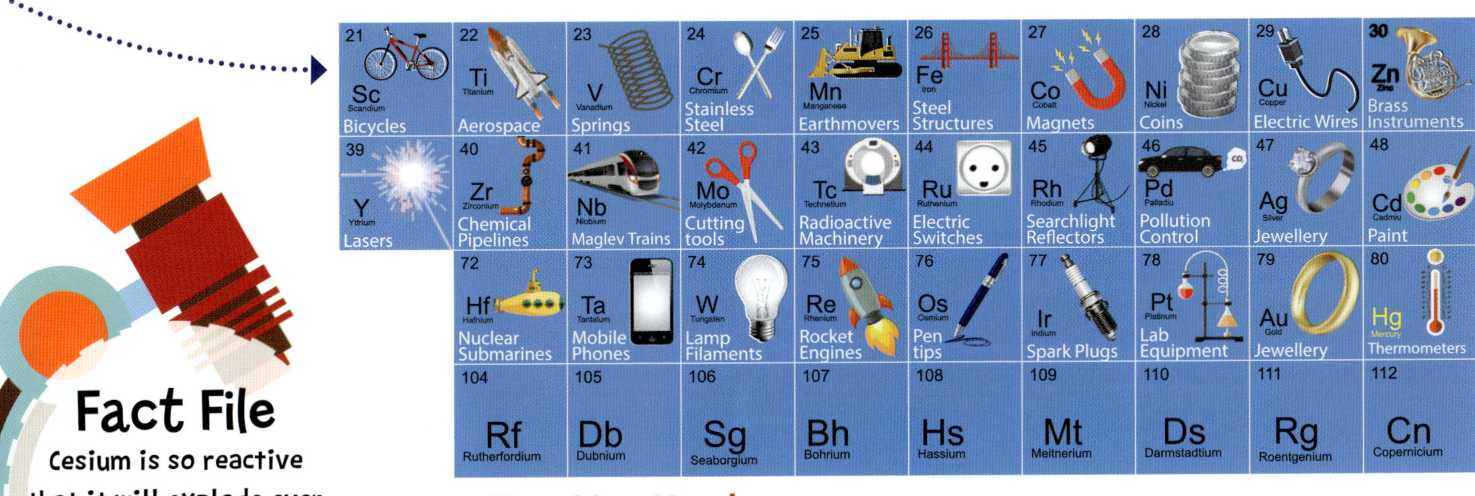

Transition Metals

The transition metals have properties of metals but are different from the alkali metals listed under Group 1. They consist of the elements between Groups 2 and 3. Iron, copper, gold and silver are the most well-known transition metals.

Fact File

Cesium is so reactive that it will explode even if it comes in contact with ice!

Chemical Bonds

Atoms can arrange in different ways and form molecules because of their ability to form chemical bonds. The knowledge of bonding can help scientists produce new materials with desirable properties.

Formation of a Chemical Bond

When atoms come close to one another, the electrons in the outermost shells distribute themselves in such a manner that they use the lowest energy levels possible as opposed to any other alternative arrangement.

If the total energy of the combination of two atoms is lower than that of the individual components, then the atoms will combine by forming a chemical bond. The type of bond that will form between two elements can be predicted based on their location in the periodic table.

Types of Chemical Bonds

There are four major types of chemical bonds—covalent, ionic, metallic, and hydrogen. Covalent bonds form between nonmetallic elements. Ionic bonds form between oppositely charged ions. Metallic bond forms between metallic compounds and alloys.

Covalent Bond

A covalent bond is formed when atoms share electrons. The bonds between these atoms are typically very strong. Small molecules and large polymers can be formed through covalent bonds.

Diamond is an example of a giant covalent structure. The carbon atoms in diamond are held together through strong covalent bonds, making it one of the strongest materials in the world.

▲ *A carbon atom shares its electrons with four hydrogen atoms to form methane.*

Metallic Bond

Metals are made up of massive structures of atoms arranged in a regular pattern. The electrons in the outer shell of the metal atoms are capable of moving freely throughout the whole structure. The sharing of electrons across the entire structure confers the strength of metallic bonds.

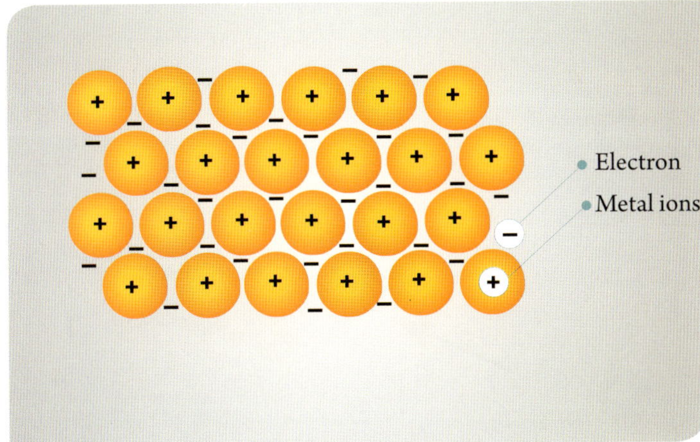

▲ *The strength of a metal comes from the strong metallic bonding.*

Hydrogen Bond

A hydrogen bond is formed between a hydrogen atom and another atom with a lone pair of electrons. Hydrogen bonds are weaker than covalent or ionic bonds. Hydrogen bonds are commonly found in DNA and proteins.

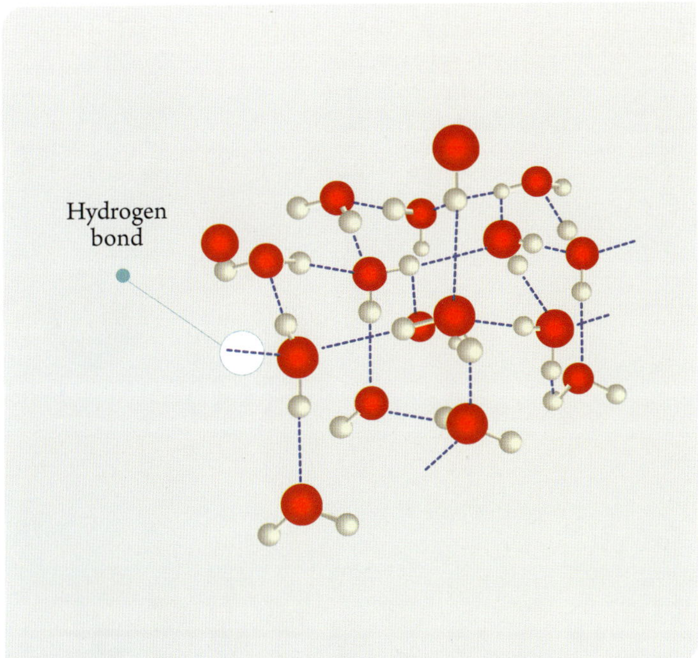

▲ *Hydrogen bonds confer shape and function to biomolecules like DNA and proteins.*

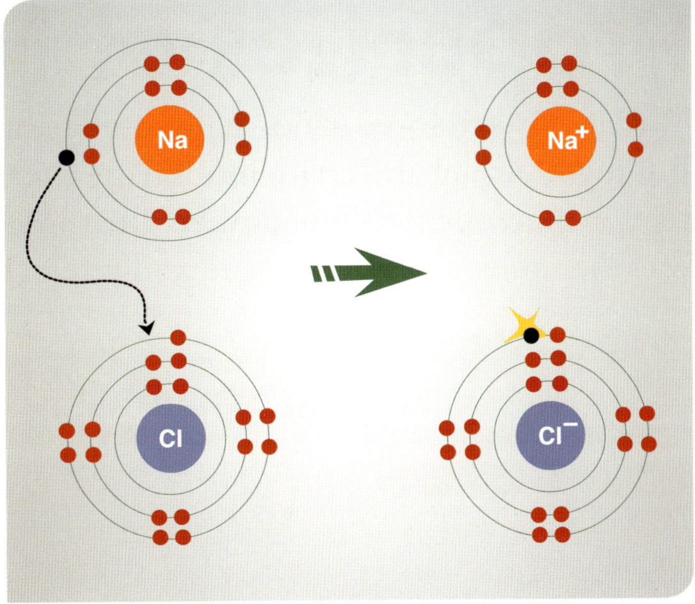

▲ *Sodium and chlorine combine through ionic bonding to form common salt.*

Ionic Bond

When a metal and a nonmetal interact, the electrons in the outer shell of the metal atoms are transferred to the nonmetal. By losing the electrons, metals become positively charged ions and the nonmetals that accept electrons become negatively charged ions. Ionic compounds are held together by strong electrostatic forces of attraction between the opposite charges. Common salt (sodium chloride) is formed through ionic bonding.

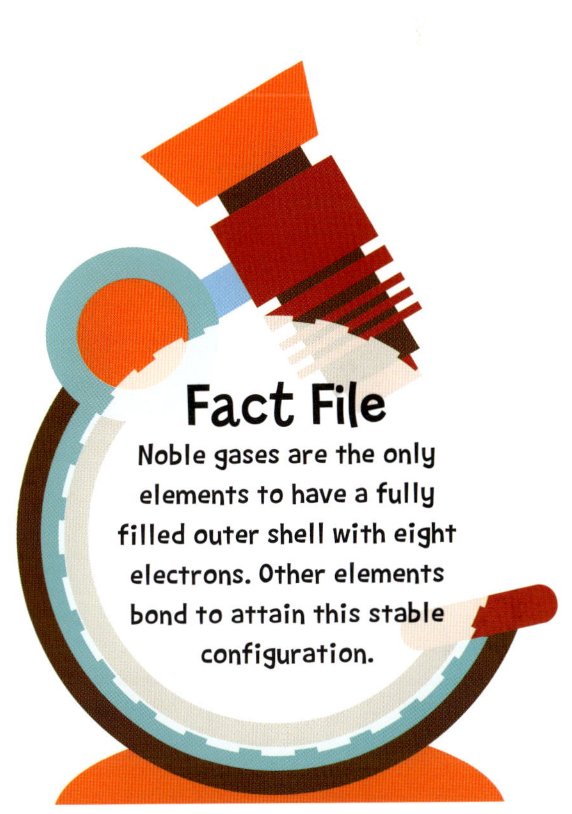

Properties of Matter

Matter exists in three major states on Earth: solid, liquid and gas. Boiling, freezing and condensation are the three methods of converting matter from one form to another. The three states of matter differ in the way the molecules are arranged and interact with each other.

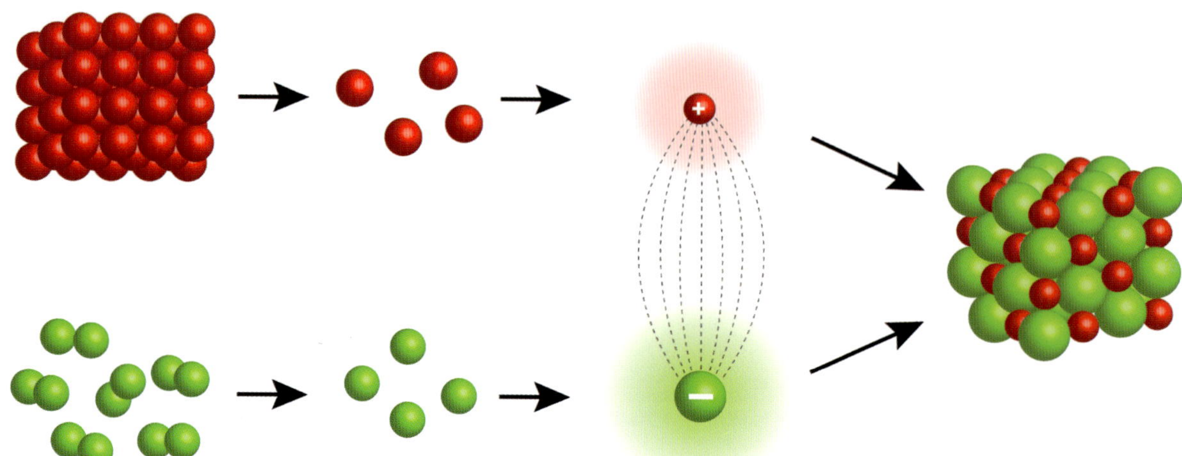

A regular lattice structure is a characteristic feature of ionic compounds.

Properties of Different Matter

Depending on the type of matter, the properties vary greatly.

Ionic compounds are highly regular structures made up of 'lattices' in which strong electrostatic forces hold oppositely charged ions from all directions, conferring strength and rigidity. As a result, ionic compounds have high melting and boiling points; they have to be heated to a very high temperature, and large amounts of energy are needed to break the strong bonds. Ionic compounds are capable of conducting electricity when dissolved in water because they can move freely and allow flow of charge.

Polymers are large molecules made up of molecules with atoms linked to other atoms through strong covalent bonds. As a result of the intermolecular forces between the molecules, polymers are relatively strong and are solid at room temperature. There are many naturally occurring polymers like cellulose, proteins and DNA. Teflon is an example of an artificial polymer, used in making nonstick wares.

Small molecules are most commonly found in liquids and gases. Oxygen, nitrogen, hydrogen, and water are examples of small molecules. They have very low melting and boiling points, as it is easy to break apart the weak bonds that hold the atoms together. The intermolecular forces increase with increasing size of molecules. Since the molecules do not have any overall electric charge (positive or negative), they do not conduct electricity.

Water is an example of a small molecule that is abundant on Earth.

Polymers are made of hundreds and thousands of repeating units.

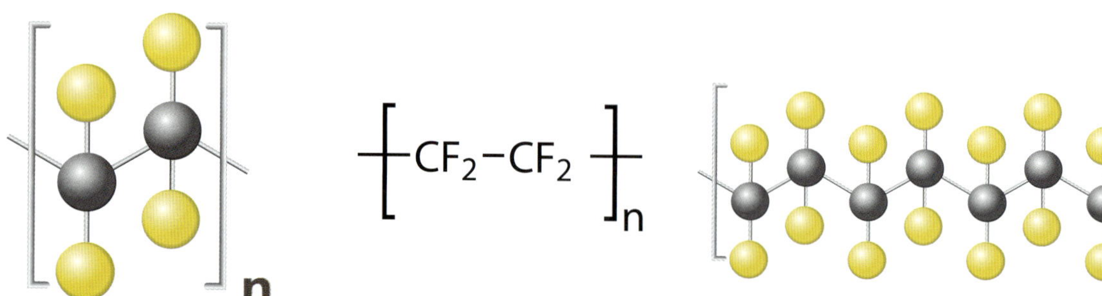

Giant covalent structures are solids with very high melting points. As the name suggests, the atoms in such structures are linked together by strong covalent bonds. Some of the best examples of giant covalent structures are graphite, diamond and silica.

Metals and alloys are made up of massive structures of atoms held together by strong metallic bonds. In pure metals like gold or silver, atoms are arranged in layers, allowing them to be bent and shaped. Metals have high melting and boiling points. Since pure metals are soft, they are usually mixed with other metals to make alloys that are harder and more useful. Metals are good conductors of heat and electricity, as the electrons in the metal can move around and carry electrical charges or thermal energy across the surface.

▲ *Metals like copper conduct electricity and are used in electric cables.*

Carbon Compounds

Diamond is formed when a carbon atom forms four covalent bonds with other carbon atoms, giving rise to a massive covalent structure that is very strong. As a result, diamond is one of the hardest substances found on earth. It has a very high melting point.

Graphite is formed when carbon forms three covalent bonds with three carbon atoms, forming a layer of hexagonal rings which do not have covalent bonds between the layers. Graphite, though strong, is not as strong as diamond with all four electrons in each atom linked through covalent bonds.

▲ *Diamond is one of the hardest substances occurring naturally on Earth.*

Fullerenes are hollow shapes made up of carbon atoms arranged as hexagonal rings. The first fullerene discovered was known as buckminsterfullerene, which is spherical in shape.

Carbon nanotubes are cylindrical structures with large lengths and small diameters with properties useful in making nanomaterial and in nanotechnology and electronics.

▲ *A fullerene is a spherical structure made of a hexagonal arrangement of carbon atoms.*

Fact File

Graphene is a structure made up of a single layer of graphite and is used in electronics.

Chemical Changes

A systematic approach is used for testing the reactions of different elements and compounds to observe different chemical changes. This knowledge helps scientists predict exactly how substances will react, and helps develop different materials and industrial chemical processes.

Reactive Elements

Not all elements interact with other substances and produce reaction. Rare gases (Group 0), which includes helium, neon, argon, krypton, and xenon, do not usually interact with other substances and for this reason they are also referred to as 'inert gases.'

▲ *Heliox is a mixture of helium and oxygen used by professional deep-sea divers who dive to depths of 300 feet or more.*

Metals, particularly the alkali metals, are very reactive and interact with water, acids, and many other substances. They readily undergo chemical reactions and this reactivity has led to extensive study of their usefulness.

The reactivity of an element depends on its atomic structure. Metals usually have one or more free electrons in the final orbit that can interact with other atoms.

When metals react with other substances, the metal atoms lose one or more electrons and become positive ions. How reactive a metal is depends on its tendency to form positive ions. Arranged in their order of reactivity are caesium, rubidium, potassium, sodium, lithium, calcium, magnesium, zinc, iron and copper.

Certain nonmetals like hydrogen and carbon are also included in the list of reactive elements, as they readily react with many substances.

▲ *Alkali metals are very reactive—sodium, for instance, explodes upon contact with water.*

Elements undergo oxidation and reduction. Oxidation is the process by which electrons are lost, while reduction results in the gain of electrons. Sometimes oxidation and reduction occur in the same reaction, and this is known as a redox reaction. One substance gets oxidised by losing electrons while the other substance accepts electrons and gets reduced.

Metals react with oxygen to form metal oxides. They also react with water and acids. When metals react with alkali (base), they form the respective salt and hydrogen.

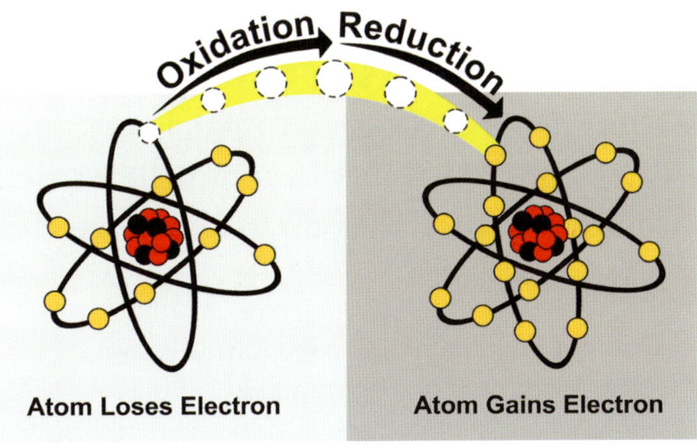

▲ A redox reaction results in the oxidation of one substance and the reduction of another.

Salts

Soluble salts are formed when insoluble solid substances are mixed with acids. The insoluble substance could be a metal oxide, hydroxide or carbonate. Salt solutions can be crystallised to produce solid salts.

When acids and bases interact with each other, they get neutralised and form salt and water. The volume of acid and alkali solution interaction can be measured in the laboratory using titration.

◄ The reaction of an acid and a base results in the formation of a salt.

Fact File

Gold is an inert metal that does not readily react with most substances.

The pH Scale

Acids produce hydrogen ions (H+) when dissolved in water while aqueous solutions of alkali or base contain hydroxide ions (OH-). The pH scale, ranging from 0 to 14, measures whether a solution is acidic or basic.

A solution with pH 7 is considered to be neutral. Those that have a pH value less than 7 are acidic while those over 7 are basic.

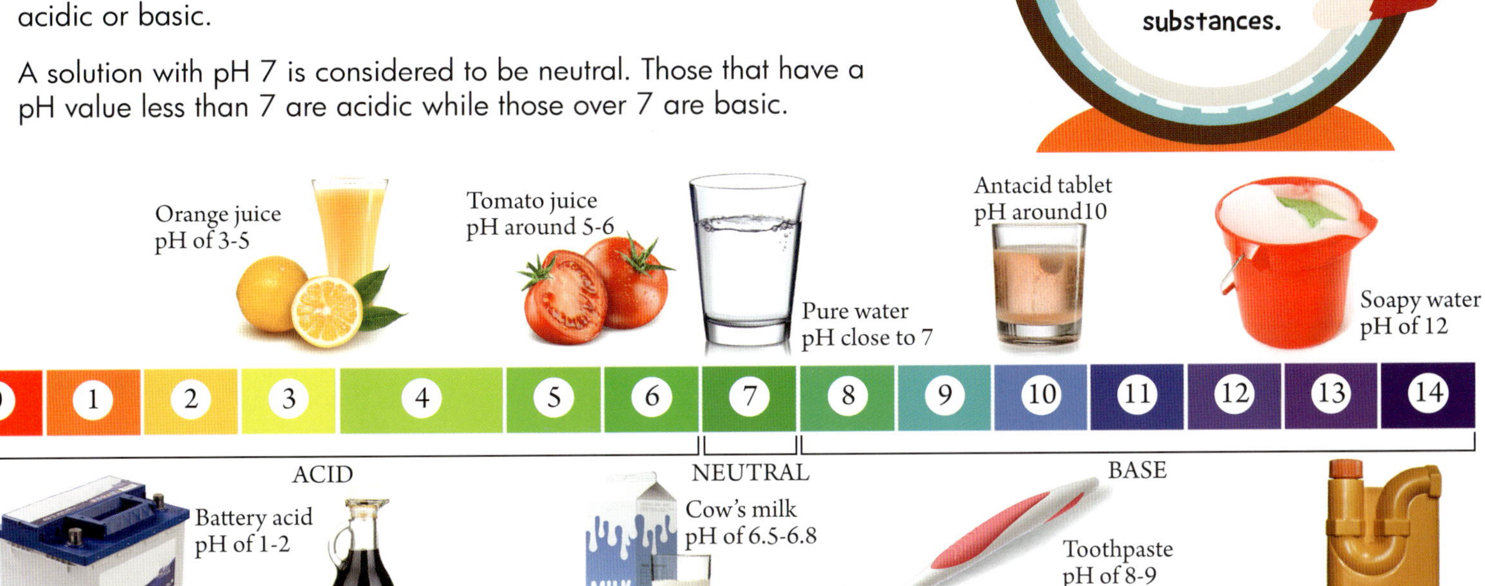

Electrolysis

Electrolysis is the process by which an ionic compound that is dissolved in water gains the ability to conduct electricity. This is possible due to the ions in the solution that are free to move about.

Electrolysis Process

The dissolved liquid containing the ions is known as the electrolyte. When an electric current is passed through the electrolyte solution, the ions move to the electrodes depending on their charge. Positive ions move toward the negative terminal, also known as the cathode. Negative ions move toward the positive electrode, called the anode. As the ions get discharged at the electrodes, they produce elements and this process is known as electrolysis.

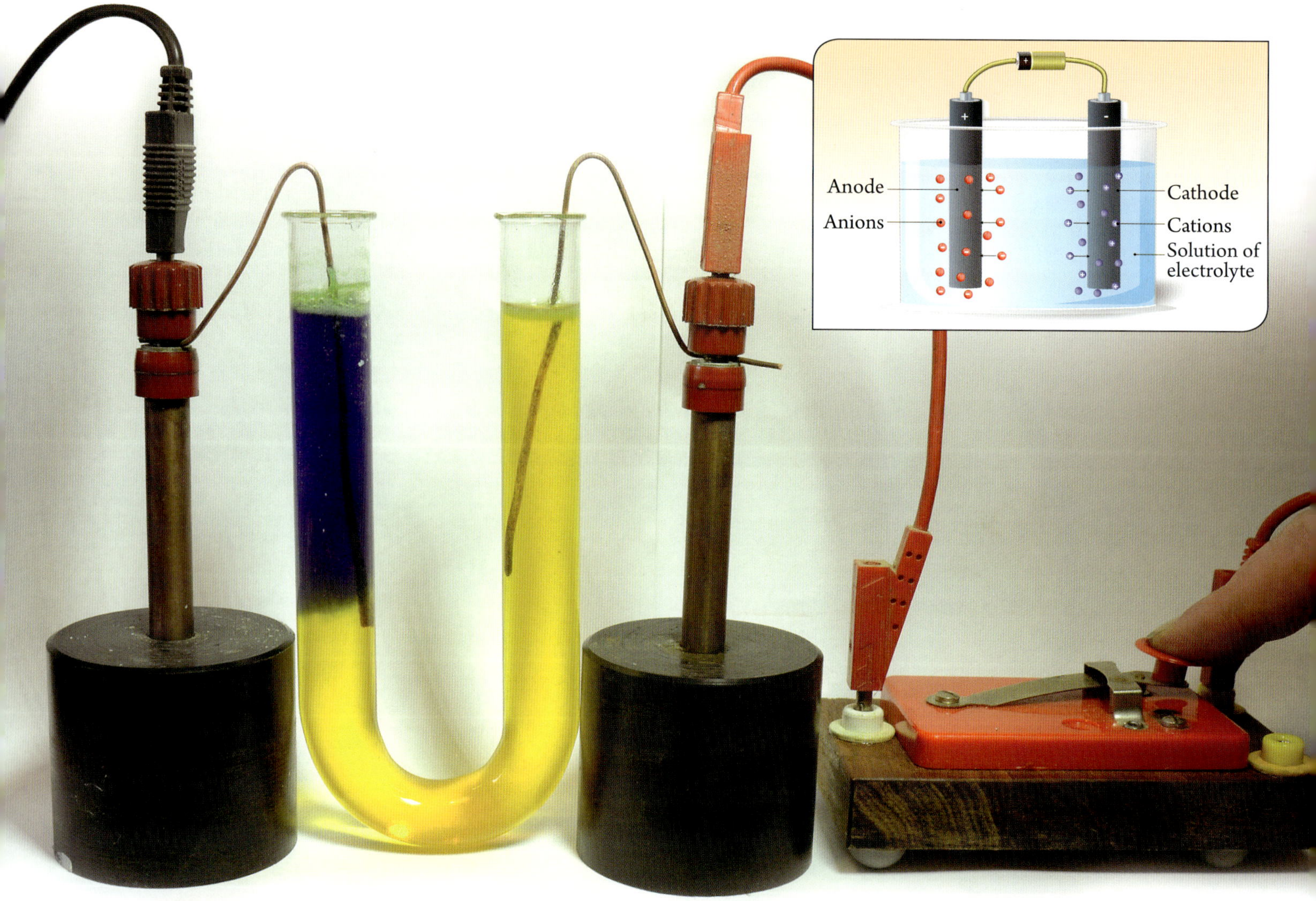

Electrolysis of Aqueous Solutions

Water cannot conduct electricity unless it contains ions. When an ionic compound is dissolved in water, the aqueous solution can be used for conducting electrolysis. Inert or nonreactive electrodes are used. At the cathode, positively charged ions gain electrons and such a reaction is reduction. At the anode, negatively charged ions lose electrons and this process is known as oxidation.

◄ *Electrolysis can be conducted using a simple apparatus in the laboratory.*

Electrolysis of Molten Ionic Compounds

When an ionic compound undergoes electrolysis in its molten state using inert electrodes, it results in the metal being produced at the cathode and the nonmetal being produced at the anode. An example of a molten ionic compound is lead bromide. Lead, as the metal, is produced at the cathode while bromine is produced at the anode.

Metal Extraction

Electrolysis is useful in the extraction of metals. If the metal is too reactive to be traditionally extracted by reacting with carbon, electrolysis is the preferred option. Aluminium is produced by electrolysis when aluminium oxide and cryolite undergo electrolysis when using carbon as the positive electrode.

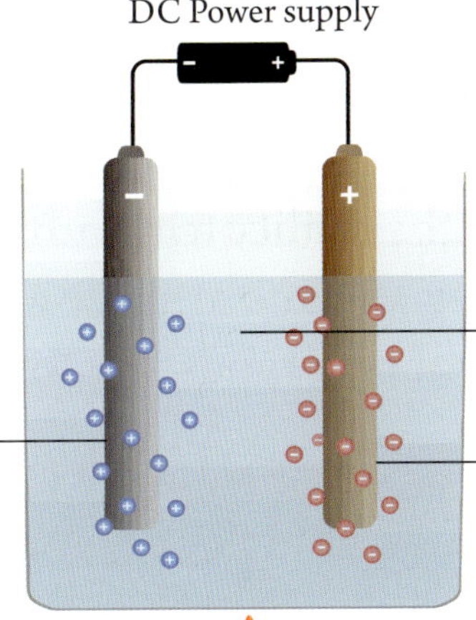

▲ *Electrolysis of lead bromide results in production of lead in the cathode and bromine at the anode.*

Uses of Electrolysis

Many metals like aluminium, magnesium, sodium, and calcium are produced through the process of electrolysis. Other metals like gold, silver, and copper are purified through this process. Hydrogen is produced by the electrolysis of water and used as the fuel in fuel cells.

Electroplating

Electroplating is the process by which a metallic object is coated with a thin layer of another metal through the process of electrolysis. The process is done by passing electric current through an electrolyte solution. The two electrodes are metals, and the metal that is to be coated over the object is used as the electrolyte solution.

If a brass spoon is to be coated with copper, the brass spoon is the cathode, copper is the anode, and copper sulphate solution is the solution through which electric current is passed through. As the copper ions leach out of the solution, the brass spoon will get coated with a thin layer of copper.

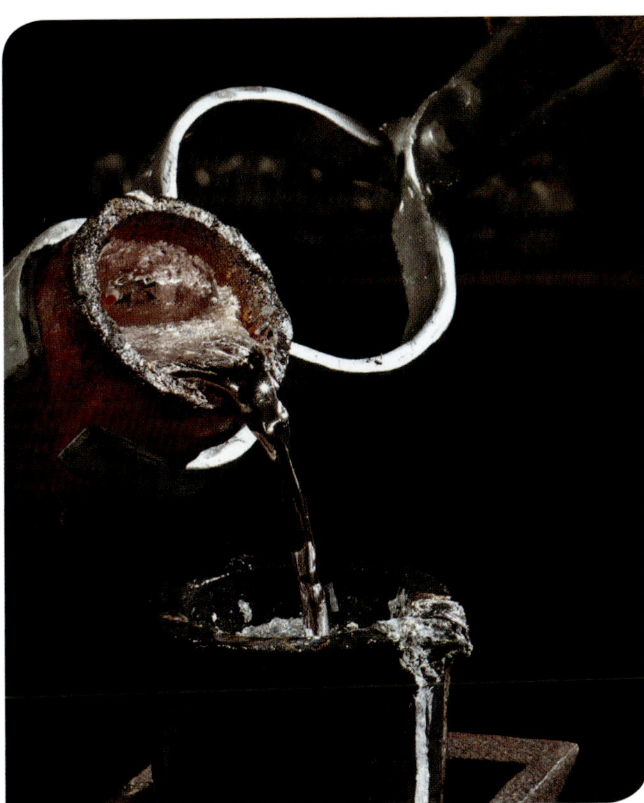

▲ *Aluminium is one of the metals produced through the process of electrolysis.*

Fact File

Did you know that astronauts, and divers in submarines, use oxygen obtained through the electrolysis process?

▶ *Electroplating can be used for producing attractive cutlery.*

Energy Changes

Energy changes occur as a normal effect of chemical reactions. When elements interact with each other, energy is transferred due to breaking and re-formation of chemical bonds. The energy change is one of two types, exothermic or endothermic.

Chemical Reaction and Energy Change

When chemical reactions occur, energy is conserved so that the amount of energy at the end of a chemical reaction is the same as before the reaction. A reaction can occur only when the reacting particles collide with each other and possess sufficient energy. The minimum energy needed by particles to react is known as the activation energy.

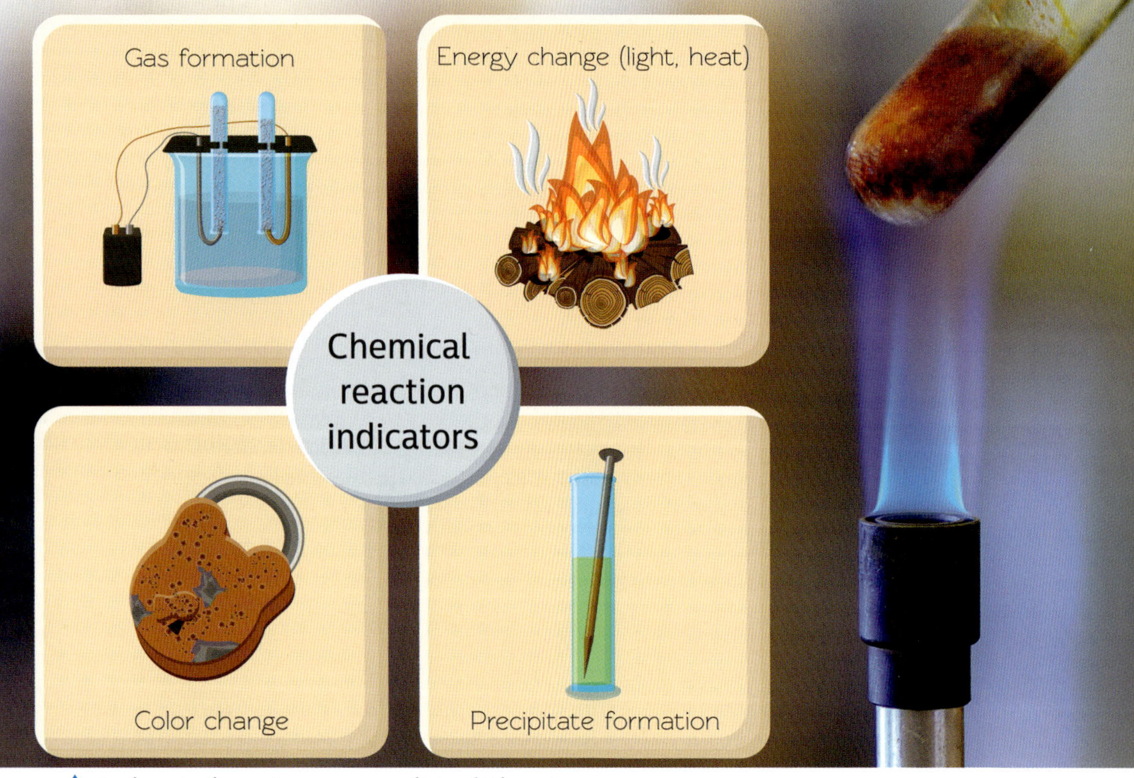

▲ *A chemical reaction can result in different observable results.*

A reaction profile gives information about the relative energies of the reactants and the products, the activation energy, and the overall energy change of the reaction.

When a chemical reaction occurs, the following events occur:

1. Energy is supplied to break bonds in the reactants.

2. Energy is released when the bonds in the products are formed.

3. The energy that is required to break bonds and the energy released when bonds are formed can be calculated from bond energies.

4. The overall energy change of a reaction is the difference between the sum of the energy needed to break the bonds in reactants and the energy released when bonds are formed in products.

5. In an exothermic reaction, the energy released while forming new bonds is greater than the energy needed to break existing bonds.

6. In an endothermic reaction, the energy needed to break existing bonds is greater than the energy released from forming new bonds.

Exothermic and Endothermic Reaction

An exothermic reaction is one in which energy is transferred to the surroundings. As a result, there is an increase in the temperature of the surroundings. In an endothermic reaction, energy is taken up from the surroundings and as a result the temperature decreases.

Cells and Batteries

Cells contain chemicals that can react and produce electricity. A simple cell can be made by connecting two different metals in the presence of an electrolyte. A battery usually consists of two or more cells connected together in a series so that it can provide a higher voltage.

In nonrechargeable cells, the chemical reactions halt when one of the reactants is completely used up. Alkaline batteries are examples of nonrechargeable batteries. Once they're used up, they are discarded. Rechargeable batteries can be used again and again or recharged because the chemical reaction is reversed when supplied with an electric current. Such batteries can be placed in a battery charger unit and connected to a power outlet for recharging.

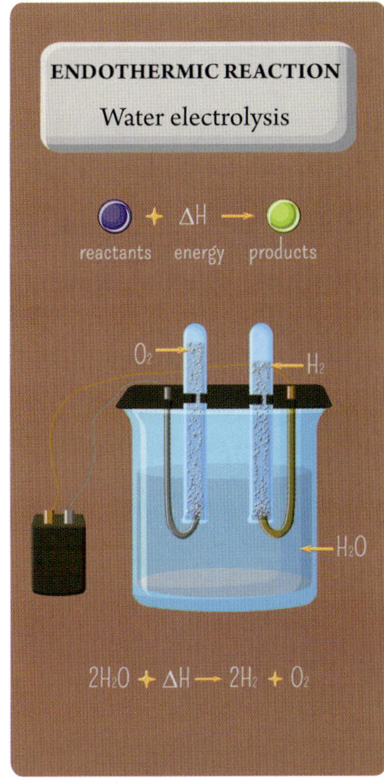

▲ *An exothermic reaction releases energy while an endothermic reaction takes up energy.*

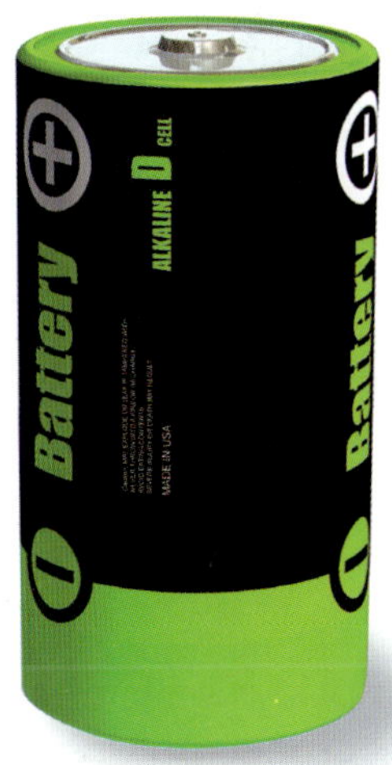

▲ *Rechargeable batteries are widely used for powering different electronic equipment.*

◄ *Electrochemical reaction is the primary working principle of fuel cells.*

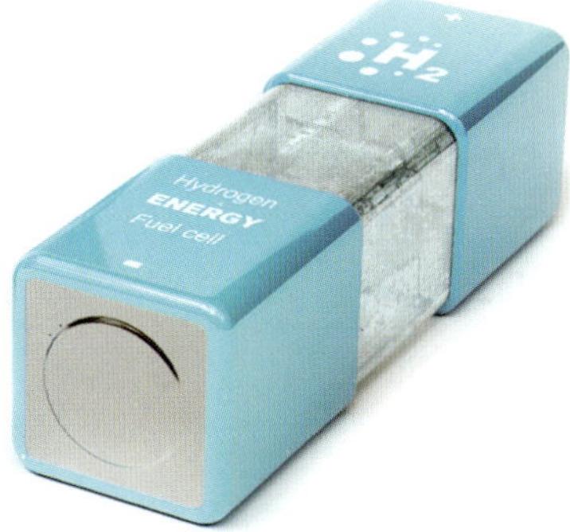

Fuel cells consist of a supply of fuel like hydrogen and oxygen or air. The fuel undergoes electrochemical reaction and produces a potential difference. Fuel cells are an alternative to regular cells and batteries.

Fact File

The smallest battery in the world is about the size of a grain of sand and was made using a 3-D printer.

Chemical Reactions

Different chemical reactions occur, each at a different rate. Chemical reactions can be manipulated to make them occur slower or faster than usual. Scientists study the different variables that affect the yield of product so that it will be useful when applied at a large-scale industrial level.

Rate of Chemical Reactions

The rate of a chemical reaction is measured by knowing the quantity of reactants and the quantity of the product formed over a given time. The factors that affect the rate of a reaction are: concentration of reacting liquids, pressure of reacting gases, or surface area of reacting solids; temperature; and the presence of catalysts.

Collision Theory

The collision theory is useful in identifying how different factors play a role in the rate of a chemical reaction. Based on this theory, a chemical reaction can occur only when the reactant molecules collide with each other with sufficient energy. This minimum energy needed for the reaction to occur is known as activation energy.

When the concentration, volume, or surface area of the reactants is increased, the frequency of collision—and thus the rate of the reaction—increases. When the temperature of the reaction is increased, the collisions become more energetic and thus it increases the rate of the reaction.

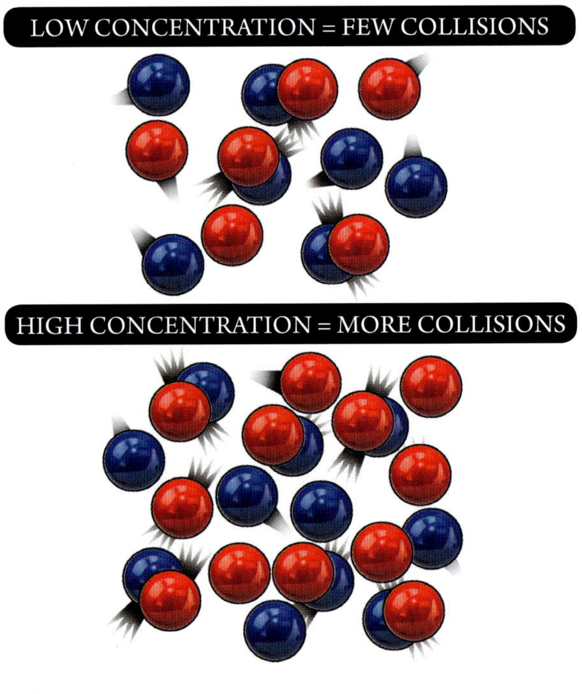

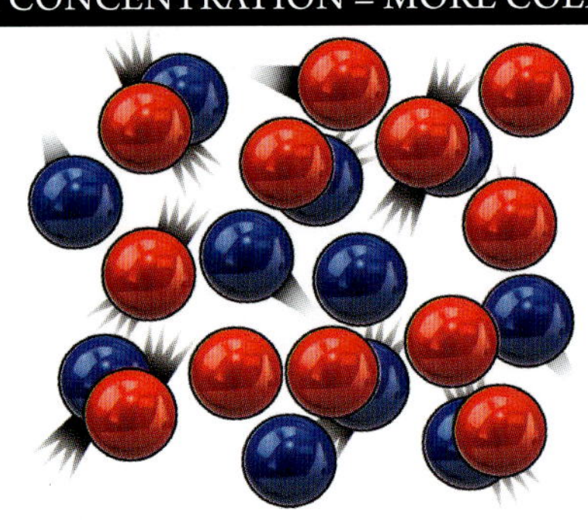

▲ *The frequency of molecular collision determines the rate of a reaction.*

Catalysts

Catalysts are substances that increase the rate of chemical reaction without getting used up. Different chemical reactions need different catalysts. Enzymes are the most important catalysts in biological systems.

Catalysts can speed up a chemical reaction by providing an alternative pathway for the reaction to occur with lower activation energy. Not all catalysts speed up a reaction. Catalysts that slow a reaction are called inhibitors.

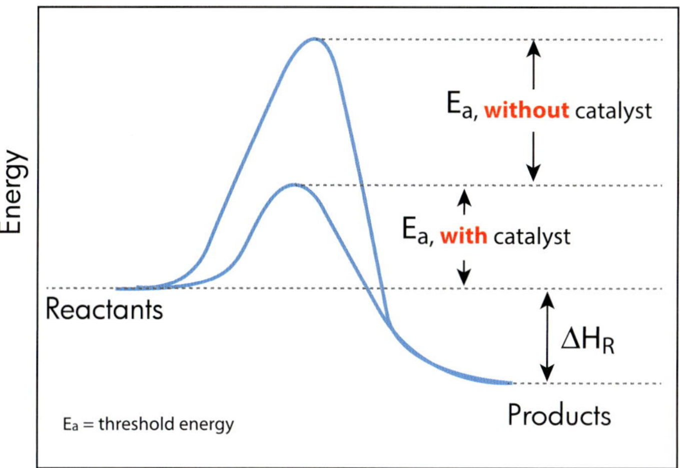

▲ *Catalysts are used to increase the speed or rate of a reaction, as seen in the graph.*

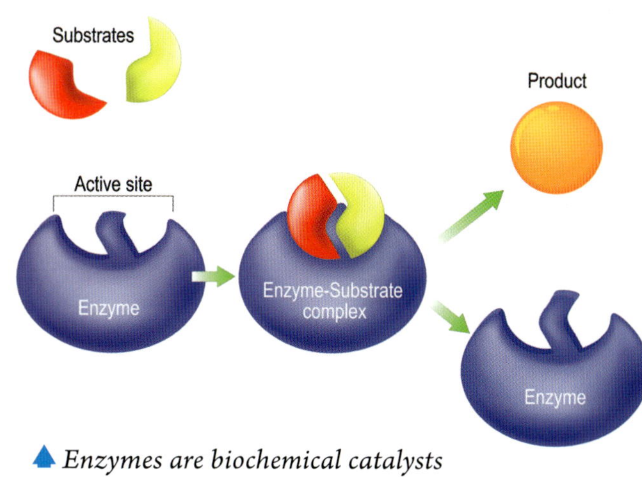

▲ *Enzymes are biochemical catalysts that are crucial for many life processes.*

Reversible and Irreversible Reactions

In certain chemical reactions, the products that are formed can react to produce the original reactants. Such a reaction is known as a reversible reaction. Chemical reactions in which the products formed cannot produce the original reactants under any circumstance are known as irreversible reactions.

It is also true that if a reversible reaction is exothermic in one direction, it is endothermic in the reverse direction. Different conditions like temperature, pressure, and concentration of reactants or products can have an effect on the rate of the reaction.

REVERSIBLE REACTIONS

IRREVERSIBLE REACTIONS

▲ *Reversible and irreversible reactions can be observed in common everyday examples.*

Organic Compounds – Hydrocarbons

Organic compounds are made up of carbon bonded with other elements, most commonly hydrogen, oxygen, and nitrogen. There are many types of organic compounds because of the ability of carbon to combine with other atoms to form different families of compounds.

Common Organic Compounds

Organic compounds make up a major portion of living organisms and are crucial for all biological activities. Many organic compounds are also synthesised artificially or extracted for different purposes. Some of the important organic compounds include:

- Fossil fuels
- Pharmaceuticals
- Perfumes
- Flavouring substances
- Dyes
- Detergents

Hydrocarbons and Crude Oil

Crude oil is formed from the biomass buried under the Earth's surface millions of years ago. It is a mixture of different compounds, most of which are known as hydrocarbons. Hydrocarbons are molecules made up of only carbon and hydrogen atoms.

Alkanes are the most common type of hydrocarbons. Alkanes are represented by the general chemical formula C_nH_{2n+2}. The first four members of the alkane family are:

- Methane (CH_4)
- Ethane (C_2H_6)
- Propane (C_3H_8)
- Butane (C_4H_{10})

◄ Crude oil is pumped out from oil wells and distilled into different products.

Separation of Hydrocarbons

The hydrocarbons in crude oil are separated through a method called fractional distillation. The hydrocarbons in the oil are separated into fractions, each containing a similar number of carbon atoms. Petrol, diesel, kerosene, fuel oil, liquefied petroleum gas, and other products are obtained from the distillation of crude oil.

The physical and chemical properties of hydrocarbons depend largely on the size of the molecules. The boiling point, viscosity, and flammability of hydrocarbons increase with molecular size.

The properties of hydrocarbons also decide how they are used as fuels and how much energy they release upon heating. The complete combustion of hydrocarbons yields water and carbon dioxide.

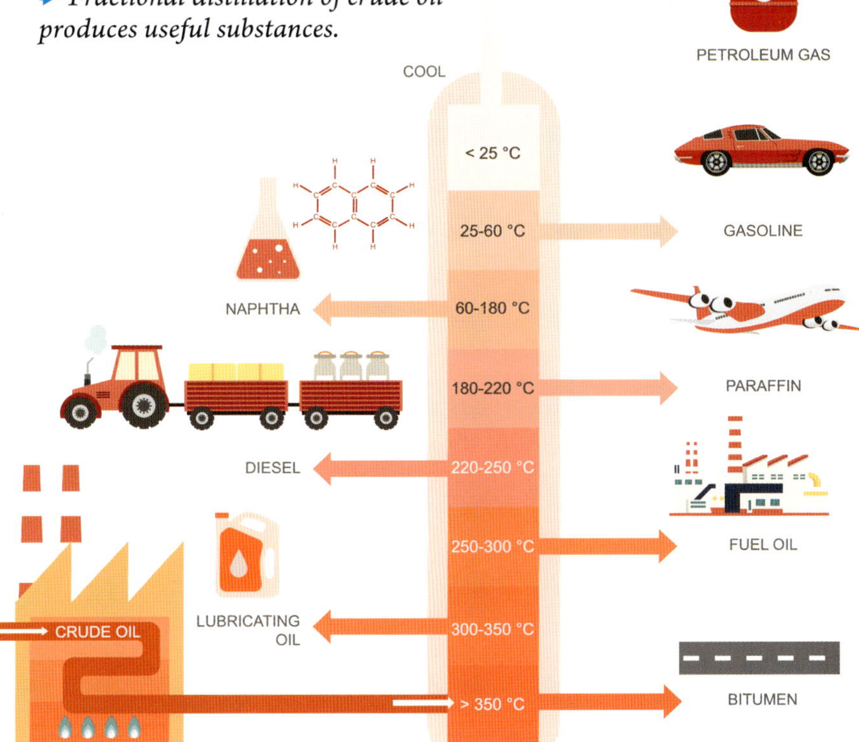

Fractional distillation of crude oil produces useful substances.

Cracking of Hydrocarbons

Large chain hydrocarbons can be broken down into smaller and more useful molecules. This process is known as 'cracking.' There are two common methods of cracking: steam cracking and catalytic cracking. The process produces alkanes and another class of molecules known as alkenes.

Alkenes are more reactive than alkanes and are useful as fuels. They are also used for producing different types of polymers and chemicals. Alkenes are hydrocarbons with double bonds between two carbon atoms. Alkenes have the general chemical formula C_nH_{2n}. The first four members of the alkene family are:

- Ethene (Ethylene) (C_2H_4)
- Propene (Propylene) (C_3H_6)
- Butene (Butylene) (C_4H_8)
- Pentene (Pentylene) (C_5H_{10})

Alkenes do not undergo complete combustion like alkanes. As a result, when alkenes are heated, they burn with smoky flames.

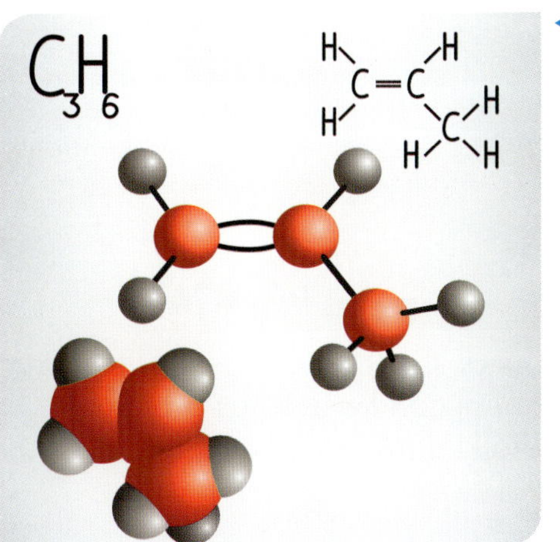

Propylene is a type of alkene.

Ethylene is the first member of the alkene family.

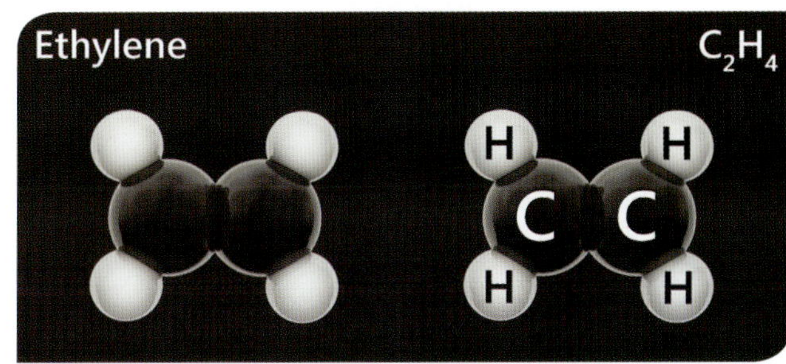

Organic Compounds – Alcohols and Carboxylic Acids

Alcohols and carboxylic acids are other classes of important organic compounds. These two classes of compounds are capable of interacting with each other to produce compounds called esters.

Alcohols

Alcohols are the simplest hydrocarbons with a hydroxyl group (-OH) attached. The general chemical formula of alcohols is $C_nH_{2n+1}OH$. The first four members of the alcohol family are:

- Methanol
- Propanol
- Ethanol
- Butanol

Uses of Alcohols

Methanol and ethanol are the most common types of alcohols that are used for different purposes. Methanol is used as an additive to petrol to improve its combustion properties. It can also be used as a fuel on its own.

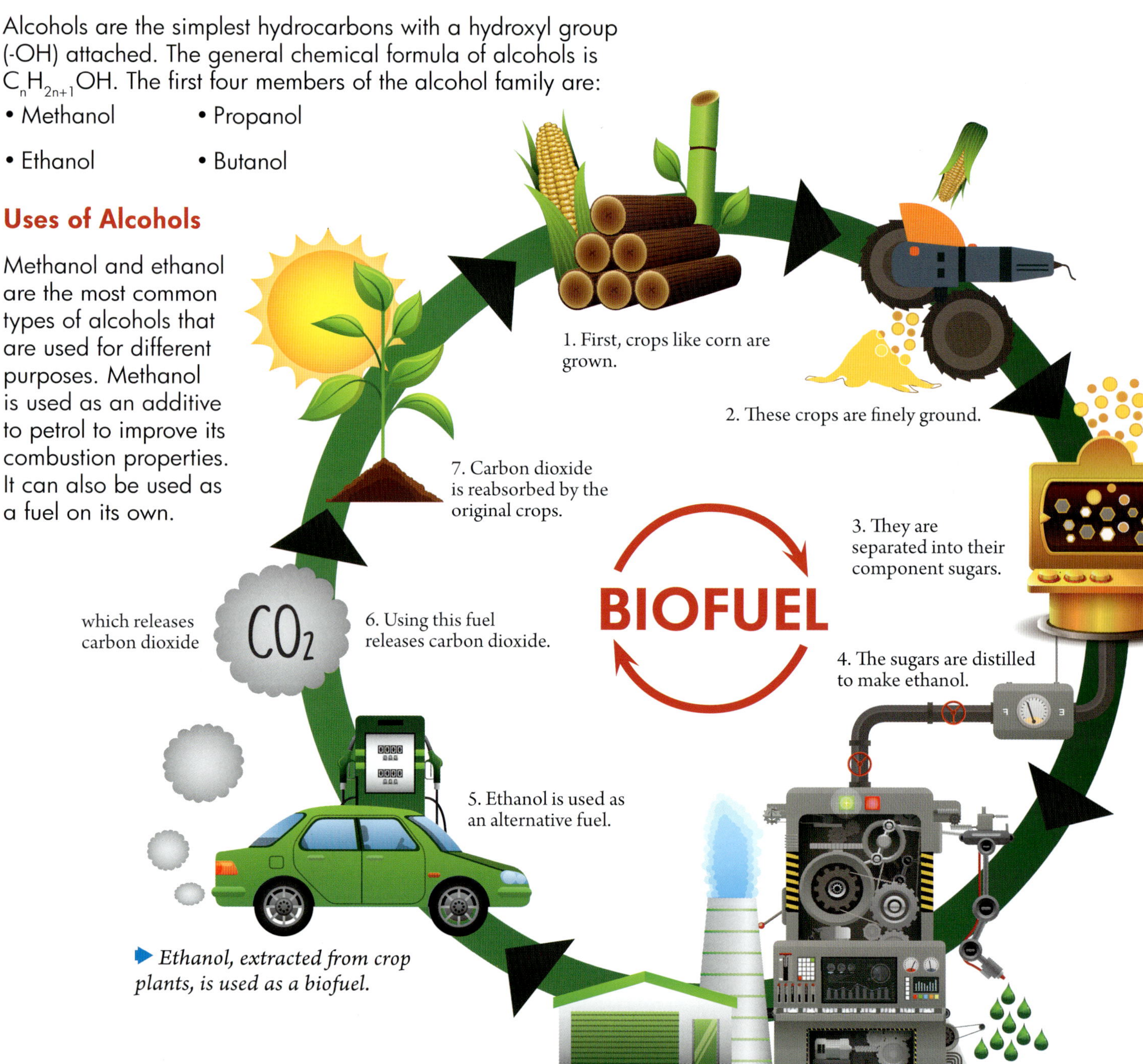

▶ *Ethanol, extracted from crop plants, is used as a biofuel.*

Ethanol is the most commonly used solvent for dissolving many organic compounds that do not dissolve in water. It is used widely in perfumes and cosmetics. Mixed with petrol or gasoline, ethanol can be used as a biofuel extracted from different sources. Ethanol is primarily employed in making alcoholic drinks and beverages. The anesthetic ether is made from ethanol.

Carboxylic Acids

Carboxylic acids are organic compounds with a carboxyl (-COOH) group. The carbon atom is bonded to an oxygen atom through a double bond and a hydroxyl group through a single bond. Carboxylic acids are weak acids and occur in nature in the form of fatty acids, amino acids, lactic acid, butyric acid, citric acid and many others. The first few members of the carboxylic acid family include:

- Formic acid
- Acetic acid
- Propionic acid
- Butyric acid
- Valeric acid

Uses of Carboxylic Acids

Soaps are manufactured with the help of sodium or potassium salts of certain fatty acids. Many organic acids like acetic acid and citric acid are widely used in the food industry. Acetic acid is used in the production of vinegar. It is also used in rubber manufacture as a clotting agent. Sodium salts of certain carboxylic acids are used as preservatives. In the pharmaceutical industry, carboxylic acids are used for production of drugs like aspirin and phenacetin. Other acids are used in making perfumes, dyes, and the synthetic fibre, rayon. Sodium and potassium salts of certain higher acids are used in the production of soaps. Many organic acids are widely used in the food industry, especially for manufacturing soft drinks.

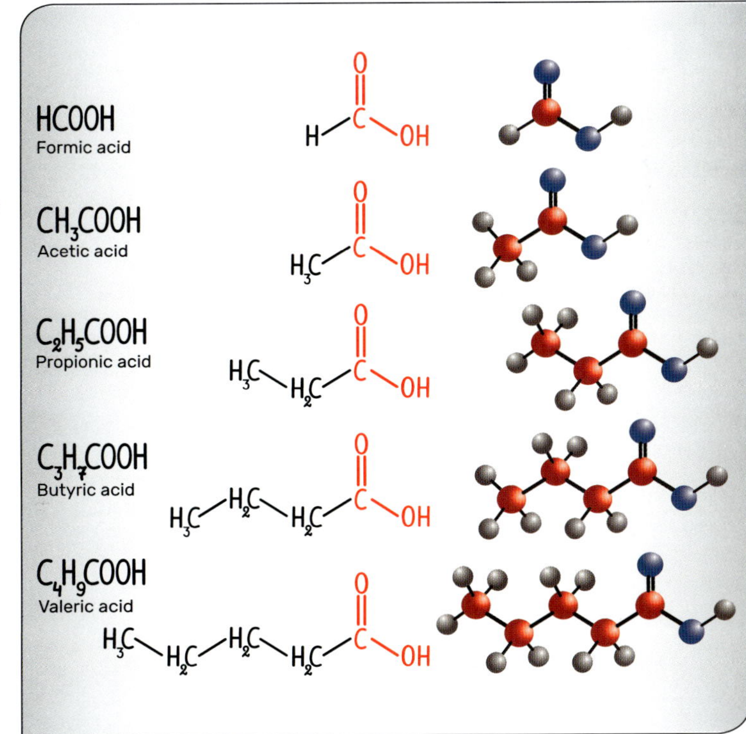

▲ *The first five members of the carboxylic acid group.*

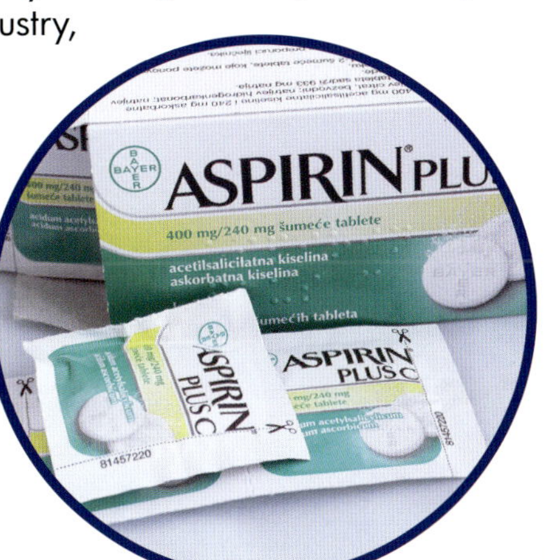
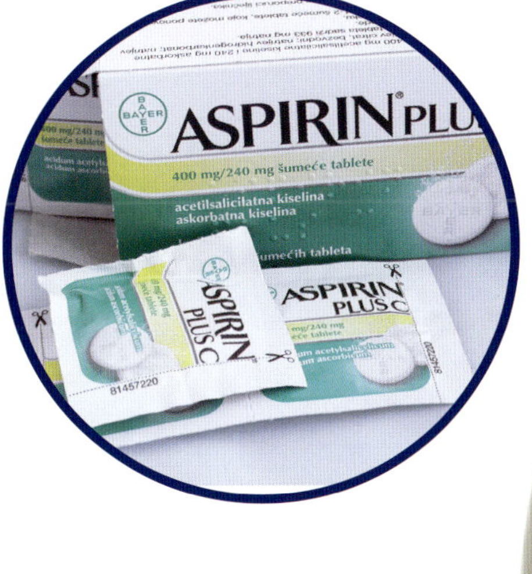

▶ *Vinegar and aspirin are produced from carboxylic acids.*

Fact File

Methanol is also called 'wood alcohol' because it is a byproduct of destructive wood distillation, a process of heating wood in the absence of air.

Polymers

Polymers are natural or artificial materials with molecular structures consisting of similar, repeating units. Plastics, resins and natural biomolecules like amino acids, DNA, starch and cellulose are examples of polymers.

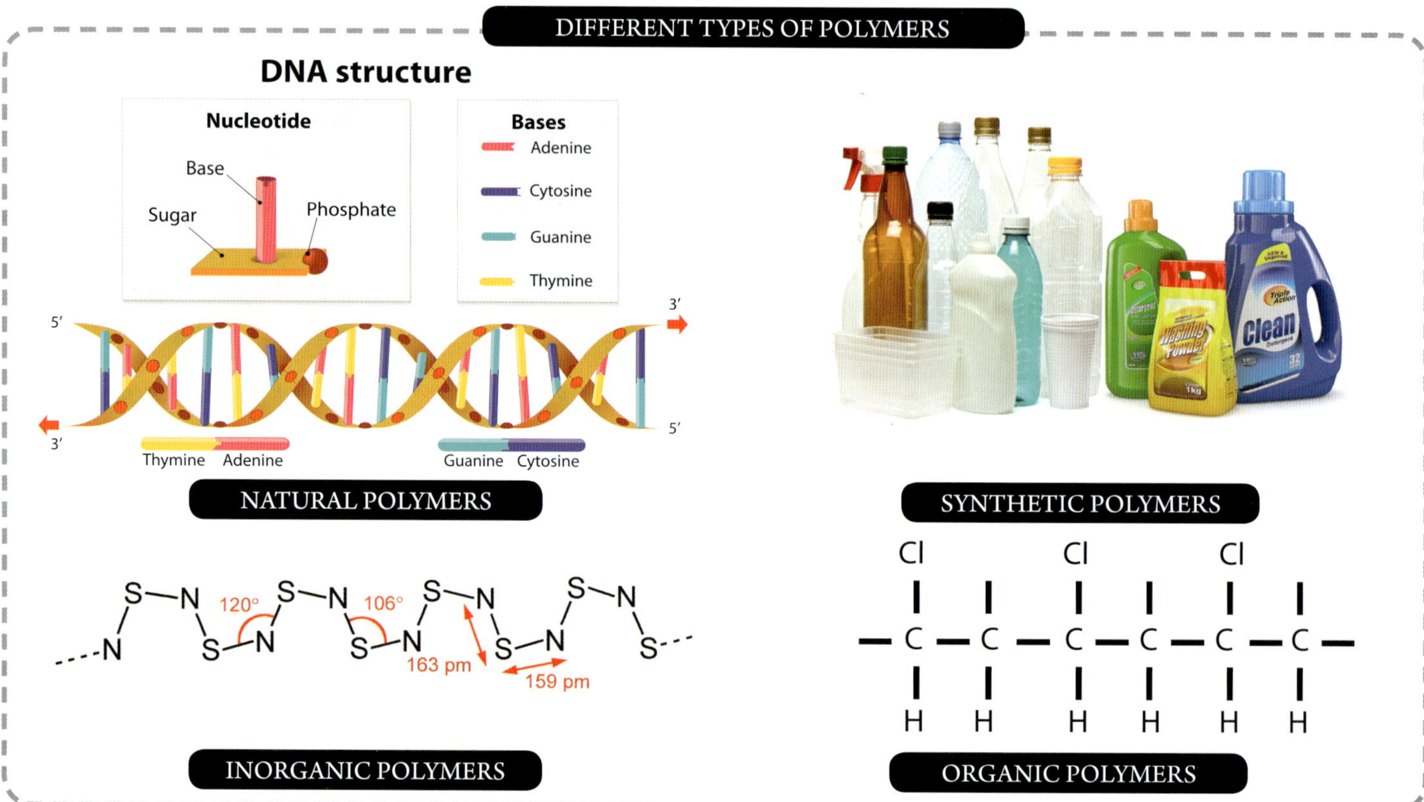

Polymerisation

Polymerisation is the process by which repeating units are added to form a macromolecule. There are two types: addition polymerisation and condensation polymerisation.

Addition polymerisation refers to the reaction that results in small molecules (called monomers) joining together to form long chains of repeating units. In polymers formed by this reaction, all the atoms are exactly the same as the monomers, as no other components are formed or added.

Condensation polymerisation occurs when monomers with two functional groups link together by losing water. Amino acids combine through condensation polymerisation, releasing water as a byproduct.

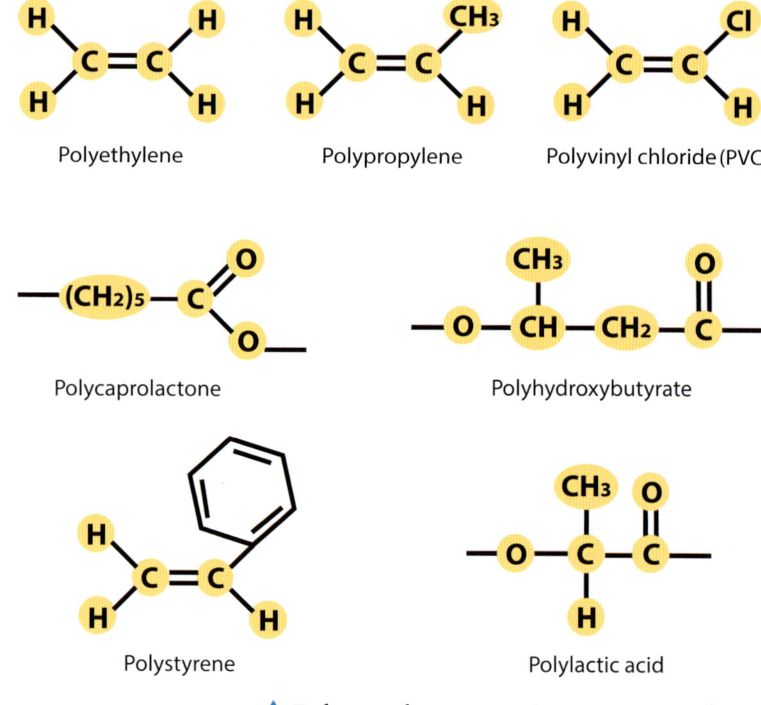

▲ *Polymers have repeating structures of different subunits.*

Natural Polymers

Amino Acids: An amino acid is a molecule with two different functional groups. There are 20 amino acids that exist in nature. These amino acids in different combinations combine to form polypeptides. The amino acids combine to form the peptide chain through condensation polymerisation. Different amino acids combine in the same chain to fold and form proteins. Insulin is an example of a protein formed by repeating units of amino acids.

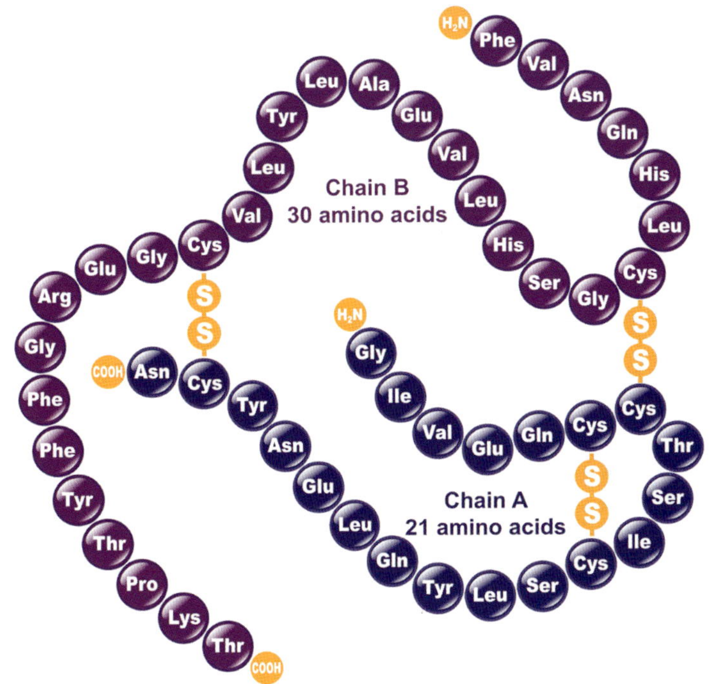

▲ *Insulin, a small protein, is a polymer of amino acids.*

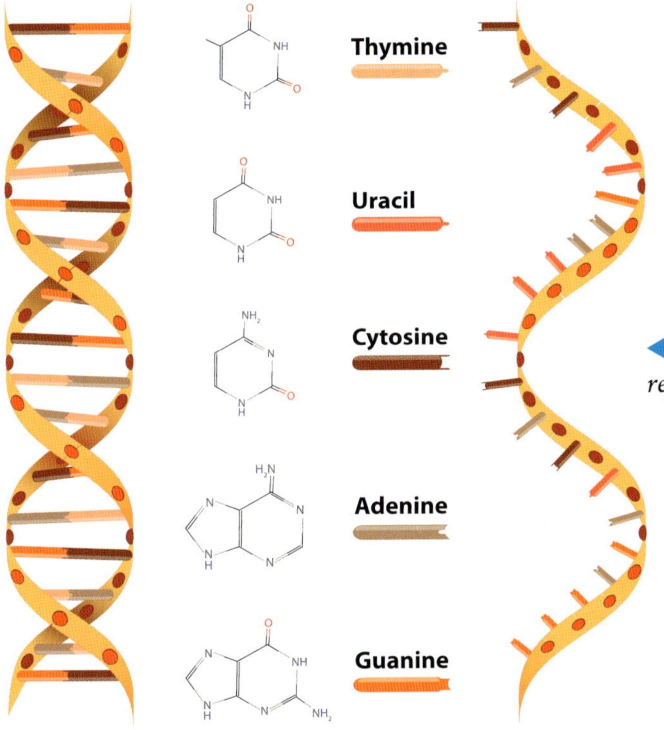

◄ *DNA and RNA are made up of repeating units of five nucleotides.*

DNA and RNA: Deoxyribonucleic acid (DNA) is a macromolecule that contains the blueprint of a complete cell's structural and functional components. It is found in all living organisms. DNA is formed by repeated chains of four nucleotides—adenine, guanine, cytosine, and thymine. DNA is made of two strands wound around each other as a double helix. The double helical structure is formed by the double and triple bonds formed between the complementary nucleotide bases. The principal role of RNA is to act as a messenger carrying instructions from DNA for controlling the synthesis of proteins.

Artificial Polymers: Synthetic or artificial polymers are those that are made by humans and do not occur in nature. Polyethylene is one of the simplest known polymers. It is made up of repeating units of ethylene. Synthetic polymers are also sometimes referred to as plastics. Nylon, Teflon, polyvinyl chloride (PVC), polyethylene, and polypropylene are some of the plastics that are commonly used for making fabrics, pipes, nonstick pans and other objects.

▲ *PVC pipes and Teflon pans are made of artificial polymers.*

Synthetic polymers have been a source of concern as they do not biodegrade easily and are considered to be environmental hazards.

Chemical Analysis

In chemical laboratories, analysts use different tests to detect the presence of chemical compounds. The tests usually rely on reactions that result in formation of precipitate, colour, odour or the release of gas with identifiable properties. Instruments are also used, especially when the quantity is less.

Identifying Pure Substances and Mixtures

A pure substance is generally a single element or a compound that is not mixed with any other substance. Formulations or mixtures are made up of more than one chemical component. A formulation consists of two or more chemical substances mixed in measured quantities for conferring certain properties.

Pure substances have a specific melting and boiling point. A pure substance can be distinguished from a mixture using the melting and boiling point data.

Chromatography is a chemical method that is used for separating the individual components of a mixture. There are different types of chromatography, the simplest one being paper chromatography. This method works on the principle of separation through distribution of substances between a mobile phase and a stationary phase.

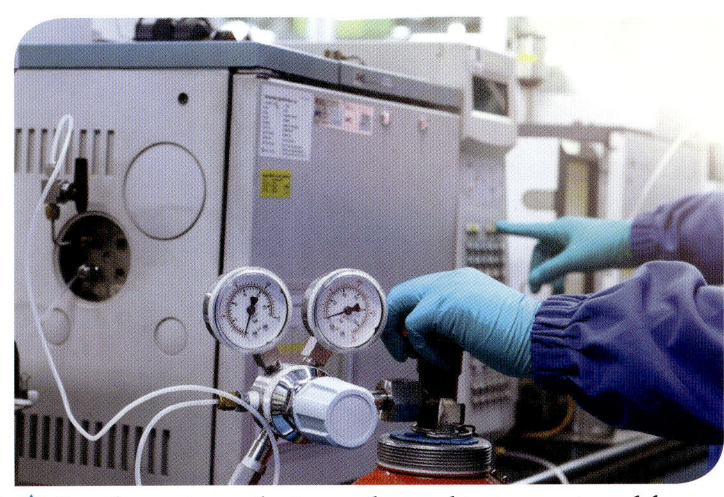
▲ *Gas chromatography is an advanced instrument used for separating compounds.*

▲ *Thin layer chromatography separates simple food colouring components.*

In a typical paper chromatography setup, the mobile phase is a solvent such as alcohol and the stationary phase is the strip of filter paper used, also called a 'chromatogram.' When a drop of coloured chemical mixture is placed on the paper, the solvent moves up and reacts with the mixture, causing spots to be formed corresponding to the components.

Fact File

Paper chromatography was a technique invented by Archer Martin and Richard Synge in 1943.

Identifying Gases

Test for Hydrogen: A burning piece of stick or splint is held near the open end of a test tube. If the released gas is hydrogen, the splint burns brightly with a popping sound.

Test for Oxygen: A burning splint, when placed near the mouth of a test tube with oxygen, will burn brighter. A glowing splint also gets relighted when exposed to oxygen.

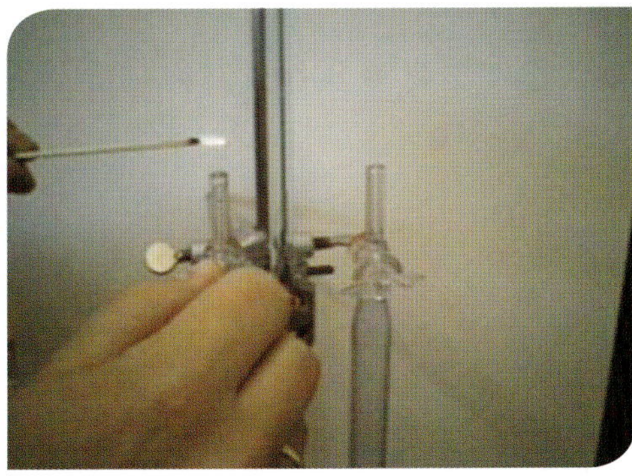

◄ *A burning splint can be used for testing the presence of oxygen.*

Test for Carbon Dioxide: When carbon dioxide gas is passed into a test tube containing calcium hydroxide solution (lime water), it turns milky or cloudy.

Test for Chlorine: Litmus paper is useful for testing the presence of chlorine gas. When damp litmus paper is dropped into a test tube with chlorine gas, the litmus paper is bleached white.

▲ *The splint burns brightly when exposed to oxygen.*

Identifying Ions

Flame tests are the easiest way to identify different metal ions. Compounds containing the metal ions lithium, sodium, potassium, calcium, and copper can be identified through this test.

Metal Ion	Flame Colour
Lithium	Crimson
Zinc	Yellow
Sodium	Deep yellow
Potassium	Lilac
Calcium	Orange-red
Copper	Green
Strontium	Red

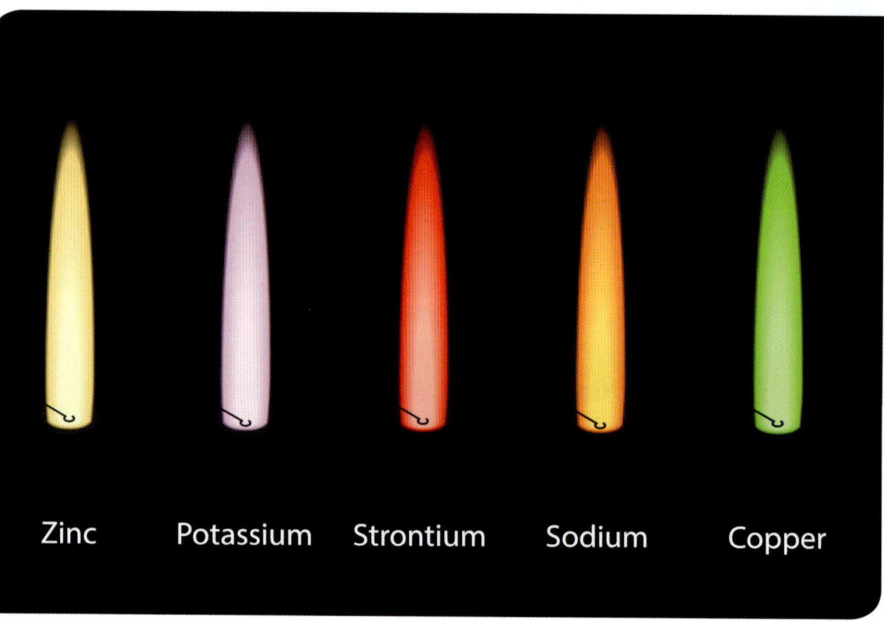

▲ *Flame tests are used for identifying different elemental ions.*

Identifying Hydroxides, Carbonates, Halides and Sulphates

Carbonates can be identified by mixing them with dilute acids. The reaction results in the formation of carbon dioxide, which in turn can be detected by passing the gas through lime water and observing for the formation of cloudiness.

Halides can combine with silver nitrate solution and dilute nitric acid to form precipitates. Silver chloride is white, silver bromide is cream, and silver iodide forms a yellow precipitate.

Sulphate ions react with barium chloride solution and hydrochloric acid to form a white precipitate.

Metal hydroxides can be tested by adding to sodium hydroxide solution.

Metal Ion	Colour of Precipitate
Aluminium	White
Calcium	White
Magnesium	White
Copper (II)	Blue
Iron (II)	Green
Iron (III)	Brown

Many elements can exist in more than one form. The numbers indicate the oxidation state. Iron (II) and copper (II) ions share two electrons with another element, while iron (III) shares three electrons.

◀ *Metals form different coloured precipitates upon reacting with sodium hydroxide.*

Flame Emission Spectroscopy

Instruments provide accurate, sensitive, and rapid detection of elements and compounds. One of the most commonly used instruments for detecting the presence of metal ions in a solution is flame emission spectroscopy. The sample to be examined is lighted and the light from the flame is passed through a spectroscope. The output is a line spectrum that identifies the ion(s) present when compared with a reference set.

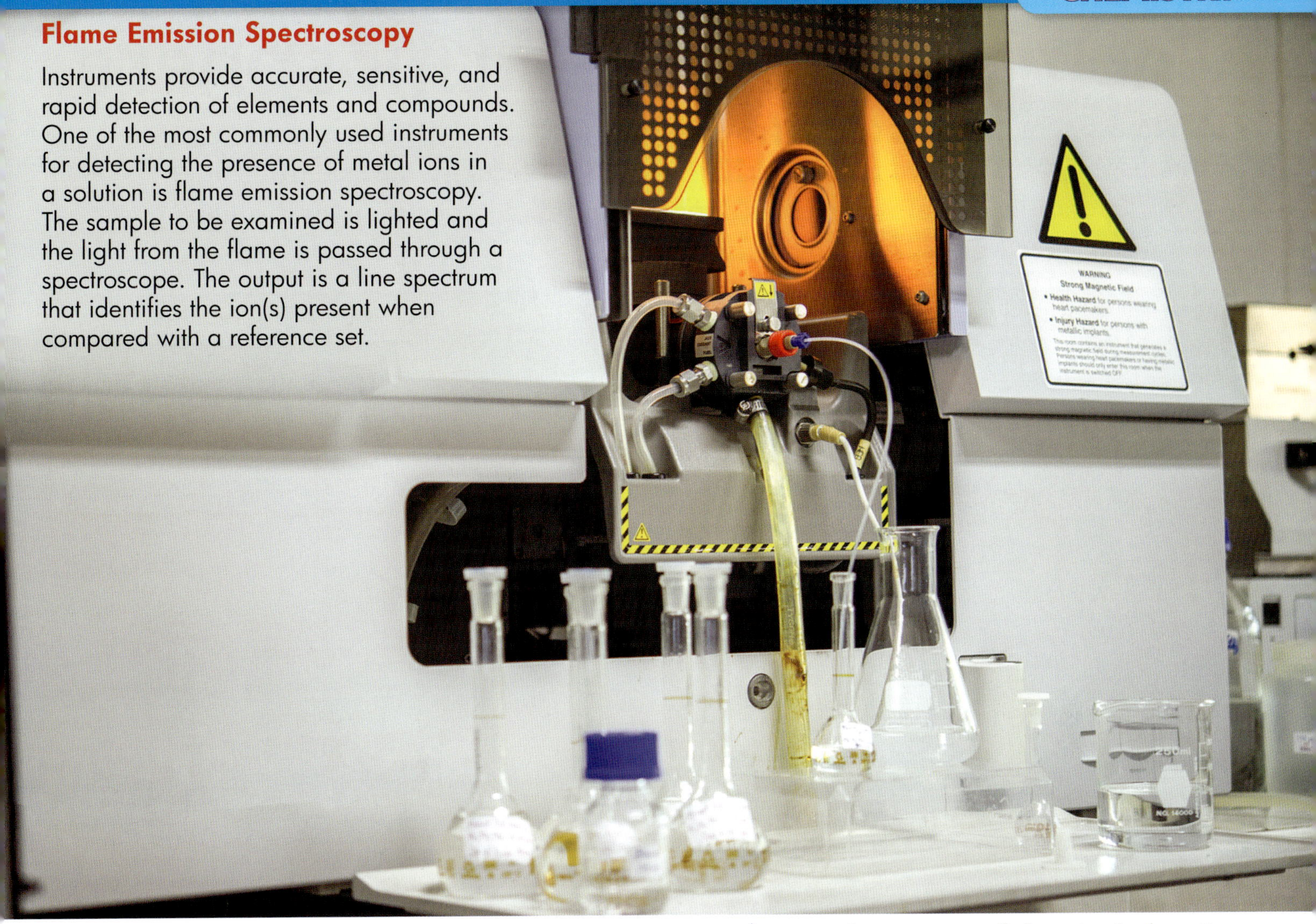

▲ *A type of spectroscope called an atomic absorption spectroscope, used for identifying metals in solutions.*

Mass Spectrometry

A mass spectrometer is used for identifying the mass of particles in a given sample. If the constituents of a particular sample are not known, the mass spectrometer can be used to find the elements in it by identifying their masses. Sometimes, it can also reveal the structure of the molecules. The sample is first ionised, that is, it is conferred positive or negative charge artificially. The electrically charged constituents are then measured for their mass to charge ratio. This is the working principle of a mass spectrometer. The first mass spectroscope was invented in 1912 by the British physicist J.J. Thomson. As with spectroscopes, there are many different types of mass spectrometers, developed for different needs.

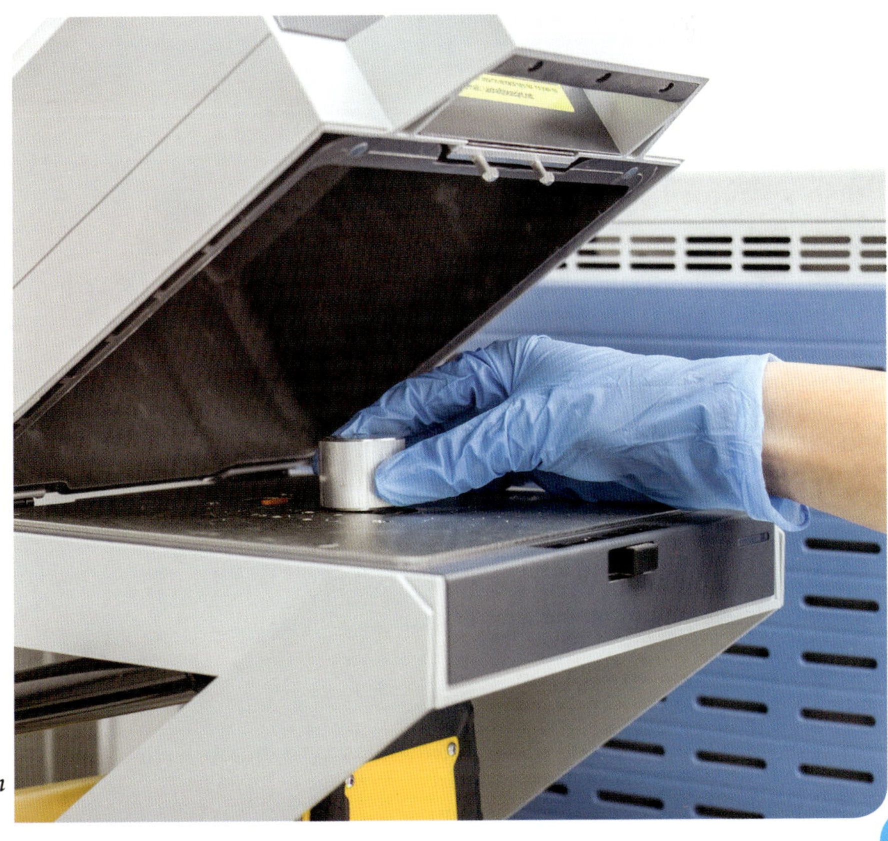

▶ *A mass spectrometer finds application in pharmaceutics, mining, and other fields.*

Chemistry of the Atmosphere

The atmosphere is a series of layers enveloping the Earth. Earth's atmosphere provides the gases needed for supporting life and protects the surface from harmful radiation. The atmosphere is dynamic and undergoes changes through natural causes as well as through human activity.

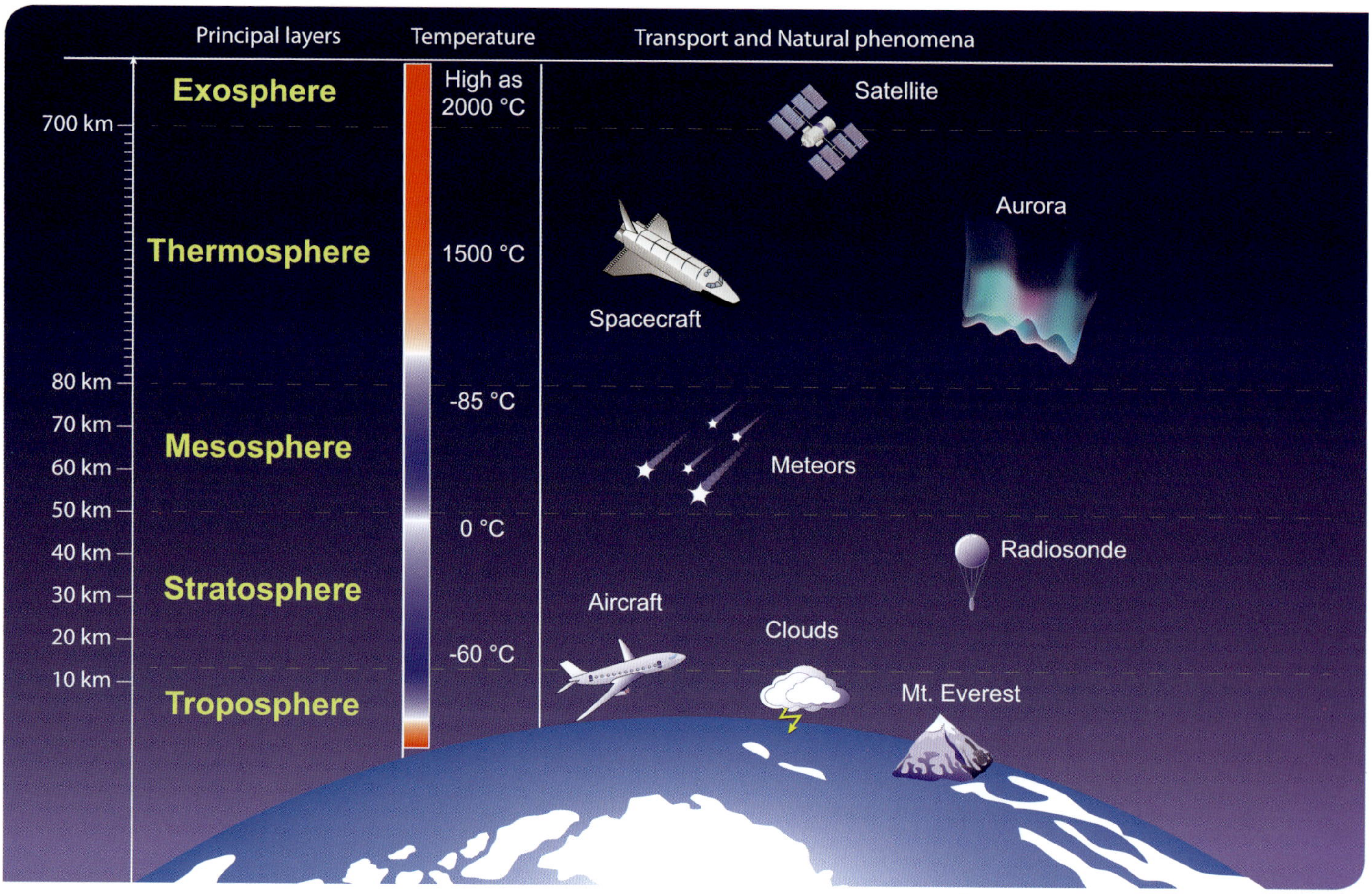

▲ *The Earth's atmosphere consists of many protective layers*

Earth's Atmosphere

For around 200 million years, the composition of the gases in the atmosphere has remained more or less constant. Nitrogen, oxygen, argon, carbon dioxide, water vapor, methane, hydrogen, helium, krypton, and neon are present in trace amounts.

The atmosphere is divided into many layers: troposphere, stratosphere, mesosphere, thermosphere, and exosphere. The troposphere is the layer closest to the Earth's surface while the exosphere is the outermost layer that gradually merges into outer space.

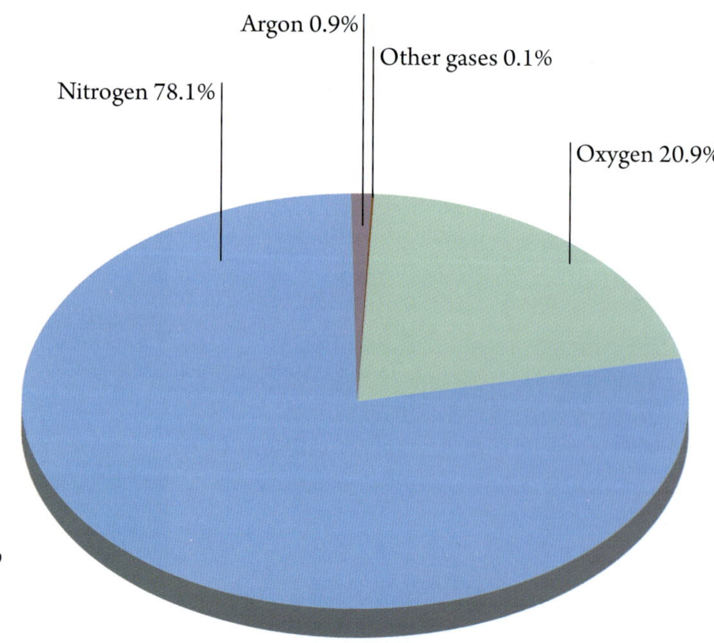

▶ *Nitrogen and oxygen make up the largest percentage of gases in the atmosphere.*

Early Atmosphere

There are many theories that predict what the Earth's early atmosphere used to be like and how it has evolved over 4.6 billion years. According to one theory, the first billion years saw violent and intense volcanic activity that released gases that made up the early atmosphere.

Carbon dioxide would have made up the majority of the composition, with little or no oxygen. The volcanic activity produced nitrogen, ammonia, and methane that built up in the atmosphere.

When the oceans formed, the carbon dioxide in the atmosphere dissolved in the water to form carbonates that formed precipitates and accumulated as sediments. This continuous process gradually reduced the carbon dioxide in the atmosphere.

▲ *Intense volcanic activity was common in the first few million years on Earth.*

Oxygen and Carbon Ratio

When algae and plants formed, they used up carbon dioxide and produced oxygen. Starting from about 2.7 billion years ago, oxygen began to accumulate in the atmosphere. Over millions of years more plant species evolved and flourished, increasing the amount of oxygen.

This also led to the development of different animals that depend on oxygen for survival and growth. The decrease in carbon dioxide was aided by other processes, such as the formation of sedimentary deposits and fossil fuels.

Fact File

Nitrogen (78%), oxygen (21%), and argon (0.9%) make up the major composition of the atmosphere.

Pollution

Human activity has resulted in pollution of air, water and soil. It has also had an effect on the composition of the atmosphere. Greenhouse gases, though essential for sustaining life on Earth, can also pose a global risk if they exceed a certain level.

Greenhouse gases

Carbon dioxide, methane, and water vapor are the greenhouse gases present in the atmosphere. They are essential for supporting life. Carbon dioxide is taken up by plants to grow. However, the level of greenhouse gases in the atmosphere has been increasing steadily due to various human activities. The biggest contribution comes from burning fossil fuels for electricity, industrial uses, and powering vehicles.

Increased vehicle use has caused high levels of air pollution

Soil and Water Pollution

Also known as land pollution, the pollution of soil is caused by chemicals like hydrocarbons, solvents, and heavy metals such as lead and mercury. When these chemicals find their way into the soil, they can pollute the top layer and make it unusable. The accumulation of plastics in the land is also a source of concern, especially for wildlife. Plastic objects typically take thousands of years to degrade. Water sources get polluted through the release of harmful effluents from industries and factories.

Untreated industrial waste completely destroys water sources.

Global Climate Change

Scientists have identified that continuation of activities that contribute to rising greenhouse gases will cause a steady rise in temperature across the globe. This, in turn, will lead to changes in climate patterns and melting of the polar caps that will flood many coastal regions.

▲ *Global warming has caused the polar ice caps to melt.*

Pollutants

The burning of fossil fuels like coal, oil, and natural gas is the major source of oil pollution. It releases carbon monoxide, carbon dioxide, sulphur dioxide, hydrocarbons, solid waste (like soot), and nitrogen oxides. Along with the other natural constituents in the atmosphere, it can lead to the formation of particulate matter.

Different pollutants have varying effects. Carbon monoxide is a toxic gas that is difficult to detect. Sulphur and nitrogen oxides cause lung irritation and different respiratory problems. Particulate matter in the air can cause a condition known as 'global dimming' and health issues.

Carbon Footprint

'Carbon footprint' refers to the total amount of carbon dioxide or other greenhouse gases that are released during a full life cycle of a service or product. Many organisations around the world are taking care to reduce carbon dioxide and methane emissions caused by manufacture or services.

▲ *Pollutants released by industries and factories pose a serious threat to health.*

Fact File

Nearly 14 billion pounds of garbage is dumped into the oceans every year, of which plastics form the major portion.

Water Treatment and Fertilisers

We depend on food and water for our very existence. Potable water and fertilisers that improve crop yield are necessities everywhere. Even though fresh water and crops are now available for our consumption, careful use, reuse and innovation is necessary to make it available for generations to come.

Potable Water

Water that is suitable for drinking should be free of microbes and have only low levels of dissolved salts. The production of potable water for consumption depends on the available freshwater sources and technology.

Usually, rainwater is the major source of fresh water and collects in the ground as well as in rivers and lakes. Not all lakes, ponds, or rivers may have suitable water for drinking purposes. The important step is to identify a safe source of water and pass it through filter beds, then sterilise it by using ultraviolet light, chlorine and ozone. In areas where fresh water is scarce, desalination is the best available option. Rainwater harvesting is also essential for collecting water that would otherwise drain into the ground.

Rainwater harvesting is an easy way of collecting water and preventing water logging.

Waste Water Treatment

Waste water is generated constantly from homes, agricultural fields, and industries in large amounts. It carries chemicals, microbes, and organic matter that need to be treated efficiently before release.

Organic matter and microbes need to be removed from sewage and agricultural waste while harmful chemicals and compounds are removed from industrial waste. In general, these processes are involved in treating waste water:

1. Screening, followed by grit removal

2. Sedimentation and removal of sewage sludge

3. Anaerobic digestion of sewage

4. Aerobic treatment of effluent

Sewage is treated in a number of different steps before release.

Fertilisers

Farmers use fertilisers to improve crop yield and health. While compost is a good natural fertiliser, it is not possible to obtain it in large quantities in a short span needed for large fields. Artificial or chemical fertilisers solve the problem. They can be mass-manufactured and available at affordable costs.

Fact File

Desalination is carried out by distillation or reverse osmosis. Since this process consumes a lot of energy, desalination itself is quite expensive.

▲ *Farmers use fertilisers to increase yield of crops.*

NPK Fertilisers

Nitrogen, phosphorus, and potassium together are referred to as NPK fertilisers. For decades, they have helped improve agricultural productivity. Ammonia is manufactured through the Haber process or from ammonium salts and nitric acid. Potassium fertilisers such as potassium chloride and potassium sulphate can be directly mined and used as fertilisers. Phosphate rocks that are mined have to be treated with sulphuric acid, phosphoric acid, or nitric acid and the salts thus produced are used in the fields.

Ammonia Manufacture

Ammonia is one of the fertilisers commonly used. The Haber process is used for manufacturing ammonia. Using raw materials, nitrogen, and hydrogen, ammonia is manufactured by passing the purified gases over an iron catalyst at 450°C and 200 atmospheres pressure. The hydrogen and nitrogen gases interact to form ammonia. The cooled and liquefied ammonia is removed and the remaining hydrogen and nitrogen gases are recycled.

▼ *Ammonia is produced on a large scale in factories for use as a fertiliser.*

Metals and Alloys

Metals are solid elements that are opaque and lustrous. Importantly, metals are capable of conducting heat and electricity. Metals and alloys are important for crafting many objects and equipment that we use.

Properties of Metals

Metals are usually hard, heavy, and have very high melting and boiling points. They are said to be malleable and ductile, that is, metals can be beaten into thin sheets and stretched into wires. Many metals are capable of combining with other metals to form alloys.

▲ Titanium is used for making strong yet lightweight bicycle frames.

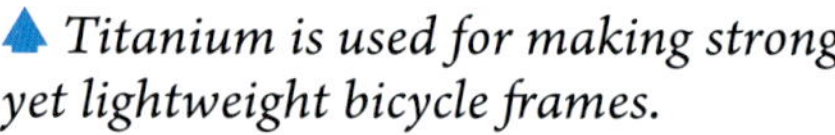

▶ Stainless steel, made out of iron, is the preferred material for making utensils.

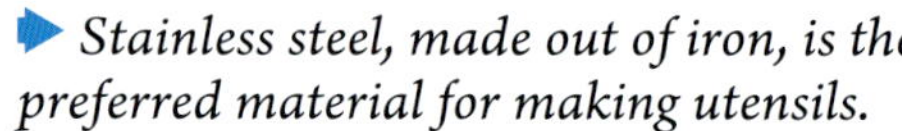

▲ Gold has always been used for decoration and doesn't fade or rust.

▲ Copper is commonly used in making taps and wires.

Metal Extraction

Earth has only a finite supply of metal ores. Copper ores are becoming scarce, and new ways are being developed to extract metals from other ores through different methods.

Phytomining is a process by which plants are used for absorbing metallic compounds. These plants are harvested, then burned to ash to produce the metal compounds.

Bioleaching is another process that employs bacteria to produce solutions with leached metal compounds that can be extracted.

Electrolysis is a process by which copper compounds are displaced from solutions under the effect of electricity.

▲ Phytomining is a unique way of using plants to extract metals.

▲ *Iron pipes can develop rust and degrade over time due to exposure to moisture.*

Corrosion

Corrosion of metal occurs though chemical reactions that occur between the elements and the environment. Rusting is the most common corrosive reaction that is observed. Iron undergoes corrosion in the presence of air and water. Corrosion can render the metal useless.

The usual way to prevent corrosion is by coating the metal with a barrier layer such as grease, paint, or through electroplating. In some cases, a metal is coated with another metal that is corrosive. An example of this is galvanised iron that is coated with zinc, which corrodes but protects iron.

Fact File

The purity of gold is measured in carats. 24-carat gold is 100% gold whereas 18-carat gold has only about 75% of gold mixed with other metals.

Alloys

An alloy is a mixture of one or more metals. Many things we use in our daily life are made of alloys. Steel is an alloy of iron with a specific amount of carbon and other metals like chromium or nickel. Carbon added in steel provides strength to it. High-carbon steel is strong but brittle whereas low-carbon steel is soft and easy to shape.

Bronze is an alloy of copper and tin. Brass is an alloy of copper and zinc. Both bronze and brass can contain traces of other elements such as aluminium, manganese, silicon, phosphorus, arsenic or lead.

▲ *Galvanised metal is resistant to corrosion.*

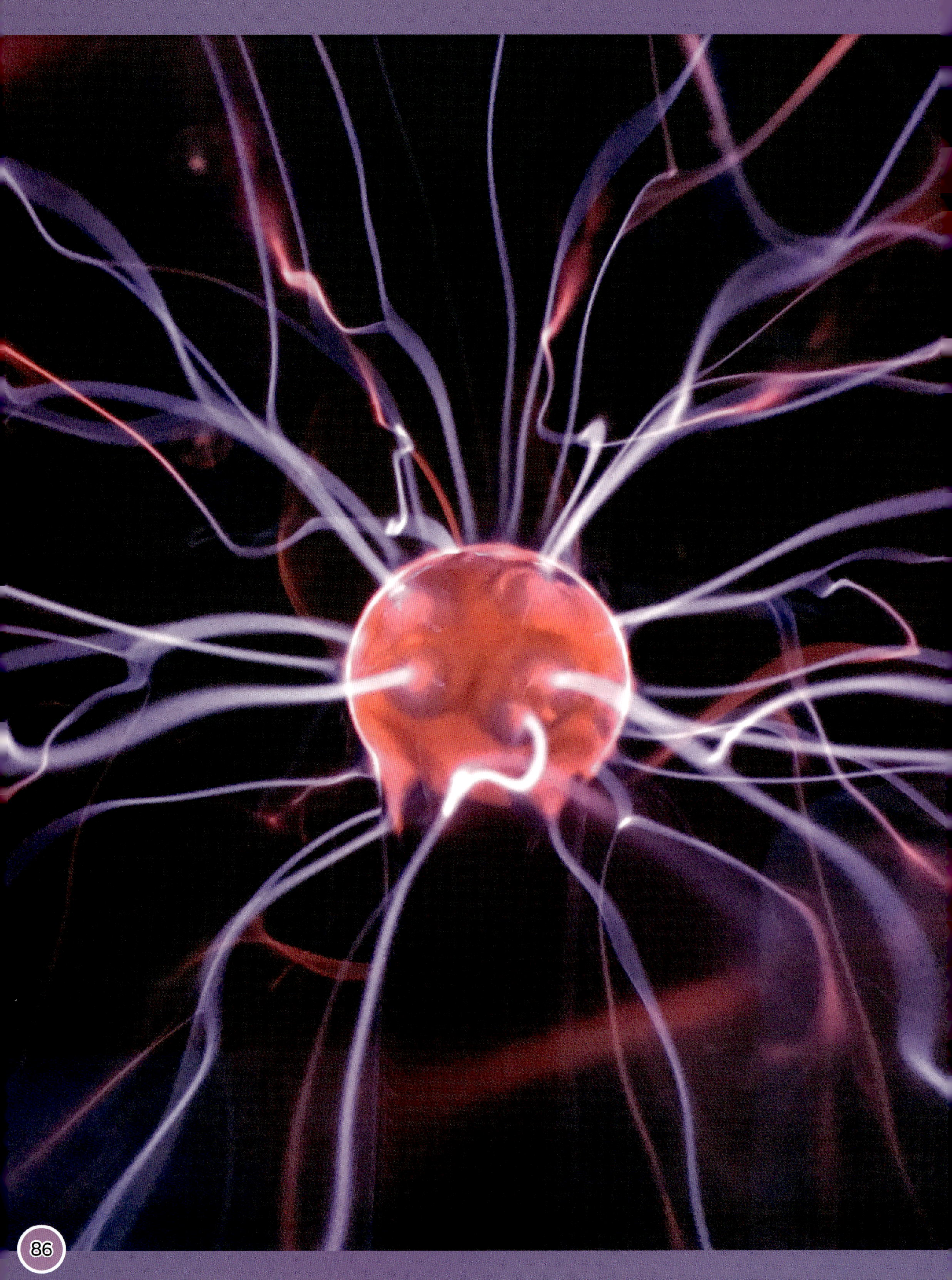

A First Introduction to Science

ENCYCLOPEDIA of LEARNING

DISCOVER
PHYSICS

Energy

Energy, in simple terms, is the ability to do work. Energy is everywhere around us and is responsible for changes, chemical reactions, biological activity, and movement happening everywhere. Energy can also take up many different forms. Energy is measured in standard units called joules.

Energy System

A system is a group of objects. When there is any change in the system, the energy stored in one or more object in it also undergoes changes. Heat, force, electricity, and work can result in a change in an energy system. A few common examples include:

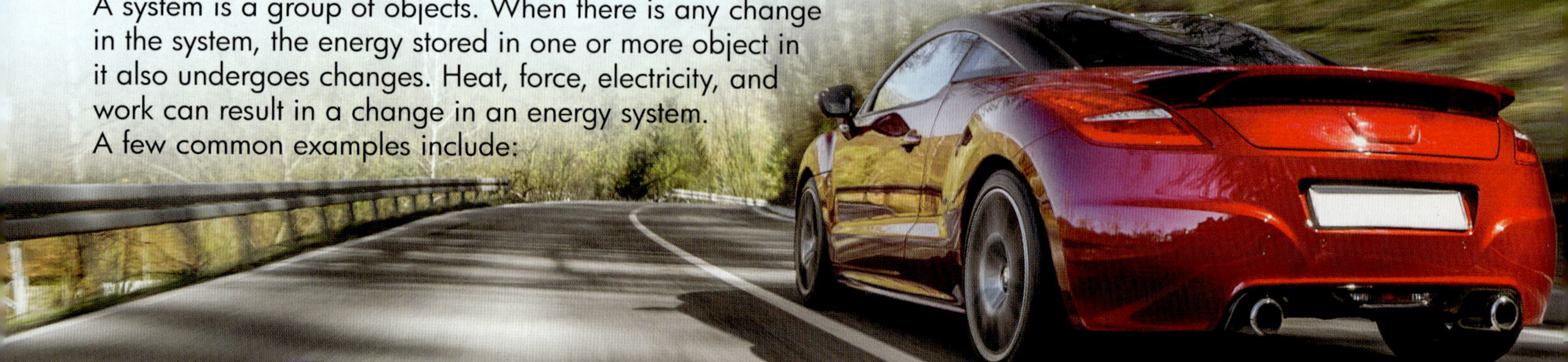

A ball hit by a bat

Boiling water in a kettle

A rock thrown up in the air

Types of Energy

All objects possess internal energy. Energy is primarily classified into potential and kinetic energy. Potential energy is stored energy. Kinetic energy is the result of movement. A rock lying on the ground might look like it does not possess energy. However, it contains stored energy known as potential energy. A moving object possesses kinetic energy as a result of the force that set it into motion.

The ability to transfer energy from one form to another has driven and continues to enable life on our planet. Plants and certain other organisms absorb energy from the Sun and convert it into food in the form of chemical energy. Organisms that consume them gain energy for their activities. Energy is never transferred wholly from one system to another. There is always wastage in the form of heat, light, or other forms.

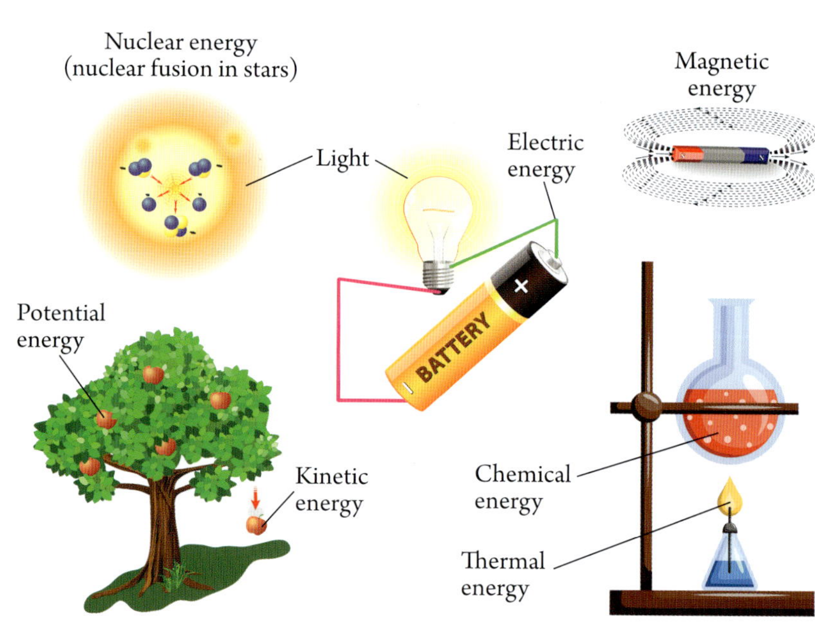

▲ *Energy comes in different forms and can be transformed from one form to another.*

There are many forms of energy we can observe around us. The Sun is a source of light and heat energy. Nuclear energy is derived from the nuclei of atoms. Energy in magnets is magnetic energy, and energy in electric materials is electric energy. Chemical energy is stored in fuels, food, and batteries. Vibrating objects can produce sound energy.

Law of Conservation of Energy

Energy can neither be created nor destroyed. It can be stored or transferred from one form to another. Before and after transfer, the total energy in a system remains constant. An example of energy transfer is the heat radiating from a hot object to a cold object that comes into contact with it. This type of energy transfer is known as conduction.

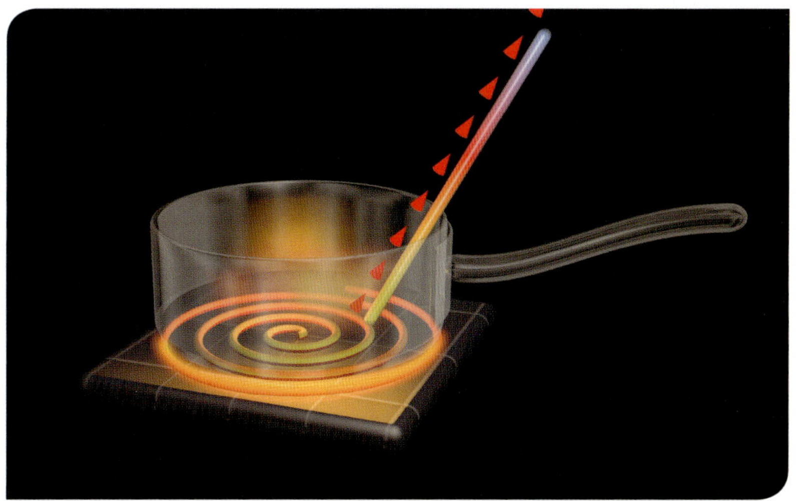

▶ *The transfer of energy from a hot to cold body is called conduction.*

Potential Energy Due to Gravity

As the name suggests, the Earth's gravitational field exerts a pull on all objects, and the potential energy arising from it is the gravitational potential energy. A rock or any object located on top of a hill has gravitational potential energy. This is because, at some point in time, an external force must have been applied to enable it to gain that height.

A simple formula is used for calculating the energy of the object:

$$E = m\,g\,h$$

m – mass of the object
g – gravitational field strength
h – height from base of hill or raised structure

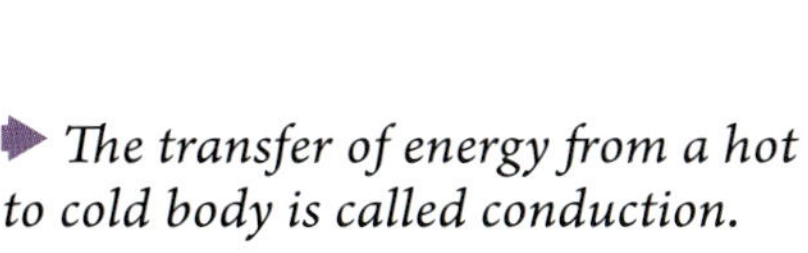

Thrilling rides in theme parks work on the principle of transfer of gravitational potential energy to kinetic energy and vice versa.

▲ *In a roller coaster ride, there is a constant transformation from gravitational potential energy to kinetic energy.*

The power consumed by a bulb is measured in watts.

Power

The rate at which energy is transferred is called power. Alternatively, power can also be defined as the rate at which work is done. Power is measured in watts. A transfer of energy equivalent to 1 joule per second is equal to the power of 1 watt. The power of light bulbs is measured in watts. The number (in watts) indicates the amount of power the bulb would consume in one hour.

Energy Efficiency

No matter how effectively a system is designed to store energy, a certain amount of energy still dissipates into the atmosphere and gets wasted. Constant innovations help design energy-efficient systems that provide maximum utilisation of the stored energy and minimal wastage.

Energy efficiency is calculated using this simple formula:

$$\text{Efficiency} = \frac{\text{Useful Output Energy}}{\text{Total Input Energy}}$$

Energy Resources

The energy resources that are available on Earth for our use include fossil fuels like coal and petroleum, biofuel, nuclear energy from radioactive elements, hydroelectricity from running water, wind energy, tidal energy from waves, solar energy from the Sun, and geothermal energy from Earth's internal heat. The energy harvested from different sources is used for electricity generation, heating, and transport.

Coal is a fossil fuel that is burned for generating energy.

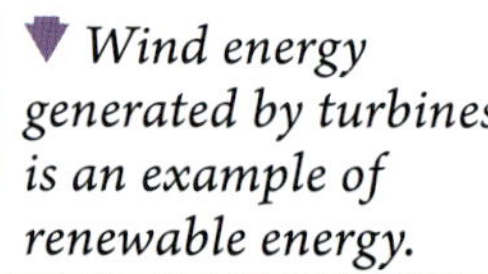
Solar panels harvest energy from the Sun for heating purposes and powering appliances.

Wind energy generated by turbines is an example of renewable energy.

Petrol and diesel that power vehicles are rapidly diminishing resources.

Not all forms of energy can be replenished. Fossil fuels are an example of nonrenewable resources. They are available in limited quantities and might not even last this century. On the other hand, solar energy is renewable as the source, the Sun, will exist for billions of years. Renewable energy sources are a better option, because most of them (solar, wind and hydrothermal energy) are also nonpolluting.

Efficiency of Different Energy Sources

At a time when many energy sources are fast diminishing, researchers across the world are trying to identify better ways to harvest and store energy. One of the most important things to be kept in mind is the energy efficiency. It is important that a large portion of an energy source or fuel should be converted into energy with minimal wastage.

While comparing different fuels and sources, wind energy is considered to be the most energy efficient. Hydroelectric power is the least polluting, in terms of carbon dioxide released into the atmosphere. On the other hand, fossil fuels like coal and oil are the least efficient, providing as little as only 30 percent energy yield. Also, the burning of fossil fuels causes pollution, so it is necessary to replace them with better sources.

Not all places in the world can harvest wind for energy production. However, different places in the world take advantage of the available physical resources and climate patterns to produce energy. At present, the cost of solar panels used for harvesting energy from the Sun is quite high. With better innovations, the cost can come down and efficiency increased. Identifying newer ways for harvesting energy is necessary for meeting the demands of a growing world population.

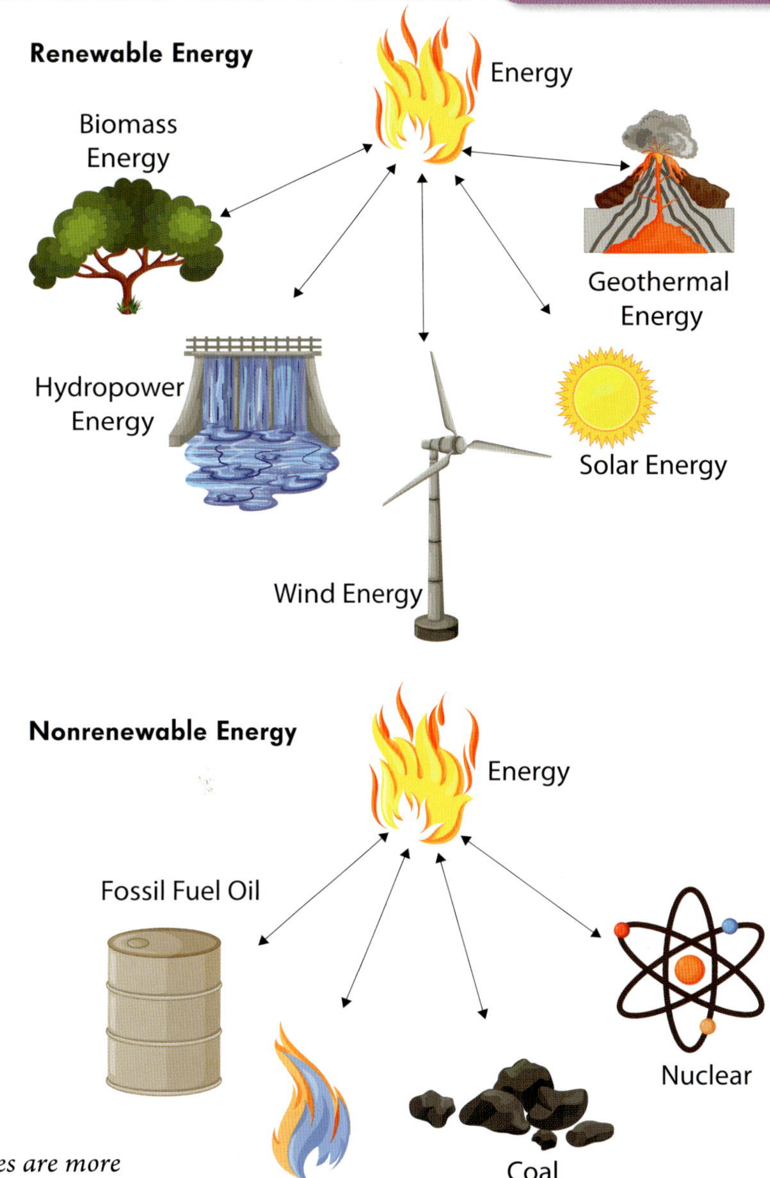

▶ *Renewable energy sources are more suitable for long-term energy demands.*

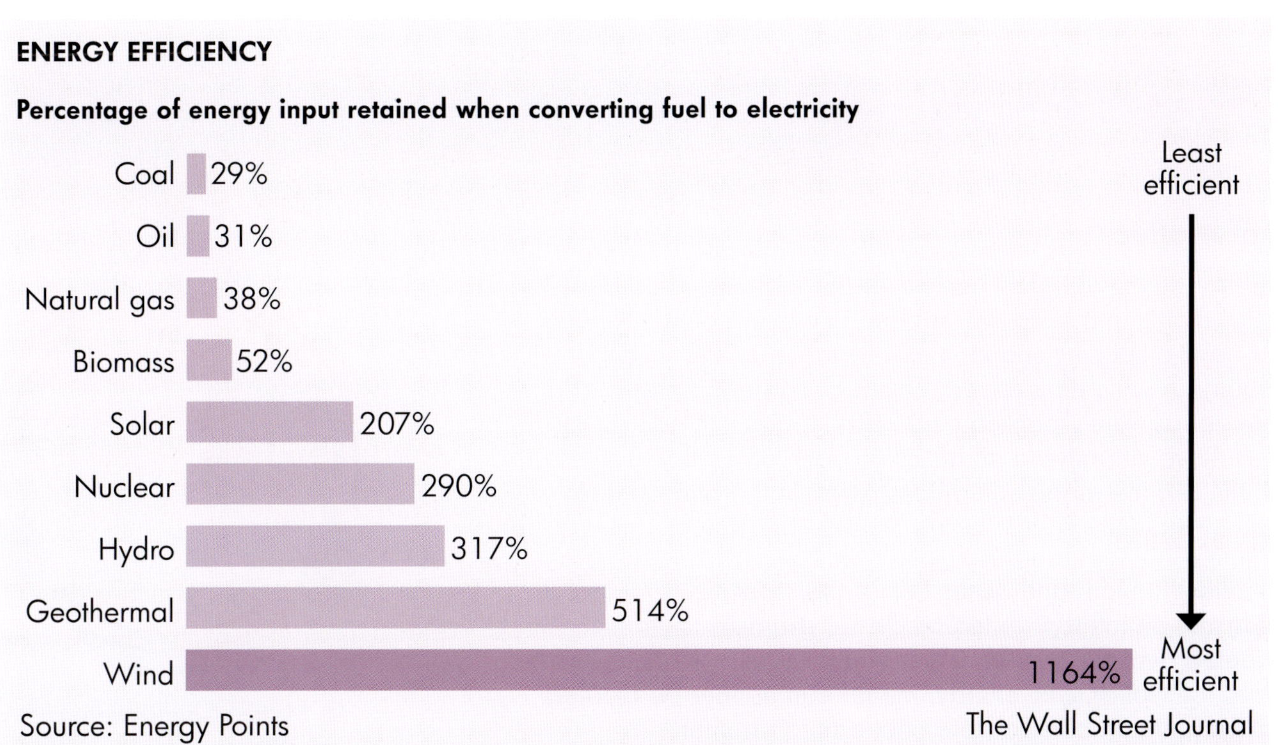

Properties of Matter

Everything present in the universe is made up of energy or matter. On Earth, matter exists in three main states—solid, liquid and gas. Plasma and Bose-Einstein condensate are two other states of matter that are achieved under specific conditions in laboratories.

States of Matter

Solids are made up of tightly packed atoms that assume a definite shape. The atoms in a solid are not free to move around. A liquid does not have a specific shape. It merely takes up the shape of the container in which it is stored. This is because the atoms of a liquid are not as tightly packed as a solid. A gas is made up of atoms that have virtually no attraction to each other. If you release a gas in the air, the atoms will diffuse away in the atmosphere.

Change of State

Certain solids, liquids, and gases can, under specific circumstances, be interconverted. A classic example is water. When heated, water becomes water vapour (gas). When cooled, it becomes ice (solid). Like energy, matter can neither be created nor destroyed. It can convert from one form to another.

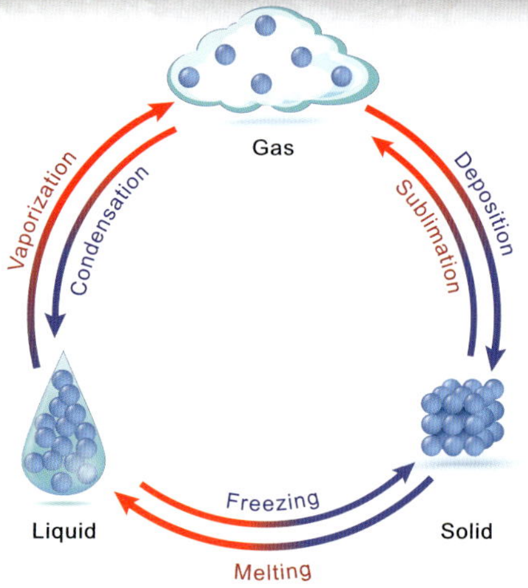

▲ *Matter can interconvert from one form to another.*

▲ *Water can change from liquid to vapour when heated (evaporation), and from vapour to liquid when cooled (condensation).*

Units of Matter

In simplest terms, mass is defined as the space occupied by any matter. Isaac Newton defined it as the quantity of matter. It is often assumed that mass and weight are the same. However, there is a difference between mass and weight. Weight is the gravitational force exerted by the Earth on a matter with specific mass. When you stand on a weighing scale or weigh an object in a weighing balance, the number of pounds shown is not only your body's mass or the object's mass, but also the gravitational pull exerted by the Earth on you or the object.

▲ *An object's weight observed in a weighing balance includes its mass and the gravitation pull on it.*

Volume is the space occupied by a solid, liquid or gas in a closed container. Density is measured as mass per volume.

Internal Energy and External Effects

The energy that is stored inside a system by the matter that makes it up is known as the internal energy. It is the sum of the potential and kinetic energy of the atoms and molecules that make up the matter.

Temperature and pressure can have an effect on the energy of the system and even change its state. Specific latent heat is a term that defines the amount of energy required to change the state of one kilogram of a substance without any change to the temperature.

The effects of various factors depend on the mass of the matter, its physical properties, and the energy input in the system. The effect of pressure is most prominent in gases. A gas stored in a container can expand or contract depending on the pressure applied.

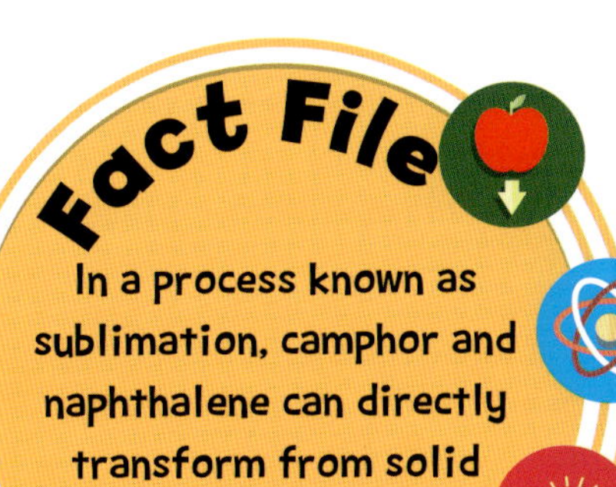

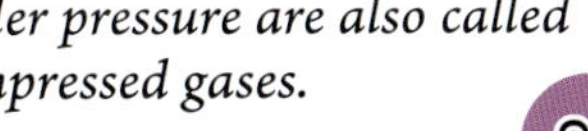

▲ *Gases stored in cylinders under pressure are also called compressed gases.*

Electricity

Electricity is a form of energy that is produced through the movement of charged particles like protons and electrons. There are two types of electricity: static electricity due to accumulation of charges and current electricity from the flow of electrons.

Uses of Electricity

In the modern world, virtually everything is powered by electricity. It is in turn produced from different sources such as wind, tides, sunlight, fossil fuels, and radioactive elements.

Materials capable of conducting electricity are classified as conductors, while those that don't conduct electricity are referred to as insulators. Semiconductors are materials that have properties of both insulation and conduction which, dependent on stimulation, can be controlled. They are therefore vital in the field of electronics as parts of a circuit.

Electrical appliances are powered directly from the main power supply from the power grid in the city or through batteries.

Electric Charge and Current

Matter is made up of atoms with electrons and protons, which are charged. A substance that has an excess of electrons is negatively charged, while another with an excess of protons is positively charged.

Since protons are bound to the nucleus, they cannot move around freely like electrons. So, a negative or positive charge in a substance occurs due to a surplus or deficit of electrons. Electric charge is measured in units called coulombs, named after the French physicist Charles-Augustin Coulomb, who developed one of the most well-known laws related to charge: like charges repel; unlike charges attract.

The flow of electric charge is known as electric current. The current is measured based on the rate of flow of electric charge. Electric current can also be defined as the flow of electrons across the atoms of the conducting material.

◀ *Copper, being a good conductor of electricity, is used in wires.*

Static Electricity

A surplus or deficiency of electrons in a localised area produces static electricity. The word 'static' means 'unmoving' to differentiate it from current electricity, which involves movement of electrons. Static electricity is caused by direct contact or friction between two materials and results in different observable phenomena like sparks, attraction, repulsion, or shocks. Devices like the Van de Graaff generator can produce large quantities of static electric charge.

Current Electricity

Current electricity is produced by the flow of electrons in a conducting medium. It comes in many forms. Batteries and solar cells produce a steady stream of electrons known as direct current (DC). Power lines transmit electricity in the form of alternating current (AC).

▲ *Touching a Van de Graaff generator causes hair to stand up straight.*

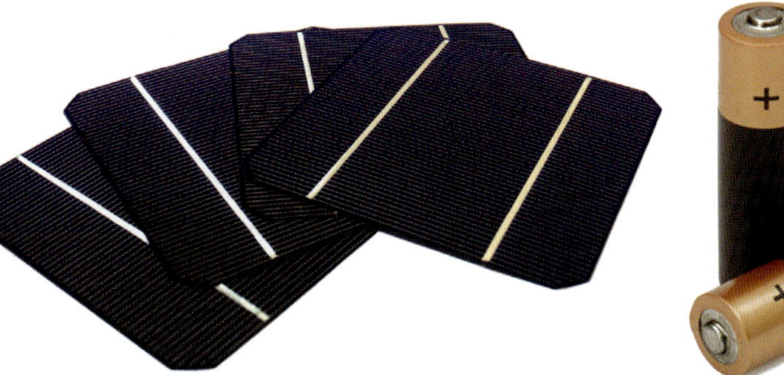

▲ *Solar cells and batteries supply electricity as direct current (DC).*

Organising the Electrons

Appliances work because of the flow of electrons inside the wires that make up the electric circuit. Wires are made of metals like copper that have loose electrons that can move around from atom to atom. In fact, when the power supply is turned off, the electrons hop haphazardly across the atoms.

When you connect an appliance to a battery, the electrons move in a steady stream from the negative to the positive terminal. This is direct current, also referred to simply as DC.

When the appliance is plugged into a power outlet, the electrons still flow, but with a little difference. Instead of flowing in a steady stream from one end to another, the electrons move forward, then reverse direction and move backward, and then forward again in repeated cycles. This type of flow of electrons is known as alternating current.

Direct current cannot be transmitted efficiently across long distances without wastage. Hence, power lines transmit electricity in the form of alternating current. The electricity in the wire moves in one direction for a short distance, then reverses and moves in the opposite direction. In one second, the current alternates 50–60 times.

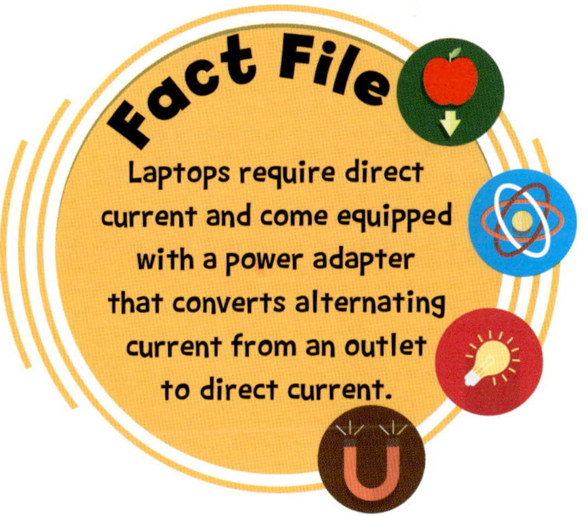

▲ *Power lines carry alternating current from stations to homes.*

Resistance and Conductance

The electrical resistance of a conducting material is the measure of how it reduces or hinders the flow of current. To give an example, a thin pipe allows only a small stream of water to trickle out, while a large pipe enables water to flow out better. Here, the thin pipe has more resistance than the large pipe. In a similar way, a thin wire that restricts the stream of electrons has higher resistance than a thick wire. Any material with high resistance will cause electrical energy to be dissipated as heat and wasted.

Conductance, the opposite of resistance, is the property of a material to conduct electric charge with ease.

Potential Difference

Electric potential is defined as the capacity of a charged object to do work. Potential difference, also referred to as voltage, is the difference in the electrical potential between two points. Current flows from one end of a circuit to another end because of the potential difference between them. In a 20-volt battery, the voltage at the negative terminal is zero, while at the positive side it is 20 volts. A circuit is created by connecting the positive and negative terminals.

Electricity always flows from a region of higher voltage to a region of lower voltage. It behaves similar to a balloon filled with air. Inside the balloon, the air is confined to a smaller space and the pressure is high. Outside, the space is vast and pressure is lower. So the air from a balloon flows out from a region of higher pressure to the lower one. In a similar way, the current flows from the positive terminal (20 volts) to the negative terminal (0 volts). When you place a component in the circuit, such as an LED bulb, the flow of electricity would make the bulb glow.

The current flowing through a component depends on the resistance and potential difference. It is given by the formula:

$$V = IR$$

V – Voltage or potential difference
I – Current
R – Resistance

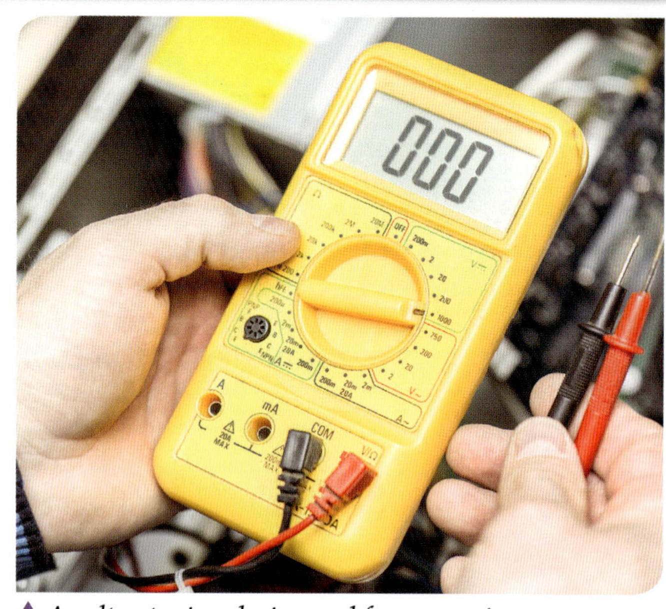

▲ *A voltmeter is a device used for measuring potential difference.*

An earth wire has a potential difference of 0 volts. It carries current only in case of a fault.

Circuits

A circuit is a closed path with electrical components through which electric current can flow. The components in a circuit can be arranged in parallel or series.

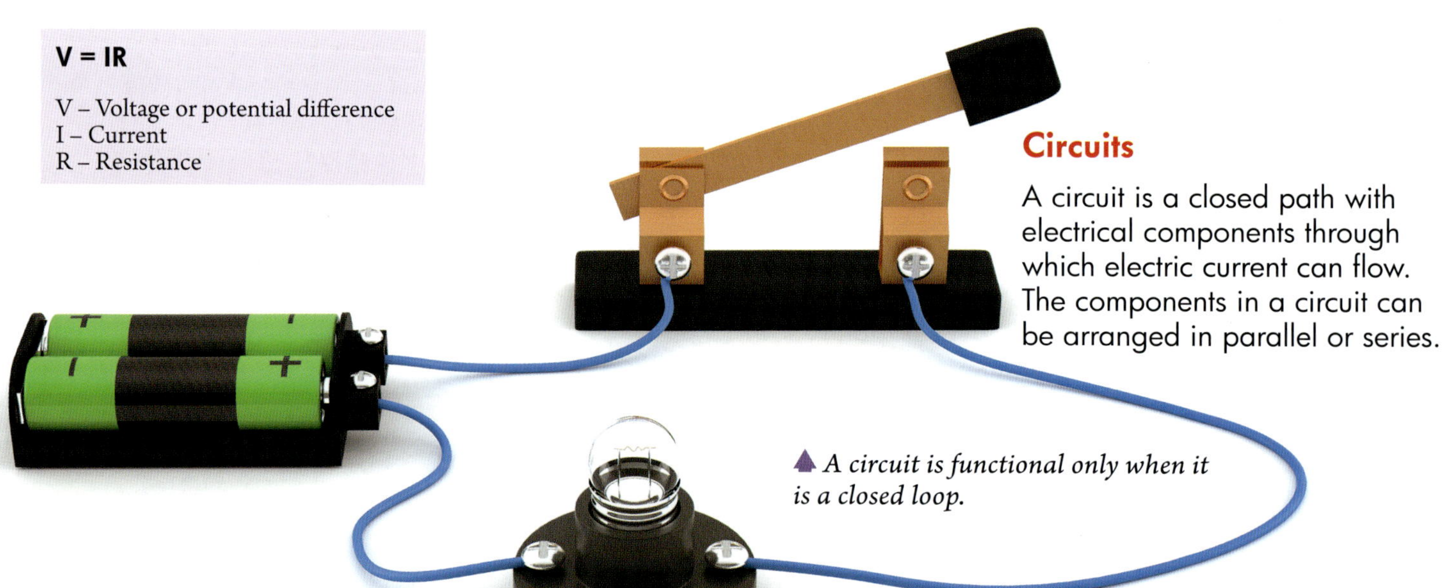

▲ *A circuit is functional only when it is a closed loop.*

In a series circuit, the same current passes through each component and the total potential difference across the circuit is shared between the components.

In a parallel circuit, the potential difference across each component is the same. The total current passing through the entire circuit is the sum of the currents through individual components.

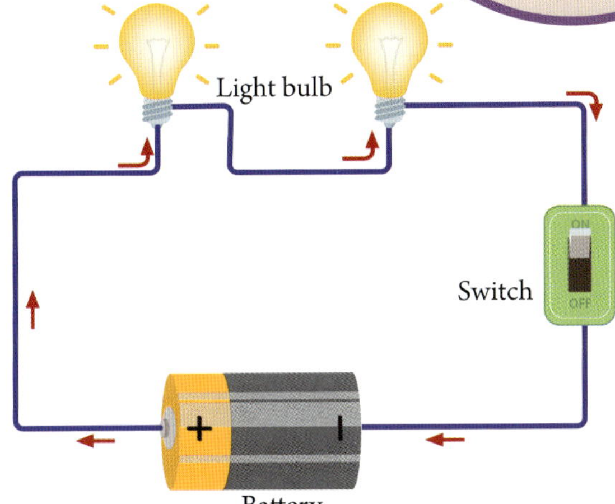

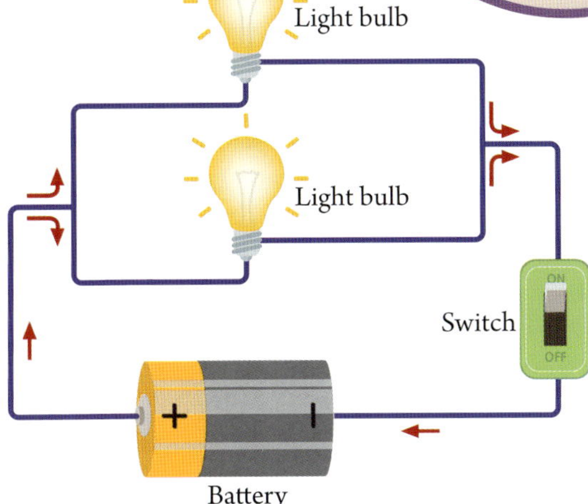

▲ *Appliances are powered or charged by connecting a cable to a power socket.*

Domestic Electric Supply

The electric supply of the main unit is alternative current with a voltage of 230V. The electrical appliances are attached to the main supply through a three-core cable that can be plugged into a power socket.

The outer part of the wire is surrounded by an insulation material like plastic or rubber. The insulation covering each type of wire is colour-coded for easy identification. Live wire has brown insulation, neutral wire blue, and earth wire has green and yellow stripes. The live wire is the one that carries the alternating current from the main supply. The neutral wire completes the circuit. The earth wire is for appliance safety purposes. In case there is a fault in the electrical supply, the earth wire provides a path back for the electric current to flow harmlessly. In the absence of an earth wire, a person can receive a severe electric shock when touching an appliance.

Power Grids

A power grid is a high-voltage power transmission network system that connects power stations and substations across a country. Power stations are equipped with transformers and electric cables that transfer power from stations to homes, workplaces, factories, and other buildings in the area. A transformer is useful for increasing or decreasing potential difference transmitted from power stations through cables.

▶ *Power stations and substations transfer power to all houses and factories in their vicinity.*

Nuclear Radiation

The nucleus of an atom consists of the protons and neutrons surrounded by an electron cloud. Almost the entire mass of the atom is concentrated in the nucleus. The nuclei of certain heavy atoms are unstable and emit radiation to achieve stability. This process is known as radioactive decay.

Radioactivity

Generally, it is the electrons of atoms that interact with each other and result in different reactions and form molecules. The nuclei of small atoms are more or less stable. The stability of a nucleus is determined by the number of protons and neutrons in it. In heavy atoms, there are many protons and neutrons. Since all protons are positively charged, the binding energy of the nucleus that holds together the protons and neutrons in the small space is not enough.

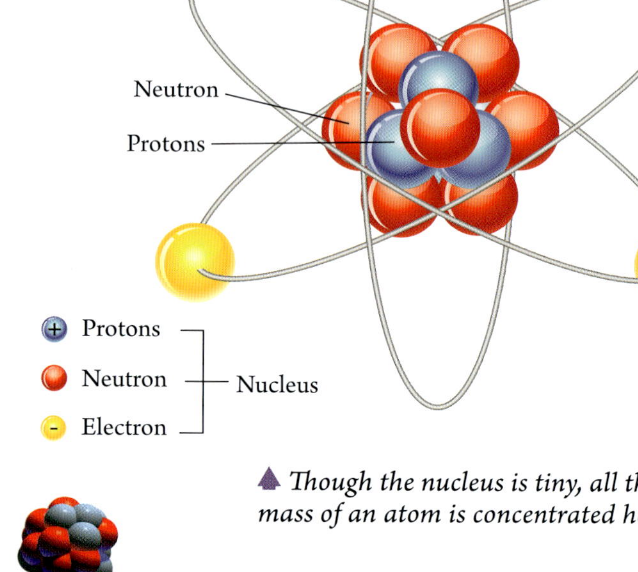

▲ *Though the nucleus is tiny, all the mass of an atom is concentrated here.*

▲ *Unstable nuclei of heavy atoms undergo fission and split into smaller atoms*

Unstable nuclei usually have excess protons and neutrons and try to lose them to achieve stability. The decay of the nuclei by emitting ionising radiation (such as alpha, beta, or gamma rays) is known as radioactivity. It is measured at the rate at which the unstable nuclei decay.

Ionising Radiation

When unstable nuclei decay, the radiation emitted is one of the three kinds: alpha or beta particles, or gamma rays.

Alpha particles: Each alpha particle consists of two neutrons and two protons and is similar to the nucleus of a helium atom.

Beta particles: A beta particle consists of a high-speed electron emitted from the nucleus when a neutron turns into a proton.

Gamma rays: Unlike alpha and beta particles, gamma rays are merely a release of energy from the nucleus to stabilise it. The release of gamma rays is almost always followed by the emission of an alpha or beta particle.

Any emission of ionising radiation changes the structure of the nucleus, and as a result the physical and chemical properties of the element. This phenomenon is known as transmutation of matter.

▼ *Penetrating power of various types of radiation: comparison of penetrating ability of alpha, beta, and neutron particles, and gamma rays and X-rays.*

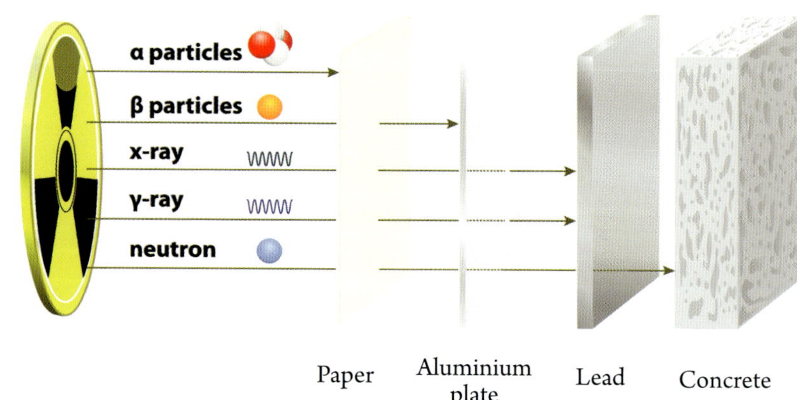

Radioactive decay is represented as nuclear equations. The emission of different types of radiation from the nucleus can have different effects. Alpha particle decay results in a change in the mass and charge of the nucleus—that is, both the mass and charge decrease. Beta particle decay does not affect the nucleus's mass, but increases the charge of the nucleus. Gamma ray emission does not change the charge or the mass of the nucleus.

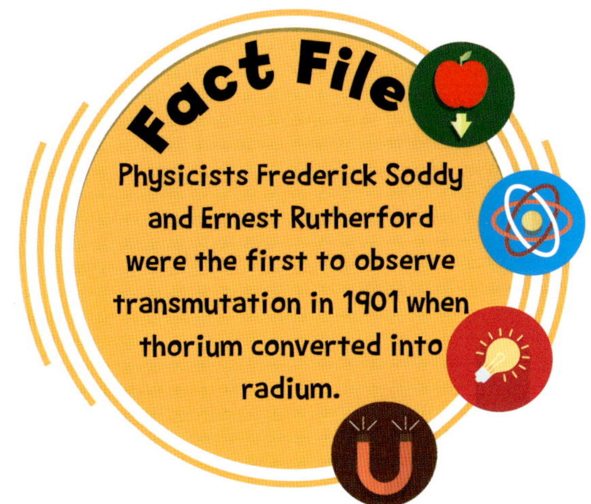

▲ *Radioactive isotopes are stored in specially designed containers with warning labels.*

Half-Life of Radioactive Elements

Radioactive elements are those elements that are capable of undergoing radioactive decay. The half-life of an isotope of a radioactive element is the time taken for the decay of half the number of atoms in a sample.

For example, consider barium-139, which has a half-life of 86 minutes. If you have 100 grams of barium-139, after 86 minutes, 50 grams of the sample would have decayed and converted into another element. After another 86 minutes, you will observe that you are left with only 25 grams of the original sample. This goes on continuously until virtually all the atoms of barium-139 have decayed and converted into another element.

Different radioactive isotopes have different half-lives. Polonium-215 has an extremely short half-life of about 0.0018 seconds, making it very unstable. On the other hand, uranium-238 has a half-life of 4.5 billion years. Radioactive isotopes are stored in containers with a specific symbol to indicate that they have to be handled with caution.

Radiocarbon dating is a procedure that uses a particular isotope of carbon, carbon-14, with a half-life of 5,730 years. It is useful for identifying the age of ancient artifacts and fossils that are less than 40,000 years old. For identifying age of older specimens, uranium isotopes (which have longer half-lives) are used.

◄ *Radiocarbon dating is one useful application of radioactive isotopes.*

Nuclear Fission and Fusion

Nuclear fission is the process by which the large and unstable nucleus of a heavy atom such as uranium is split into smaller nuclei. Nuclear fission occurs when an unstable nucleus absorbs a neutron. It is very rare for nuclear fission to occur spontaneously. The nucleus undergoing fission splits roughly into two equally sized nuclei and releases about two or three neutrons and gamma rays. Tremendous amounts of energy are also released during the nuclear fission process.

Since the products of a fission reaction possess kinetic energy, the neutrons usually start a chain reaction. This chain reaction can be designed to occur in a controlled manner inside a nuclear reactor to harvest the energy produced for electricity generation. Uncontrolled nuclear fission chain reaction causes massive explosion and widespread damage, as in the case of nuclear weapons.

Nuclear fusion is the opposite of fission and is the process by which two light nuclei fuse together to form a heavy nucleus. This process results in the conversion of mass into energy and radiation. Nuclear fusion occurs continuously in the Sun.

Much of the energy generated by the Sun is the result of nuclear fusion of hydrogen nuclei into helium, continuously. About 620 million metric tons of hydrogen inside the Sun is converted into helium every second.

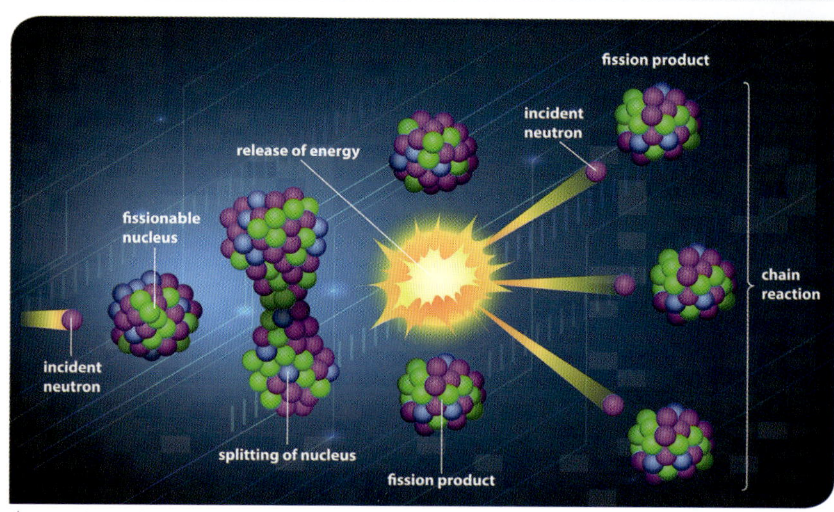

▲ *Nuclear fission results in the splitting of big nuclei into smaller ones.*

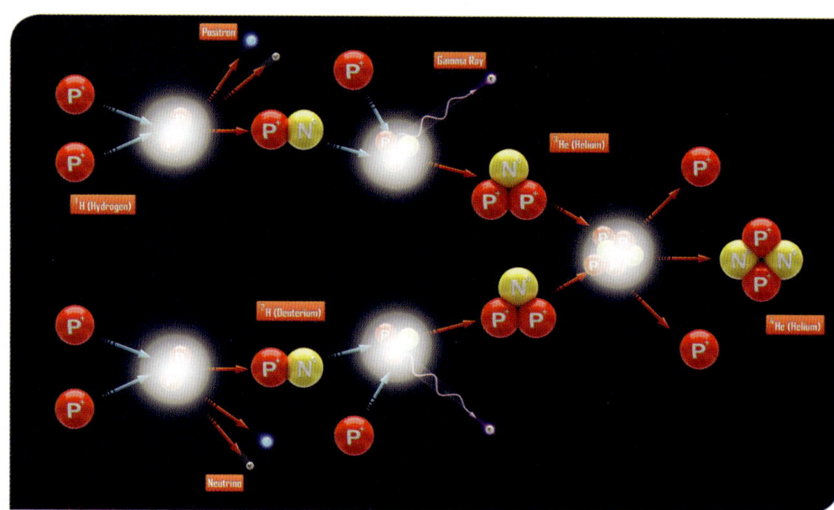

▲ *Nuclear fusion is the opposite reaction of fission.*

▲ *Nuclear power plants have to be operated safely to avoid dangers.*

Nuclear Reactor

Nuclear power plants consist of one or more nuclear reactors that use the mechanism of nuclear fission on heavy atoms like uranium and plutonium to produce nuclear energy. The energy results in a lot of heat that is used to convert water into steam, and the steam is used for powering electric turbines to produce electricity.

Nuclear energy generation has its advantages and disadvantages. It does not cause pollution and is more energy-efficient than many other fuel sources. Producing nuclear energy does not cause air pollution.

However, building a nuclear power plant is very expensive because many safety features have to be constructed for safe handling of the radioactive material. Any accidents in the nuclear plant can cause large-scale destruction and endanger lives. The Chernobyl nuclear accident that occurred in Russia in 1986 is one of the worst nuclear disasters in history. Presently, there are 451 nuclear reactors across different parts of the world, contributing about 5 percent of the total global energy produced.

Earth is surrounded by cosmic radiation but is protected by its magnetic field and atmosphere.

Background Radiation

We are surrounded by background radiation. The cosmic rays from outer space and artificially constructed sources of nuclear radiation (from weapons and reactor accidents) can cause physical damage to living tissues. The quantum of damage and risk depends on the dosage of the radiation. Radiation is measured in units called sieverts.

Radioactive Contamination and Hazards

Close proximity or contact with radioactive elements is dangerous because of the ionising radiation they emit. The process of exposing an object to nuclear radiation is known as irradiation. An irradiated object cannot become radioactive. Usually the different parts of the body can tolerate about 0.15 to 0.5 sieverts of radiation without causing any considerable harmful effects.

Radioactive waste generated in nuclear reactors is disposed of with great care and precaution.

Radioactive waste is stored and disposed of in special containers

Storage of Radioactive Materials

Radioactive isotopes as well as waste from nuclear reactors have to be stored in suitable containers. Usually, lead is the choice of material for containers. Lead provides protection against radiation mostly because it is dense and thick. Sometimes, steel containers with concrete casing can also be used as an alternative for lead. For an additional degree of safety, the materials are stored in rooms or spaces with locks or limited access. The radioactivity symbol is prominently displayed to warn people from handling the containers.

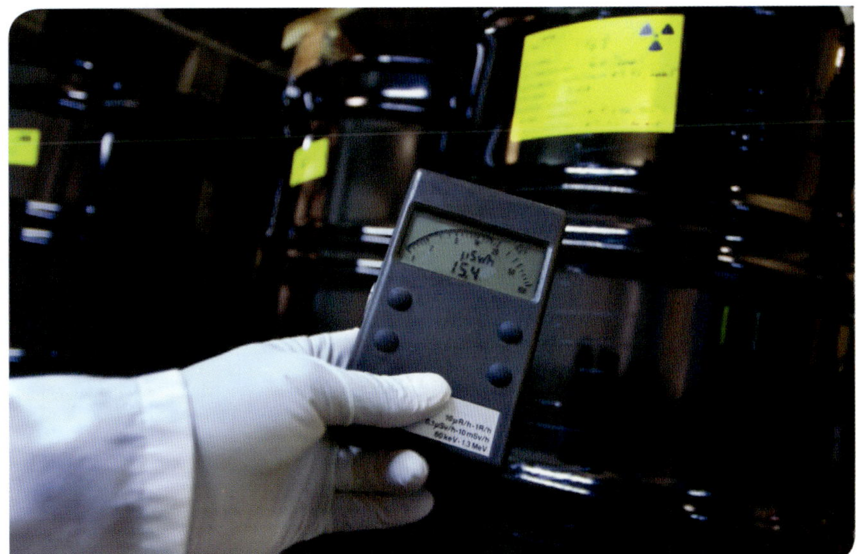

A Geiger counter is used for checking radiation levels of radioisotopes.

A Geiger counter is a device used for detecting and measuring radiation from radioactive materials. People who work in such laboratories routinely assess the radiation levels using this device as a safety precaution.

The best method, currently used, for the disposal of radioactive waste is to dispose of it deep underground in specially designed facilities. This is known as geological disposal and is done to ensure that the radioactive waste does not contaminate groundwater or soil.

Forces

Force is defined as an interaction such as a push or a pull with an object which, when not opposed by anything else, will change an object's motion. While constructing machines and mega projects, engineers analyse the effect of force and design accordingly.

▲ *A footballer kicking a ball is an example of contact force.*

Contact and Noncontact Forces

All forces between objects are contact or noncontact forces. Contact forces are physically in contact with the object, while noncontact forces are physically separated. There are many different kinds of forces that one can observe.

A few examples of contact forces include friction, air resistance, and tension. Gravitational force exerted by the Earth and electrostatic force are examples of noncontact forces.

▲ *Gravity is a noncontact force that pulls any object toward the ground.*

Gravity

An object's weight is the force exerted by gravity on the object. The force from gravity is the result of the gravitational field around the Earth. The weight of an object depends on the gravitational field strength with respect to the object's location. An object's weight is directly proportional to its mass.

Weight can be calculated using the formula:

$$W = m\,g$$

W – Weight
m – Mass of the object
g – Gravitational field strength

Types of Force

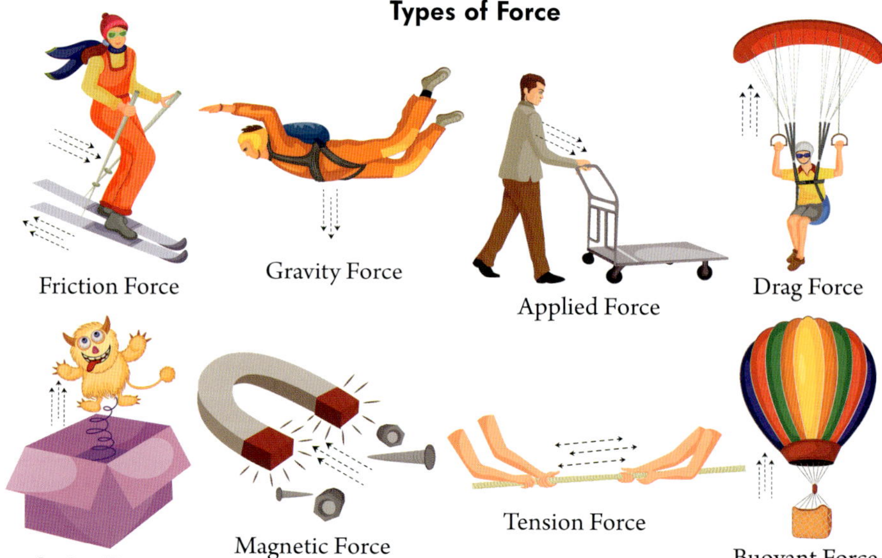

Resultant Force

An object can be acted upon by a number of forces at the same time. If a single force could have the same effect as the sum total of all other forces, then such a force is called a resultant force. A resultant force can be equal to many other forces acting together. On the other hand, the resultant force can be zero when the net total forces cancel out.

Work and Moment

When the application of a force causes an object to move across a certain distance, then work is said to be done.

Work done = Force x distance moved

W = F s

W – Work
F – Force
s – Distance from original position

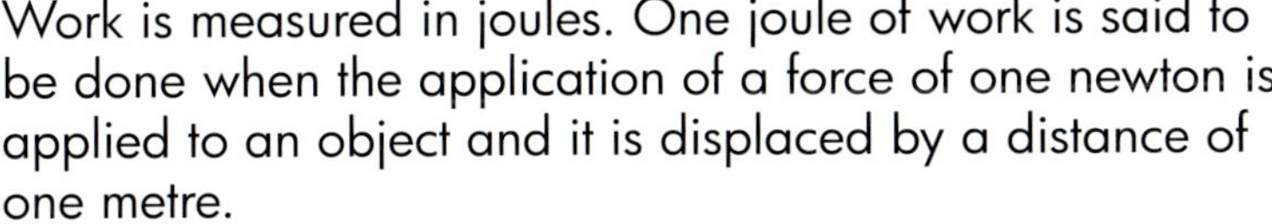

Work is measured in joules. One joule of work is said to be done when the application of a force of one newton is applied to an object and it is displaced by a distance of one metre.

Sometimes, a force or a group of forces may cause an object to rotate instead of moving. The turning effect of the force is called the moment.

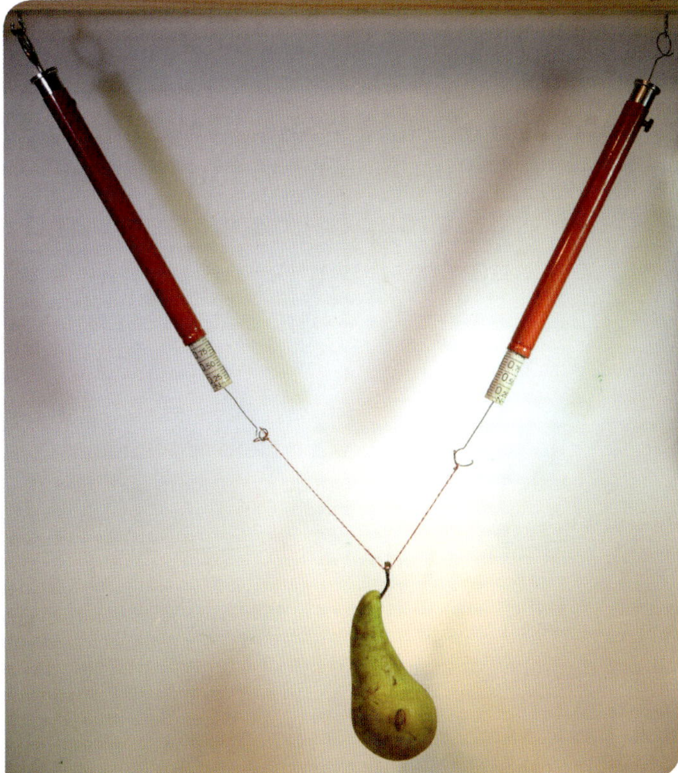

▲ *When two or more forces act on a body, they cancel out or add up.*

◀ *Work is the result of force applied and distance traveled.*

Atmospheric Pressure

The atmosphere is a thin, protective layer around the Earth. It has many layers, and with increasing altitude, the air becomes less dense. The number of air molecules above a surface decreases with an increase in height. The force applied by the entire body of air in the atmosphere is known as atmospheric pressure or barometric pressure, which can be measured using a device called a barometer.

◀ *A barometer is used for measuring atmospheric pressure.*

Motion

Even as you observe your surroundings, you will realise that most things you see are in motion. Even though we do not sense it, Earth is hurtling across space around the Sun at an incredible speed. Motion is an important phenomenon in the universe, and different kinds of forces are responsible for motion.

Types of Motion

Motion can be classified as simple or complex. Simple motion consists of an object moving along a straight line, or a pendulum swinging to and fro at a fairly constant rate.

Some of the common types of motion include:

Linear motion: An object moving along a straight line is said to be in linear motion. This is one of the most fundamental types of motion. A moving object, when not subject to any external force, will continue to move in a straight line with constant velocity.

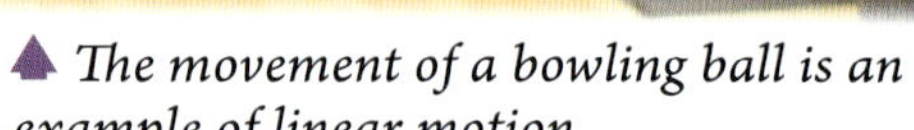
▲ *The movement of a bowling ball is an example of linear motion.*

Circular motion: The movement of an object in a circular path. The orbit of a planet around the Sun is a classic example of circular motion.

Rotary motion: The rotation of an object around a fixed point is rotary motion. A Ferris wheel and the rotation of a planet around its axis are examples of this type of motion.

▲ *A ferris wheel exhibits rotary motion.*

Random motion: Movement of any object that is not easy to predict, fixed or regular, is called random motion.

▲ *The action of a saw is a reciprocating motion.*

Reciprocating motion: The to-and-fro rhythmic movement of an object, like a saw cutting wood, is known as reciprocating motion.

Oscillation: The movement of an object from one end of its central position to the other end and then back to the central position and further on is known as oscillation. The pendulum exhibits oscillatory motion.

▲ *This device, Newton's cradle, exhibits oscillatory motion.*

Measuring Motion

Distance travelled by an object is how far it travels. Displacement, measures the distance travelled in a straight line from one point to another along with the direction. Speed is measured as the rate at which an object travels. No object ever travels at a constant speed, and it varies continuously.

The speed of a person depends on the terrain, fitness level, age and other factors. Different activities are done at different speeds. On average, a person can walk a distance of 1.5 metres per second, run 3 metres per second or cycle at 6 metres per second.

Even the speed of wind or sound is never constant. The speed of sound in air versus its speed in water varies.

Speed can be measured using the formula:

$$\text{Speed} = \frac{\text{Distance Travelled}}{\text{Time Taken}}$$

Velocity is a measure of how fast an object moves in a particular direction. The rate of change of velocity is called acceleration.

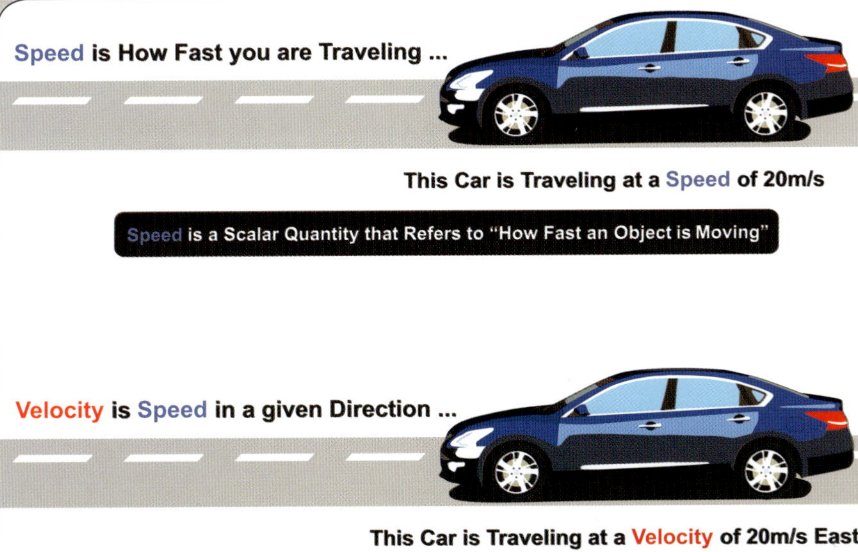

Speed denotes how fast one travels, while velocity also gives direction.

Gravity and Motion

Close to the Earth's surface, any object that is falling freely is under the influence of Earth's gravitational force and has an acceleration of 9.8 metres/second. If a body is falling through a fluid, it will initially accelerate due to the effect of gravity and gradually slow down (or decelerate) due to the buoyant force of the liquid that acts upward, in the opposite direction of gravity.

Gravitational force acts on a body and pulls it toward the Earth.

Newton's Laws

Isaac Newton was one of the most influential scientists in history and made major contributions in the understanding of important physical phenomena, especially gravity and planetary motion. He set forth a set of three laws to describe the relation between mass and motion.

Newton's Law of Motion

Newton put together a set of three laws of motion that make up the foundation of mechanics: the study of motion of objects in the universe. The laws were developed to predict and describe the relationship between an object and the forces acting upon it, and how the object's motion is affected by the forces.

Isaac Newton compiled the laws in his work *Principia Mathematica*, first published in 1687. Newton's laws have been observed and experimentally verified for over two centuries.

Newton's First Law of Motion

"Every object continues in its state of rest or uniform motion in a straight line unless it is forced to change the state due to the action of external forces."

The tendency of an object to remain unchanged at rest or in motion is called inertia. The state of inertia is affected only when one or more forces act on the object. Even if there are multiple forces acting on an object, the object can continue in its state of inertia if the forces cancel each other out.

▲ *Isaac Newton was among the most influential physicists in the world.*

Newton's First Law of Motion

An object at rest stays at rest.

An object acted upon by a balanced force stays at rest.

An object acted upon by an unbalanced force changes speed and direction.

An object at rest stays at rest.

An object acted upon by an unbalanced force changes speed and direction.

An object in motion stays in motion.

An object acted upon by an unbalanced force changes speed and direction.

Astronauts sometimes travel to the International Space Station to conduct repairs or routine maintenance. They can place the tools beside them in space and the tools will stay, without falling down or moving away. This is because there is no force acting on them (such as gravity) to interfere with their state of rest. Similarly, if the tool is pushed away, it will continue moving unless stopped by some external force.

Newton's Second Law

"The greater the mass of an object, the more force it takes to accelerate it."

Acceleration of an object is the effect of some force acting on it. It is inversely proportional to the object's mass. The greater the mass of the object that is being accelerated, the more force that is needed to accelerate it. Newton's second law of motion gives the relationship between force, acceleration, and mass through a mathematical formula:

Resultant Force = Mass x Acceleration

Newton's Second Law of Motion

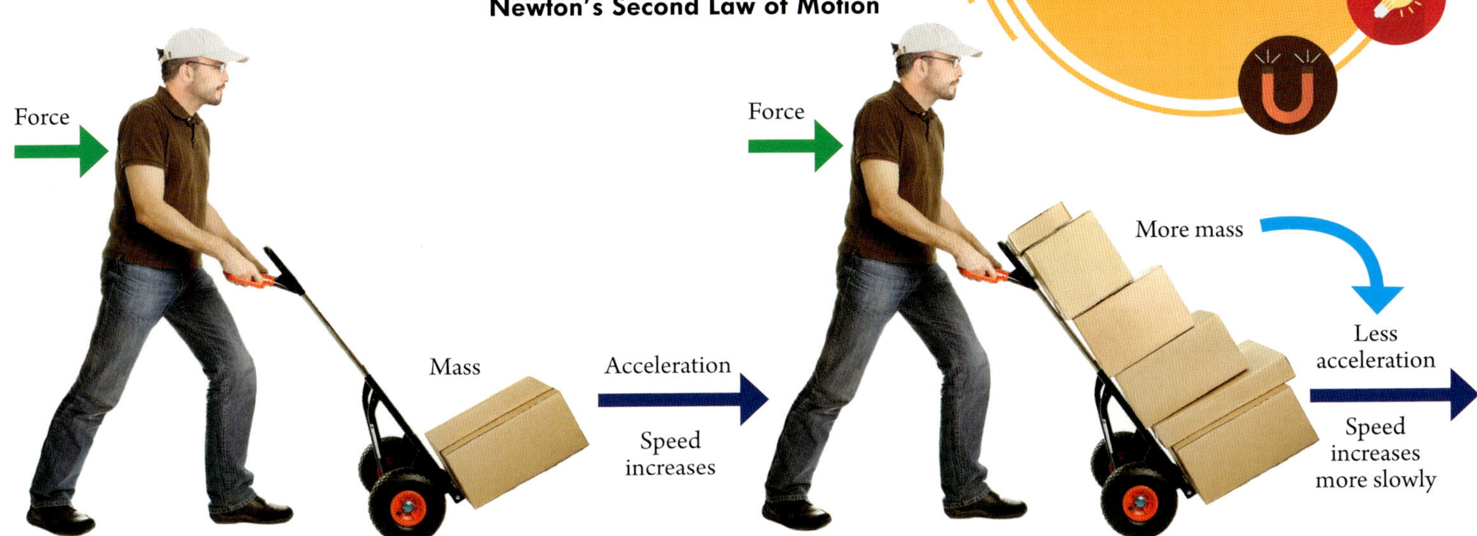

Newton's Third Law

"For every action, there is an equal and opposite reaction."

In every interaction, a pair of forces acts on the two bodies or objects. The size of the force of the first object is equivalent to that of the second object acting in the opposite direction. According to this law, all forces come in pairs.

A rocket that is preparing to be launched into space pushes against the ground, applying the force using its powerful engines. The ground applies an equal and opposite force to push the rocket away from it in the upward direction.

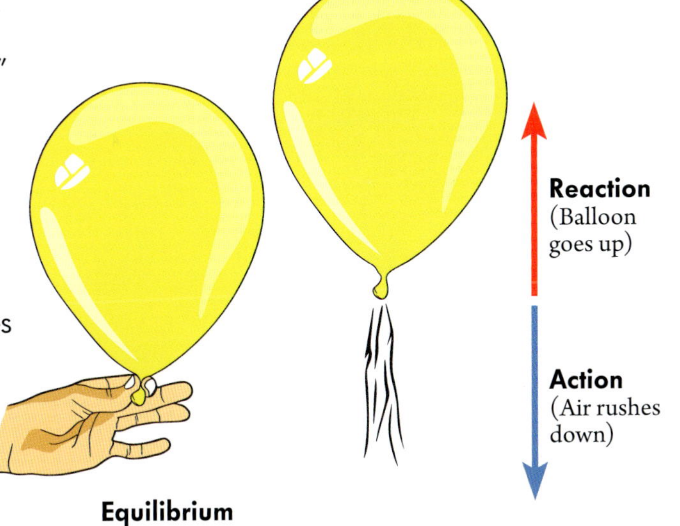

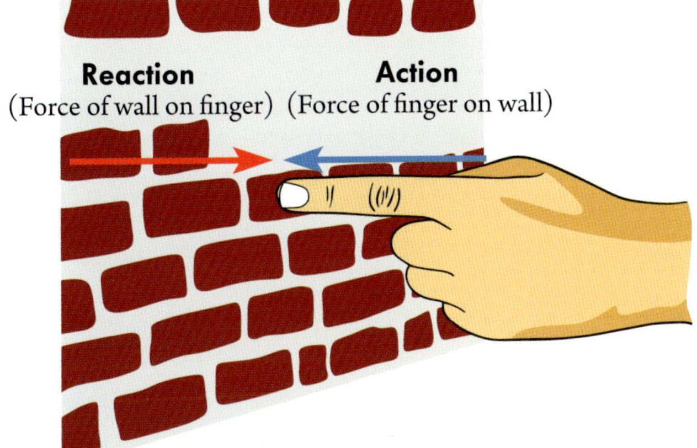

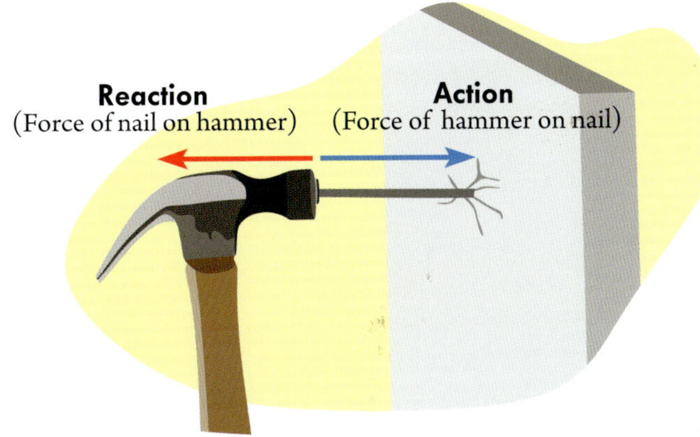

Physics of Driving

All moving objects, such as vehicles, are subject to different laws of physics. Many factors are involved in the driving of a vehicle—gravity, friction, inertia, potential energy, and kinetic energy. These factors decide how the vehicle moves and interacts with objects around it.

Driving Uphill and Downhill

The two major factors acting upon a moving vehicle are gravity and traction. Gravity is a force that pulls all objects closer to the Earth. Friction is a force that resists motion when two materials slide against each other.

Traction is caused due to friction between the road and the weight of the car upon the tires. Traction is essential because it is the interaction between the road and the tires that enables a driver to steer the car.

Gravity can aid or hinder a vehicle depending on whether it is being driven uphill or downhill. When a driver drives a vehicle uphill, gravity works against it, as its natural tendency is to pull it down toward the Earth. The driver needs to accelerate the vehicle more to work against the gravitational force. While driving downhill, gravity aids the vehicle instead of being a hindrance. Gravity will enable the vehicle to move faster.

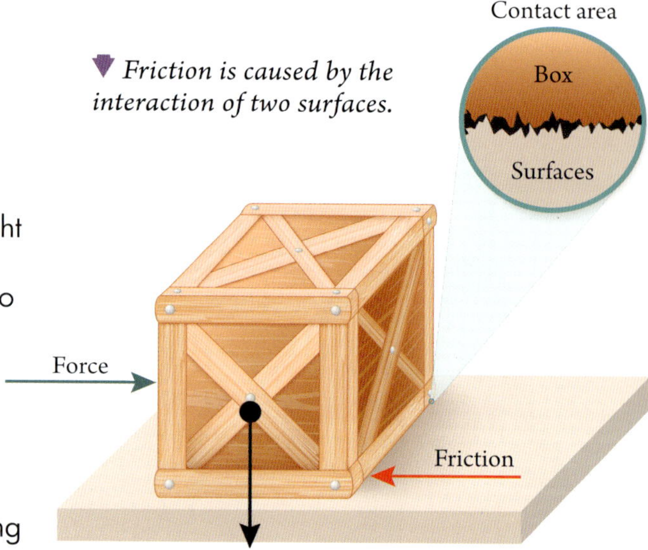

Friction is caused by the interaction of two surfaces.

Braking

All vehicles are designed for acceleration. It is important for them to be equipped with a braking mechanism that enables their movement to come to a halt by gradually slowing them down. The brakes slow down a moving vehicle by using friction between the wheel and another object. When a force is applied to the vehicle's brakes, the frictional force between the wheels and the braking mechanism reduces the kinetic energy of the vehicle.

The greater the speed of the vehicle, the higher the braking force has to be to bring it to a halt. Consequently, the greater the braking force, the larger the deceleration will be. Large and sudden decelerations can often cause the brakes to heat up and even lose control.

A driver's reaction time is defined as the time taken to respond to a particular situation. As this is a variable factor, the reaction time varies greatly from person to person. Also, different factors can affect the reaction time of an individual.

The stopping distance of a vehicle is calculated as the sum of the distance travelled by the vehicle during the driver's reaction time and the distance traveled after applying the brakes, also called the braking distance.

Potential Energy and Momentum of a Vehicle

When a bicycle is on top of a hill, it possesses potential energy due to gravity. The stored potential energy is converted into kinetic energy while riding it downhill.

The force of a moving vehicle is called its momentum. The vehicle's momentum depends on its weight and speed. A driver doubles a car's momentum when he increases its speed from 10 kilometres per hour to 20. When a speeding vehicle is stopped, the momentum is overcome by the friction of the brakes applied between the wheels and the road.

▶ *Potential and kinetic energy interconvert when a person rides uphill and downhill.*

▲ *Brakes slow down a moving vehicle.*

▲ *A fast-moving vehicle needs a higher braking force to stop.*

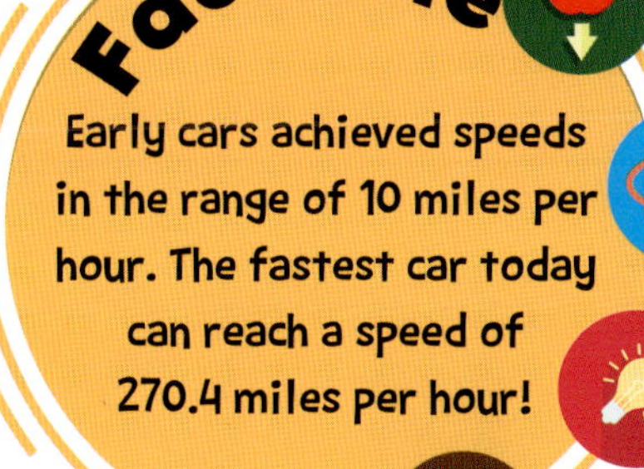

Magnetism

People have known about magnetism since ancient times. Lodestones that were capable of attracting iron objects were used for navigation because of their ability to always align toward the north.

Principle of Magnetism

Originally, the domain theory was used to explain magnetism. According to the theory, a strongly magnetic substance has tiny pockets called domains. There is no magnetism when the domains are arranged randomly. However, when the domains align in the same direction, the net effect produces a magnetic field.

With a better understanding of atoms and their constituents, scientists identified that magnetism arose as a result of the rapidly spinning motion of electrons. Since electrons have electric charge, the spinning motion generated a magnetic field. The sum total of the magnetic fields generated by all the electrons in a material confers its magnetic property.

▲ *Lodestones were used for navigation in ancient times.*

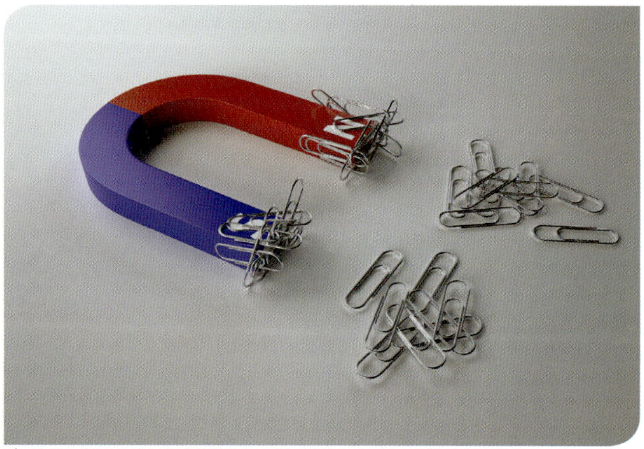
▲ *Ferromagnetic materials are used for making permanent magnets.*

Types of Magnetism

Every object or material on Earth exhibits one of the three types of magnetism: ferromagnetism, paramagnetism, and diamagnetism.

Ferromagnetism: Is considered the strongest form of magnetism and means 'magnetic like iron.' Ferromagnetism is exhibited by a few elements such as iron and rare earth metals. They can be magnetised when brought in close proximity to a magnetic field. They remain magnetised even after the magnetic field is removed. Heating or striking a ferromagnetic material can make it lose some or all of its magnetic properties.

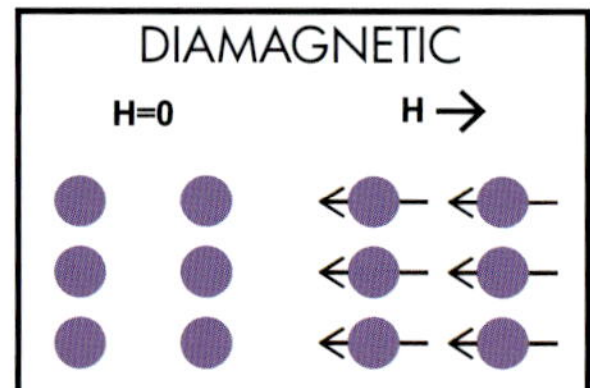

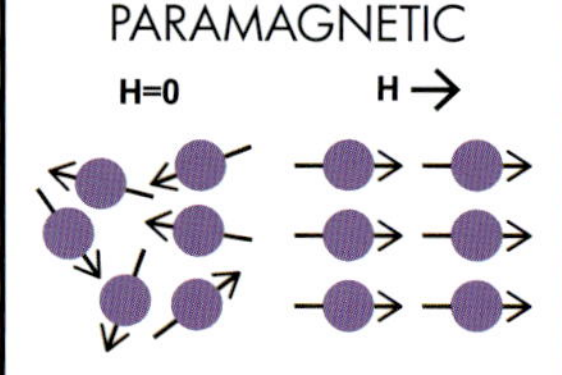

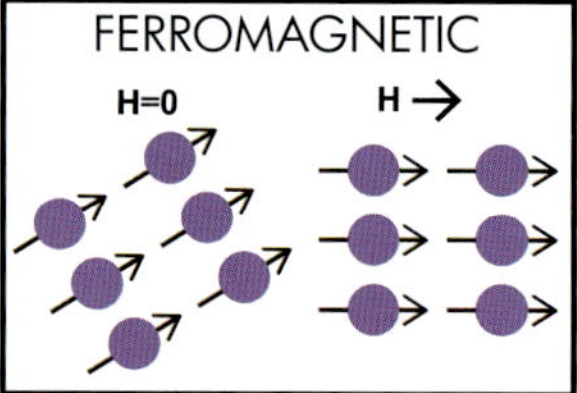

▲ *Magnetism is conferred by the direction of alignment of spinning electrons*

Paramagnetism: Is a weak form of magnetism exhibited by certain elements like gold, copper and aluminium. A paramagnetic material, when suspended from a string, aligns parallel to the Earth's magnetic field. Paramagnetism is so weak that it is nearly unobservable. Like ferromagnetism, paramagnetism diminishes upon heating.

Diamagnetism: Nonmetals and most other materials exhibit diamagnetism. Diamagnetic materials repel magnetic fields. At the atomic level, diamagnetism is caused by the net spin of electrons cancelling out and becoming zero. When a diamagnetic material is brought into a magnetic field, it aligns opposite to the direction of the magnetic field. Pyrolytic carbon is a material that is so strongly diamagnetic that it is repelled by neodymium magnets.

▲ *Strongly diamagnetic material gets repelled from a strong magnet.*

Magnetic Field

A magnetic field is the space around a magnet where its magnetism is the strongest. Generally, the magnetic force is strongest near the poles of a magnet. Two magnets, when brought in contact, exert magnetic force on each other, which could result in attraction or repulsion. The magnetic force is an example of a noncontact force.

Fact File

Magnets are an important component of all laptop and desktop computers.

▲ *Two magnets can attract or repel each other.*

A permanent magnet always has its own magnetic field. An induced magnet is any magnetic material that becomes a magnet when placed within the magnetic field. It loses all or most of its magnetic properties when moved away from the influence of the magnetic field. The magnetic lines of force emanate from the north pole and converge at the south pole, and reconnect inside the magnet. The lines of force never intersect.

When a magnet is rubbed over magnetic materials like iron or nickel, it can magnetise the material. Magnets can lose their magnetic properties if heated.

▲ *Iron filings can be used to demonstrate the magnetic lines of force.*

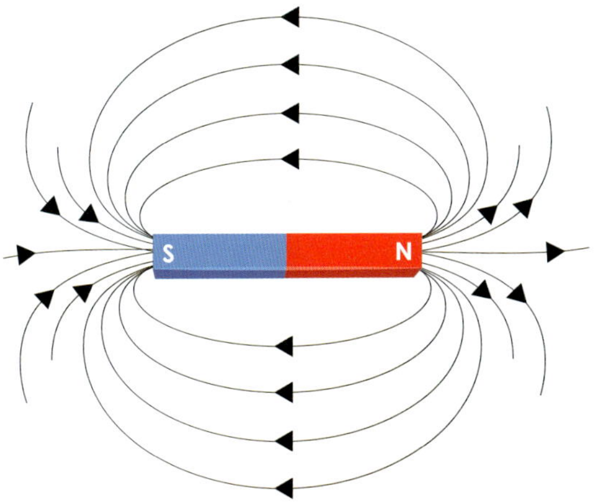

Northern and Southern Lights

The northern lights phenomenon, or aurora borealis, is caused by the interaction of charged particles with Earth's magnetic field. It can be viewed in Alaska and Iceland. The southern lights, also called aurora australis, is observed in New Zealand, Tasmania and Antarctica.

These phenomenal displays are produced when highly charged electrons from the solar wind interact with Earth's magnetic lines of force. When the electrons enter the Earth's atmosphere, they interact with the nitrogen and oxygen present in it. The colour of the lights depend on which gas the electrons interact with.

▲ *The northern lights are colourful displays of lights caused by Earth's magnetic field.*

Properties of Magnets

Any material capable of producing a magnetic field is called a magnet. The unique properties of magnets are valuable in understanding the phenomenon of magnetism and also find applications in a variety of fields.

Nature of Magnets

Natural magnets have two poles, a north pole and a south pole. No matter how many times the magnet is cut or divided, it will always have two poles. Just like electric charges, like magnetic poles repel and unlike poles attract. The north pole and the south pole attract each other. Even circular and disc magnets have two poles, one on either side or at two ends.

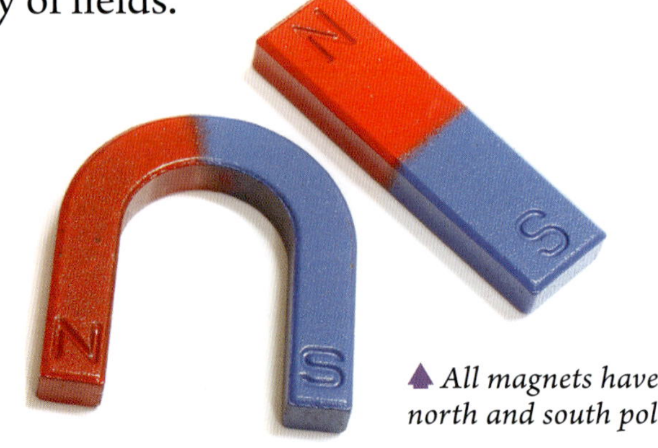

▲ *All magnets have a north and south pole.*

▲ *William Gilbert suggested that Earth was like a giant magnet.*

Earth: A Giant Magnet

A magnetic compass consists of a thin needle made of magnet that can align itself to the Earth's North Pole no matter where one stands. This phenomenon occurs only because the Earth itself behaves like a giant magnet. The Earth is rich in magnetic material like iron that gives it its magnetic properties.

The first person to suggest that the Earth behaves like a gigantic magnet was William Gilbert, in 1600. The Earth's magnetic field stretches out into space for thousands of kilometres and is known as the magnetosphere. The magnetosphere plays a crucial role in protecting us from the harmful cosmic radiation and charged particles from the Sun.

▼ *Earth has a magnetic field that extends for many kilometres into space.*

Magnetic Fields in the Solar System

The magnetic field of any object is measured in units called teslas. Earth has a considerably strong gravitational field, but its magnetic field is surprisingly weak. To give a comparison, an ordinary bar magnet has a magnetic field strength at least 100–1,000 times stronger than that of Earth. The strongest magnets ever manufactured in laboratories can have a magnetic field up to 900,000 times stronger than the Earth's magnetic field.

The Moon does not exhibit magnetism because it is not made up of a sufficient percentage of any elements that have magnetic properties. The Sun and the larger planets like Jupiter, Saturn, Uranus and Neptune have a much stronger magnetic field.

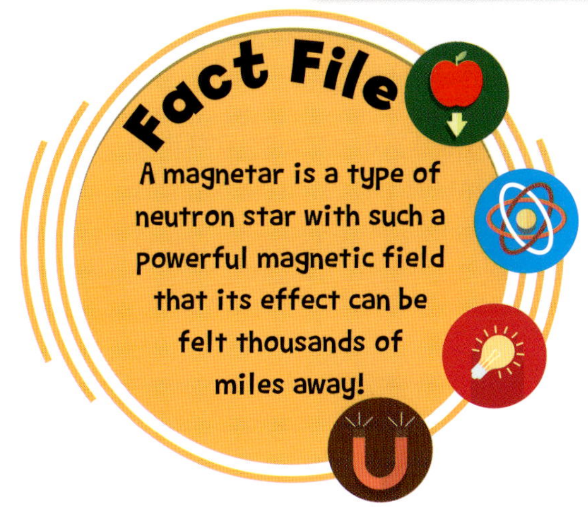

▲ *Neodymium iron boron magnets.*

▲ *Inexpensive and easily available ceramic magnets.*

Types of Magnets

Some of the most powerful permanent magnets are made by combining different magnetic materials. The four types of permanent magnets are:

1. Neodymium Iron Boron (NdFeB) Magnets: These magnets are made with an alloy of neodymium, iron and boron.

The NdFeB magnets can be made to be small and compact yet very powerful. On the downside, they tend to be brittle and have very low resistance to corrosion unless coated with a protective layer. These magnets are generally coated with iron, nickel or gold and are used in many different applications.

2. Samarium Cobalt (SmCo) Magnets: They are made using an alloy of samarium and cobalt. Like the NdFeB variety, SmCo magnets are also very strongly magnetic with the added advantages of being resistant to temperature and oxidation—and hence they are very durable. However, SmCo magnets are very expensive and tend to break easily. Both NdFeB and SmCo magnets are made from rare earth metals.

3. Alnico Magnets: The magnets are named from the first letters of the main components—aluminium, nickel and cobalt. Unlike the rare earth magnets, these magnets can be stripped of their magnetic properties very easily.

◀ *Alnico magnets are made of an alloy of aluminium, nickel, and cobalt.*

4. Ceramic Magnets: Also called ferrite magnets, they are made of iron oxide and barium or strontium carbonate. These magnets have strong magnetic properties and are cheap and easy to produce and hence are commonly used.

Electromagnetism

Electricity and magnetism were originally considered to be different and unrelated phenomena. The possibility of electricity and magnetism being interrelated was proposed and verified in the nineteenth century. The term 'electromagnetism' refers to the interaction of electric and magnetic fields.

Observation of Electromagnetism

In the year 1820, Hans Christian Oersted, a Danish physicist, discovered electromagnetism quite by accident. While switching a battery on and off, he noticed deflection in a magnetic needle placed nearby. It helped him identify that magnetic fields radiate in all directions from a wire carrying current.

▲ *Hans Christian Oersted discovered that electricity and magnetism were related.*

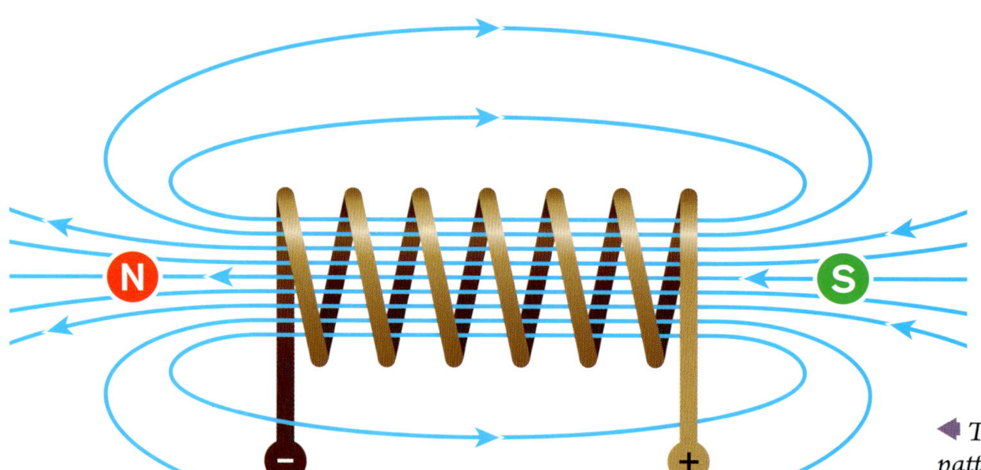

◀ *The electromagnetic field pattern around a coil of wire.*

Electromagnet

A naturally magnetic substance like iron, nickel or cobalt can be converted into an electromagnet by wrapping it tightly with coils of wire and connecting the two ends of a wire to a battery. This electromagnet temporarily acquires magnetic properties and will retain it as long as it is connected to electricity. The more coils present, the stronger the magnetic effect.

Electromagnets versus Permanent Magnets

A permanent magnet has fixed north and south poles that cannot be altered. The north-south polarity of electromagnets can be altered as and when necessary by changing the direction of the current in the coil.

Industrial-scale electromagnets are very powerful and can produce magnetic fields stronger than permanent magnets. The biggest advantage of an electromagnet is that it is possible to adjust its magnetic force strength by altering the amount of current that flows through it or the number of turns of wire.

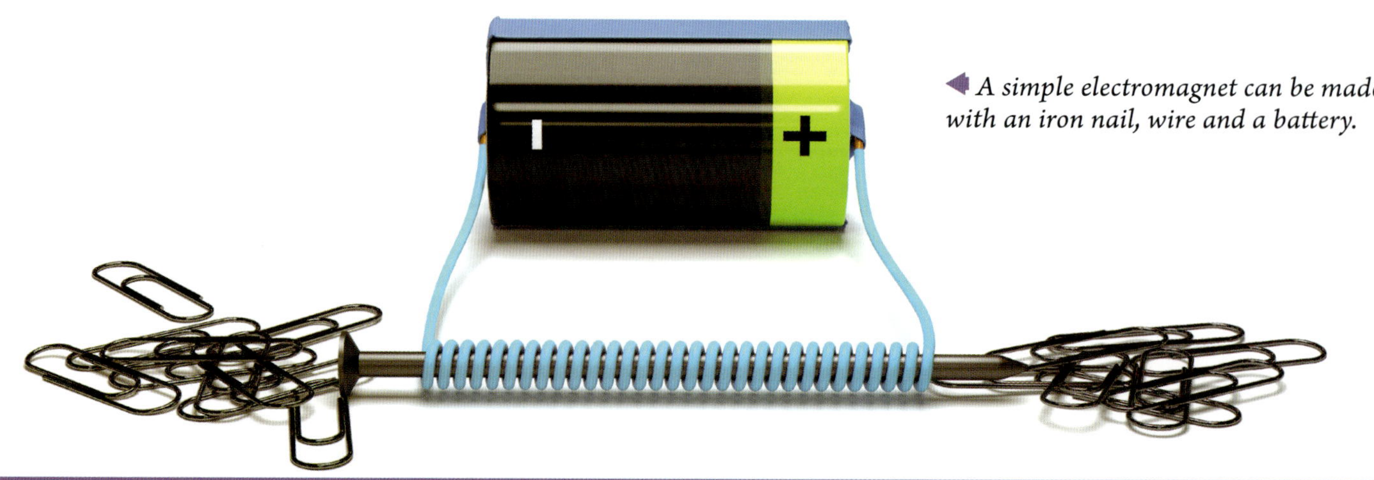

◀ *A simple electromagnet can be made with an iron nail, wire and a battery.*

Mechanism of Electromagnetism

Inside a wire, the flow of electrons results in the formation of a magnetic field. The magnetic field lines are always oriented in a direction perpendicular to the flow of electricity. The magnetic field force created by an electromagnet is also sometimes called the magnetomotive force. The strength of this force is determined by the number of coils and the amount of current passing through an electromagnet.

A cylindrical coil of wire acting as a magnet when carrying electric current is called a solenoid. A solenoid can achieve good magnetic field strength owing to its coils and shape. The magnetic field created within a solenoid is uniform and strong.

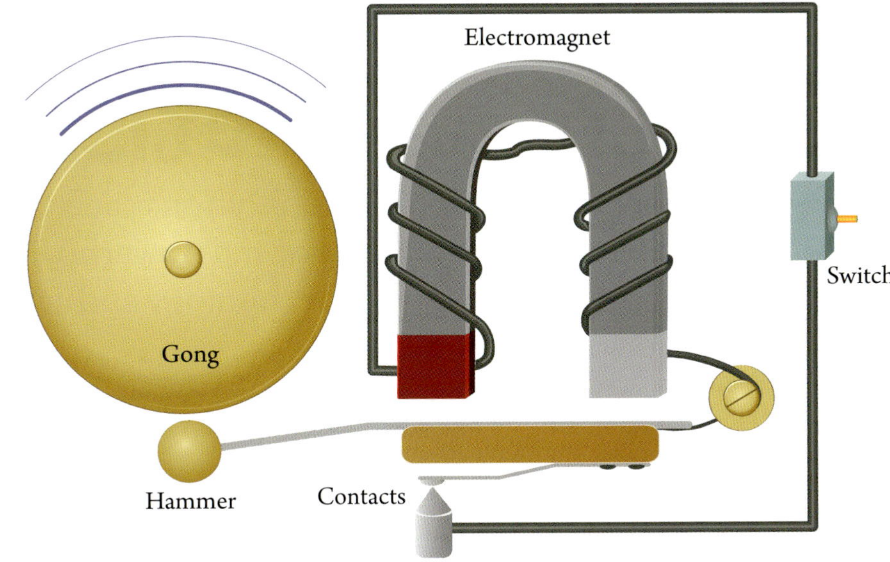

▲ *An electric bell is a device that works on the principle of electromagnetism.*

▲ *The generator effect shows that a moving electric wire in a fixed magnetic field produces current.*

Generator Effect

In the same way as an electric current flowing through a wire generates a magnetic field, the movement of an electric wire inside a magnet's magnetic field generates an electric current. This is called the generator effect. There is no physical contact between the magnet and the wire. The electric current is induced by the magnetic field.

Electromagnetic Induction

In the presence of a changing magnetic field through a current-carrying conductor, an electromotive force is generated. This process is called electromagnetic induction. Many devices like transformers, motors, and generators work on this principle.

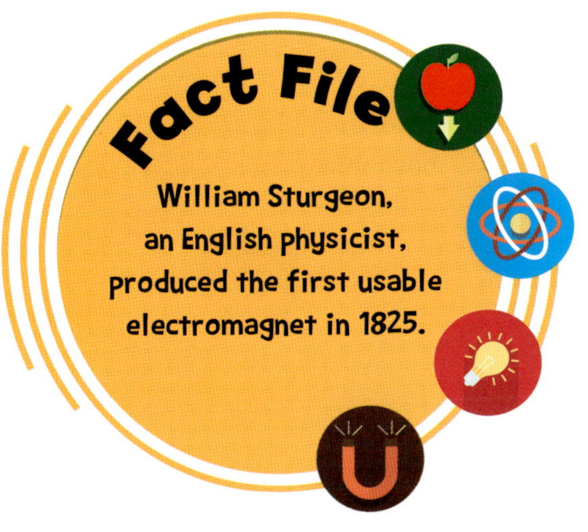

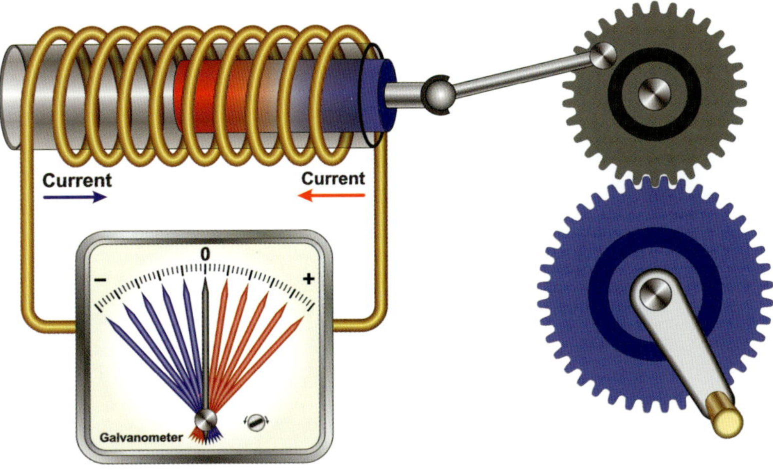

▲ *Electromagnetic induction involves a fixed conductor and changing magnetic field.*

Applications of Electromagnetism

Electromagnets have numerous applications such as the manufacture of generators, motors, transformers, loudspeakers, and powerful lifting devices. They are used in various fields of engineering and technology and are indispensable in today's world of communication and advancement.

Electric Motors

An electric motor is generally equipped with magnets, a rotating shaft, and wires. It operates on the rotation produced by a current-carrying coil of wire in a magnetic field. The rotational energy of a motor can be used for powering many different electric appliances like food processors, water pumps, vacuum cleaners, and fans.

▲ *Copper wires, rotating shaft and magnets are the major components of a motor*

Motors are also used in loudspeakers and microphones. The motor converts current variations in the electric circuits into pressure vibrations of sound waves. Microphones do just the opposite—they work on the principle of generator effect and convert pressure variations into electric current.

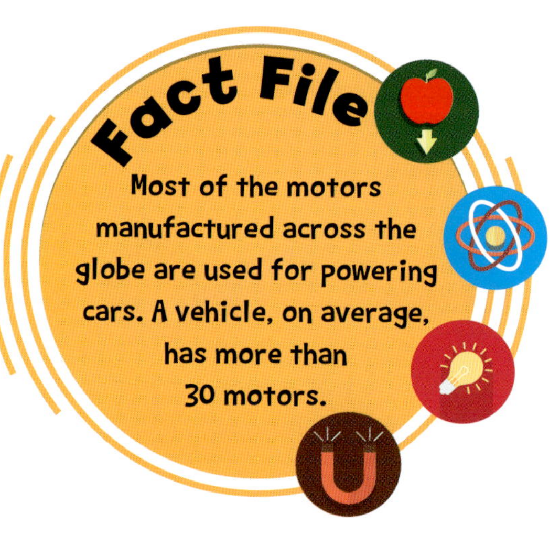

◀ *In a food processor, a motor helps power the rotating blades attached to its shaft.*

Other Uses of Electromagnets

1. Powerful electromagnets are used in scientific analysis instruments like spectrometers and particle accelerators. In a particle accelerator, electromagnets are employed for steering and focusing beams of particles traveling through a vacuum tube.

▲ *Maglev trains achieve high speeds impossible in regular trains.*

2. The ultrafast Maglev trains work on the principle of magnetic levitation. The trains, instead of running over regular tracks, instead levitate in the air due to repulsion of electromagnets in the train's underside and the guideway. Maglev trains are able to achieve very high speeds because the lack of contact with any surface greatly cuts down friction.

▲ *Magnetic separators often employ electromagnets.*

3. Strong permanent magnets, as well as electromagnets, are used in magnetic separators. Separators are employed in junkyards to separate metals from other common junk for recycling.

4. Power transformers also work on the principle of electromagnetic induction to increase or decrease voltage of the current transmitted from power lines.

▲ *Interior of a particle accelerator that employs electromagnets*

5. Electromagnets are important components of medical imaging devices such as magnetic resonance imaging (MRI) machines. The MRI's magnet is equipped in the hollow tube through which the patient enters. It generates magnetic fields much more powerful than that of the Earth's field.

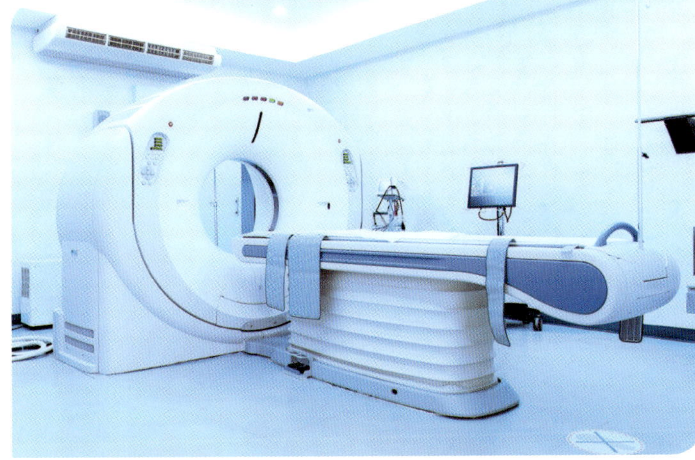

▲ *MRI machines produce powerful magnetic fields.*

6. An induction cooker consists of a ceramic plate equipped with an electromagnetic coil and works on the principle of electromagnetic induction to produce electricity and heat in the presence of a magnetic field.

▲ *Induction stoves work on the principle of electromagnetic induction.*

Waves

Any regular and recurring phenomenon is called a wave. A wave is defined by its properties like wavelength, frequency, and speed. Waves help transfer energy and carry information. Modern technology has enabled us not only to understand better about waves like electromagnetic radiation but also to make the best use of them.

Transverse and Longitudinal Waves

Waves come in different forms. All waves have certain characteristic features as well as others that distinguish them from one another. Commonly, waves are classified into two types: transverse and longitudinal. Transverse and longitudinal waves are classified based on the direction of their movement.

▲ Ripples forming in water are an example of transverse waves.

A transverse wave is a type of wave that travels in a direction perpendicular to the movement of the particles in a particular medium. The ripples forming on the surface of a pond after a pebble is dropped are an example of transverse waves. The waves form in a direction perpendicular to the movement of the pebble as it sinks down.

A longitudinal wave is a wave type that moves in a direction parallel to the movement of the particles. Sound waves traveling from the mouth of the speaker to the ears of a listener are an example of longitudinal waves.

Apart from longitudinal and transverse waves, there are also surface waves that travel along large surfaces such as oceans. A surface wave consists of particles moving in circular motion.

Apart from direction, waves are also classified based on their ability to transmit energy in a vacuum or empty space. Based on this factor, mechanical waves are those waves that cannot transmit energy in a vacuum. Sound waves, an example of mechanical waves, cannot travel in a vacuum and need a medium to travel. Electromagnetic waves, produced by the vibration of charged particles, can transmit energy in a vacuum.

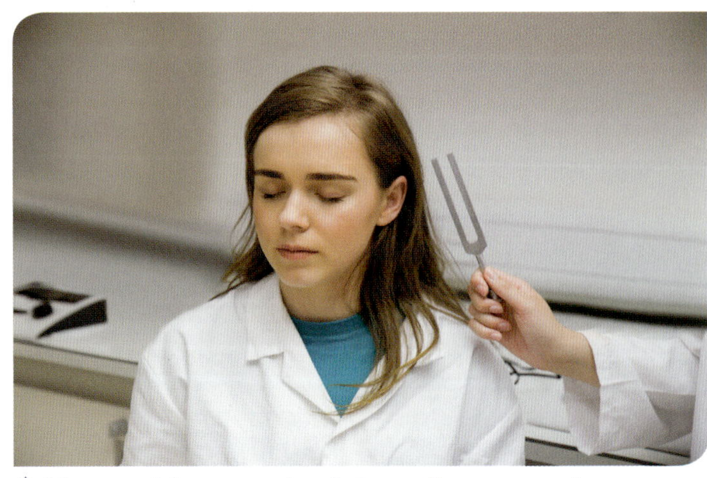

▲ The sound from a tuning fork to a listener travels as longitudinal waves.

Transverse Wave

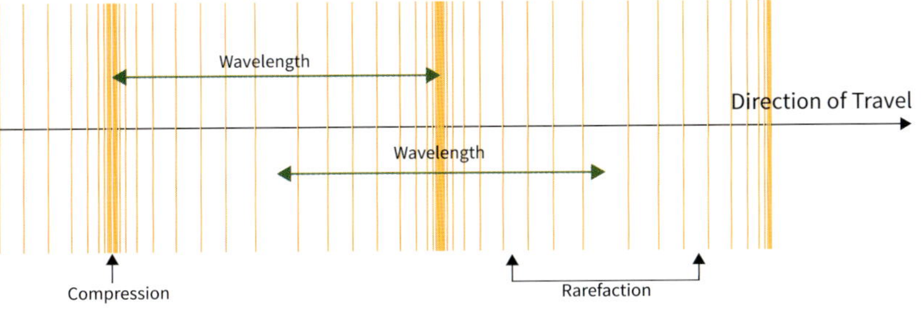

Longitudinal Wave

▲ *Transverse and longitudinal waves have different properties.*

Waves exhibit different behaviour when they encounter different mediums, and obstacles, or come in contact with other waves.

Reflection: When a wave hits a medium that acts as a barrier, it returns to the original medium. This is known as reflection.

Refraction: The change in direction that a wave encounters when it passes from one medium to another is called refraction.

Diffraction: When a wave travels through a medium, it can sometimes bend when it comes into contact with an obstacle or is forced to pass through a tiny slit.

Wave Properties

A wave motion can be described in terms of amplitude, frequency, and wavelength. A wave's amplitude is its maximum displacement away from its undisturbed position. A wave's frequency is calculated as the number of waves crossing a certain reference point in a second. The wavelength is the distance from a point on one wave to an equivalent point in the wave adjacent to it. The speed of a wave is the speed at which energy is transferred when a wave moves through a medium. The highest point of a wave is called the crest and the lowest point is called the trough. A wave can be made to oscillate in just one direction. This property is known as polarisation. Only transverse waves can be polarised.

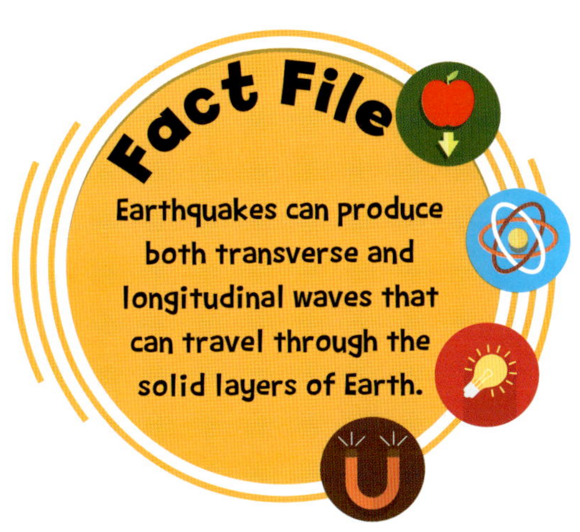

Absorption: When waves come into contact with the atoms of a medium, the atoms vibrate and absorb energy from the waves.

Scattering: Light and sound scatter or deviate from their path of travel when they encounter small particles and molecules in their path.

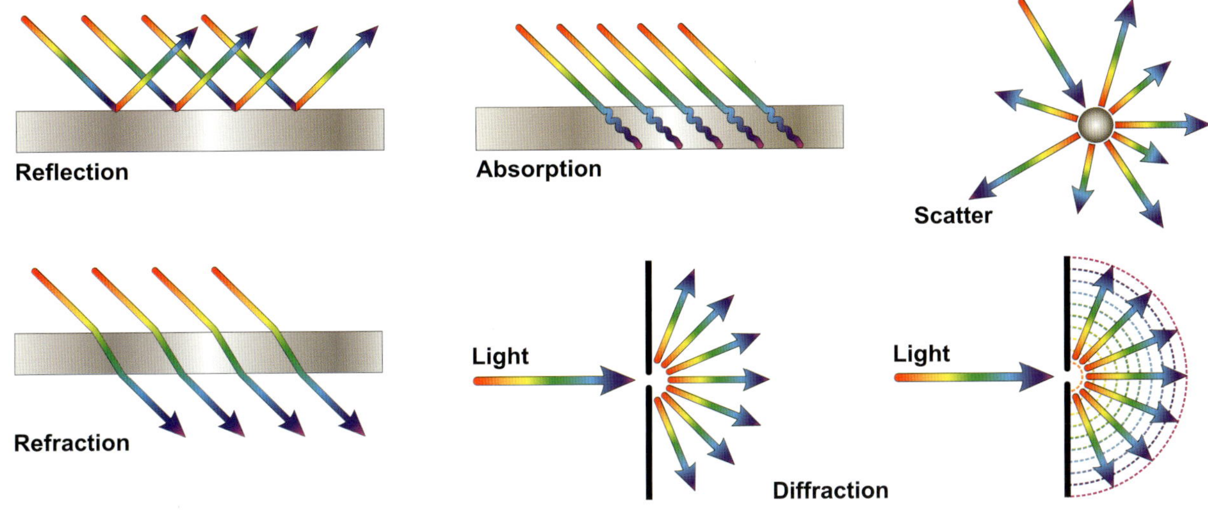

▲ *Waves exhibit different properties under varied conditions.*

Electromagnetic Radiation

Electromagnetic radiation exists in the form of waves that can transfer energy from the source to anything capable of absorbing it. Electromagnetic waves exist as a continuous spectrum ranging from short to long wavelengths.

Electromagnetic Wave Types

The electromagnetic spectrum consists of different types of waves.

Radio Waves: These have the longest wavelength, reaching about 10^3 nanometres (nm), and are used for transmitting radio and television broadcasts as well as mobile phone communications. They are also used for remote sensing and radar systems for navigation. Radio waves have the lowest energy levels in the spectrum.

Microwaves: Like radio waves, microwaves are useful for broadcasting information through space and remote sensing. They are very efficient at transmitting information because microwaves can even penetrate through clouds and rain. They are also useful for producing heat and are used in microwave ovens.

▲ *Satellite dishes capture radio waves for radio and television broadcasting*

Infrared Radiation: Can be released as heat and bounced back like visible light. In fact, infrared radiation has many similarities to visible light. Infrared sensors are useful for collecting thermal energy data and have applications in military surveillance. Infrared radiation can also be used for predicting weather conditions.

Visible Light: This is the only portion of the electromagnetic spectrum that is visible to humans, extending from 390 to 780 nm. Visible light splits into a variety of colours each representing a particular wavelength.

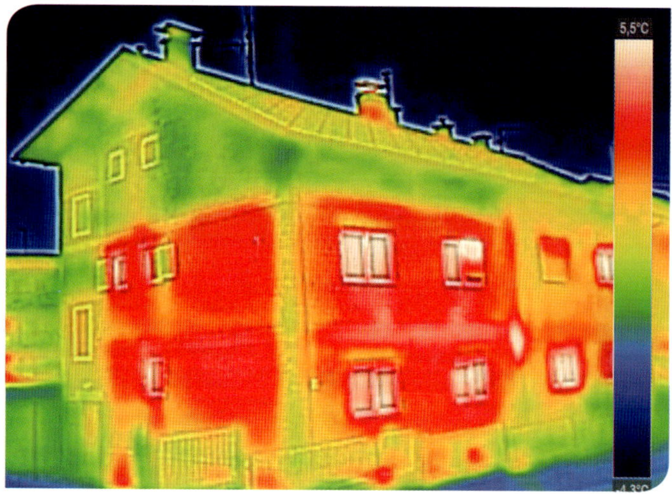

▲ *Infrared radiation can provide thermal energy data of objects and living things.*

Colour Region	Wavelength (nm)
Violet	380–435
Blue	435–500
Cyan	500–520
Green	520–565
Yellow	565–590
Orange	590–625
Red	625–740

Ultraviolet Radiation: With wavelengths in the range of 10 – 400 nm, it lies midway between visible light and X-rays. It is emitted from the Sun, constituting about 10 percent of the total light coming out. Long-wavelength UV radiation is not considered ion ng radiation, but it is still capable of producing a chemical reaction that causes glowing and fluorescence. Short-wavelength UV radiation is harmful because it can cause DNA mutation and cancer.

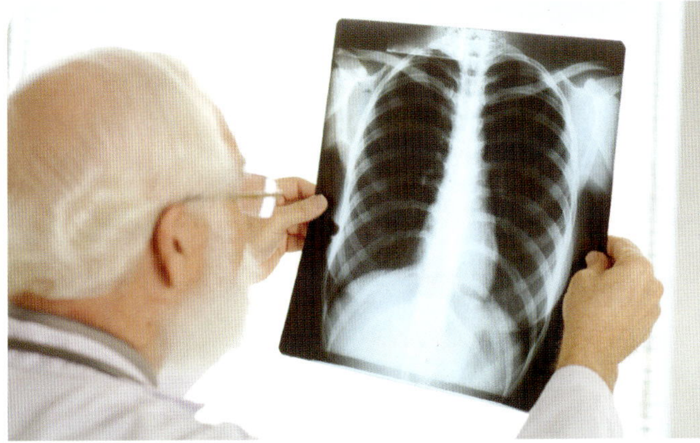

▲ *X-rays are used widely for diagnosis of problems within the body.*

X-rays: They have wavelengths in the range of 0.01–10 nm, and a high penetrating ability. Hence, X-rays are used in photographing bones and internal structures within the body. High doses of X-rays can cause cancer and other harmful effects.

Fact File

Gamma rays are the most energetic among the wave types in the electromagnetic spectrum.

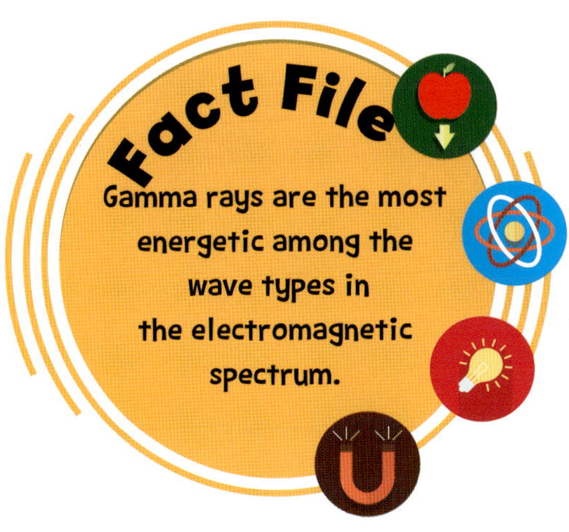

Gamma rays: They have the shortest wavelength at around 0.001 nm, and highest energy in the electromagnetic spectrum that arises from the decay of atomic nuclei. Gamma rays can only be shielded using heavy materials such as lead or concrete. In the universe, gamma ray bursts can occur during the explosion of a star. Gamma radiation dose is measured in sieverts and can cause significant harm in doses beyond the recommended limit.

▼ *When a star explodes, it can result in gamma ray bursts.*

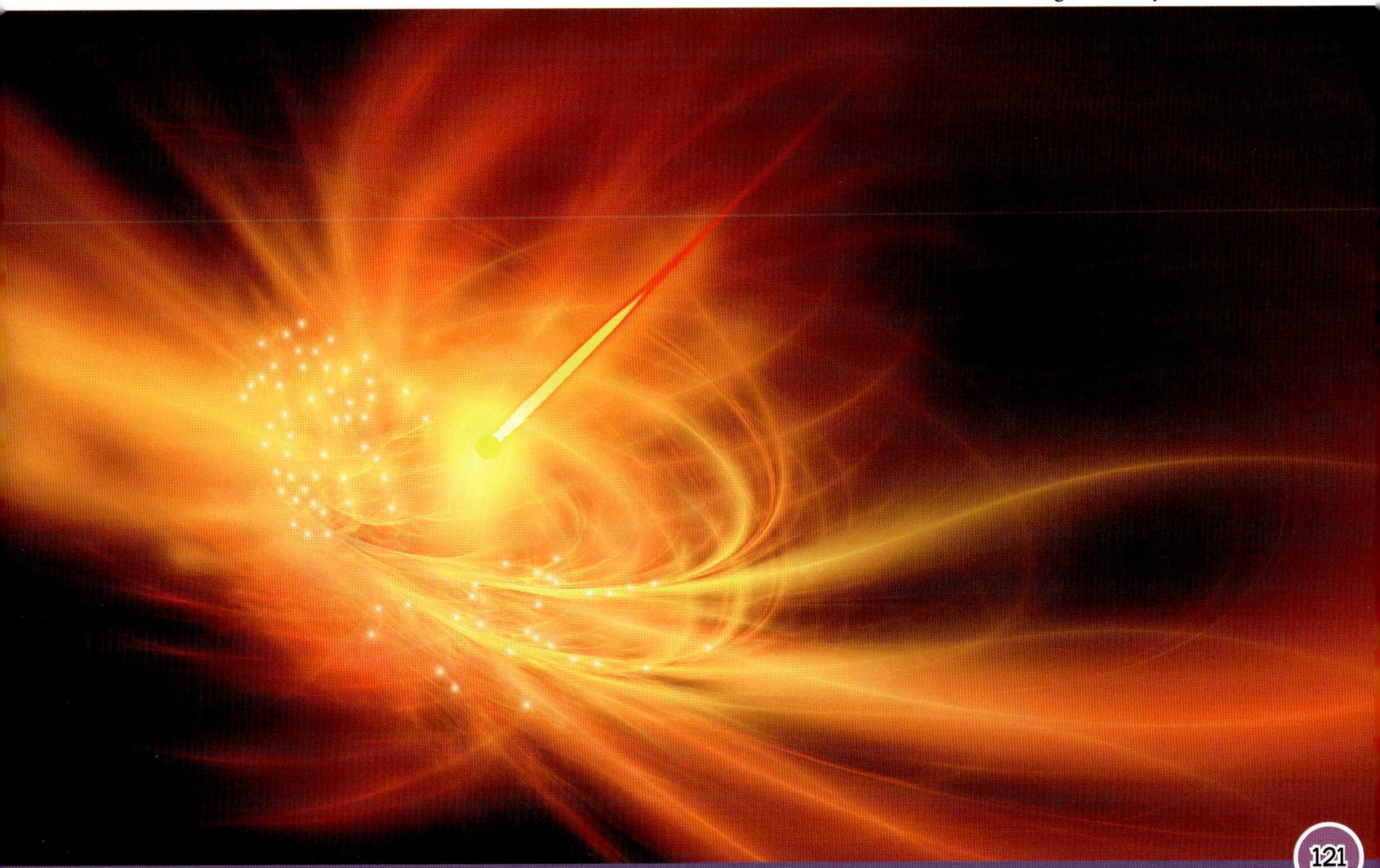

The Solar System

People have been fascinated by the features in the sky and have been attempting to seek answers about them. In the past hundred or so years, we have seen remarkable progress in our understanding of the universe.

Solar System

Our Solar System comprises the single star, Sun, and the eight planets as well as their satellites, dwarf planets and asteroids. The Solar System is merely a minuscule part of the much larger Milky Way galaxy with billions of other such star systems.

The planets in the order of proximity to the Sun are: Mercury, Venus, Earth, Mars, Jupiter, Saturn, Uranus and Neptune. Next to the Sun, Jupiter is the biggest object in the Solar System. Except Mercury and Venus, the other planets have one or more satellites also simply called moons.

Fact File

The Solar System is thought to have formed as a result of a supernova (explosion of a massive star) nearby.

▼ *The Solar System consists of the Sun, the eight planets, their moons, dwarf planets, asteroids and comets.*

Formation of the Solar System

The Sun and all the planets were formed from a cloud of gas and dust, known as a nebula. The swirling dust and gases were drawn together due to gravity after the explosion of a supernova nearby. The squeezed gases and dust spun fast, growing very hot and dense in the center and cooler around the edges.

Dust and gas began to accumulate into planets around the hot mass in the center. The icy matter in the cloud formed the cold planets, Uranus and Neptune. The light gases like hydrogen and helium floated farther from the hot mass, forming the large planets Jupiter and Saturn. The rocky material formed the four inner planets. The hot mass in the center grew hotter and eventually became a star. The remaining debris accumulated as asteroids. Most of the asteroids in the solar system are found as a belt between Mars and Jupiter.

Scientists have identified that the age of the Solar System is 4.6 billion years by studying meteorites that are considered to be remnants of the early phase of solar system formation.

The swirling gas and dust resulted in the formation of the sun and planets

Orbital Motion

The curved path taken by any object around a star or a planet is called an orbit. The planets travel around the Sun in elliptical orbits. The planets around the Sun are subject to gravity. Gravity is a force that acts between two objects with mass. The Sun, as a massive body, exerts its gravitational pull on the planets.

The planets do not get pulled toward the Sun because they are already in motion in a direction perpendicular or sideways to the Sun's gravitational pull. The forces balance out and the planets remain in their orbits, without flying out of orbit or getting pulled into the Sun and getting burned.

It is a similar principle that keeps a natural satellite such as the Moon orbiting the Earth without collapsing into the Earth's surface or moving away completely.

Artificial Satellites

Artificial satellites work on the fundamental principle of gravity. Isaac Newton predicted that if an object could be projected into space at sufficient speed, it could orbit the Earth. When launched at the right speed, the satellite would fall down at about the same rate as the Earth curves. This balance would enable the satellite to travel in a circular orbit around the Earth.

Artificial satellites orbit the Earth when launched at the right speed.

Stars

There are countless numbers of stars in the universe, and millions in our Milky Way galaxy alone. A star typically starts its life from a cloud of dust and gas and passes through many stages over billions of years before it exhausts its energy and collapses back or explodes into dust.

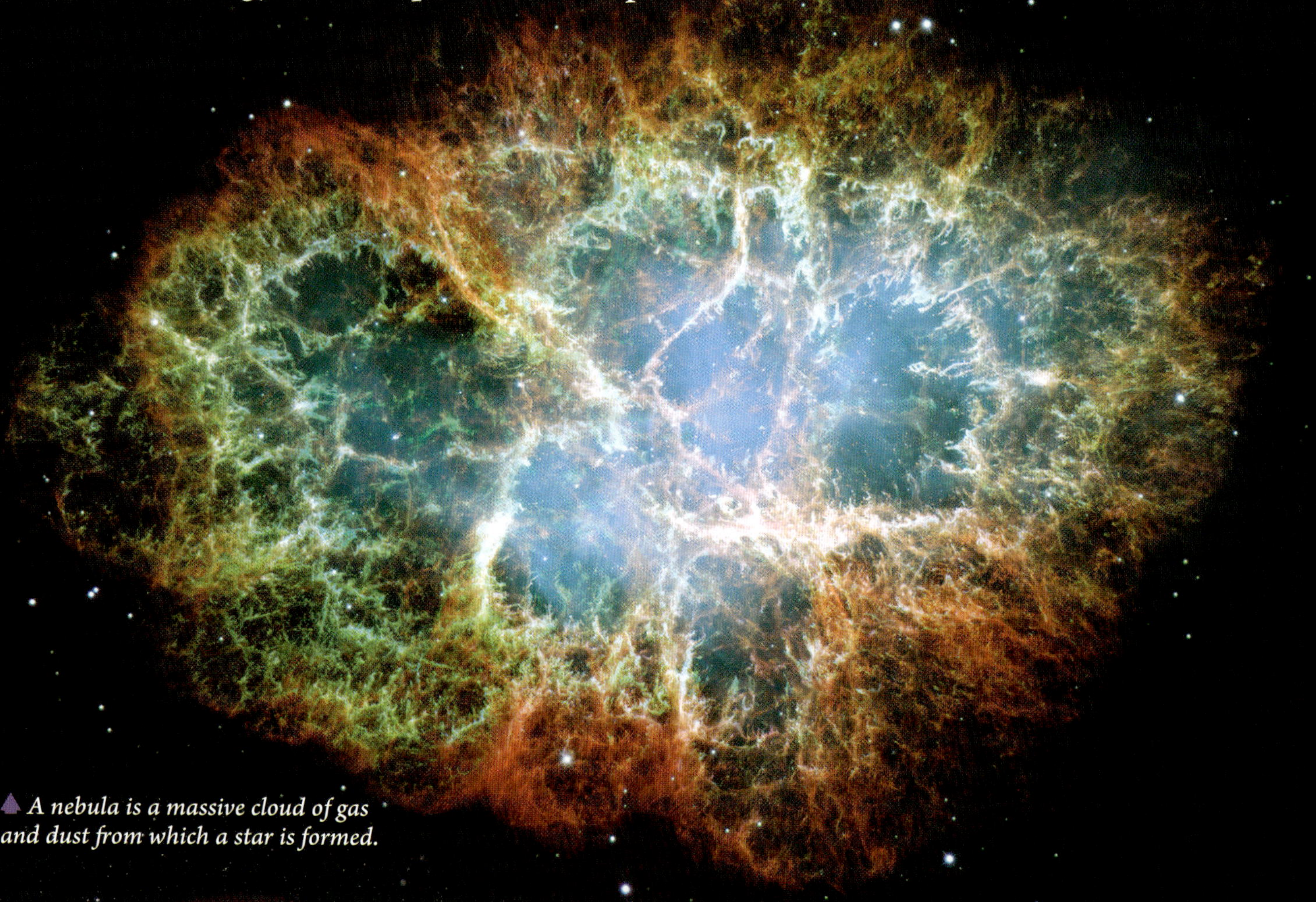

A nebula is a massive cloud of gas and dust from which a star is formed.

A brown dwarf is intermediate in size between a small star and a giant planet.

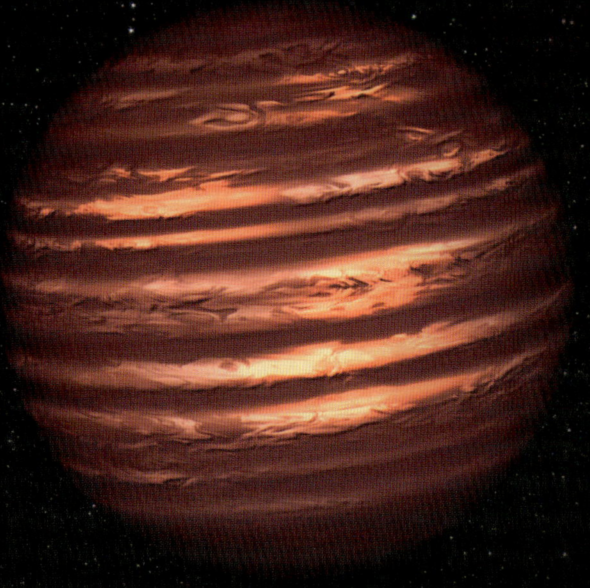

Life Cycle of a Star

A star goes through a lifecycle and its fate depends largely on its size. It begins its life as a cloud of dust and gas that is called a nebula.

The predominant gas found in this cloud is usually hydrogen. The gas cloud transforms into a protostar when the dust and gas begin to clump together due to gravity. This process of is known as accretion.

The gravitational pull attracts more and more matter toward the core, increasing the temperature and pressure. When a particular temperature is reached in the protostar's core, the process of nuclear fusion begins.

Reaching the critical temperature is essential because if it fails to achieve the right temperature conditions, the protostar will never become a star. It might instead develop into a brown dwarf that is only a little bigger than the planet Jupiter, but much denser.

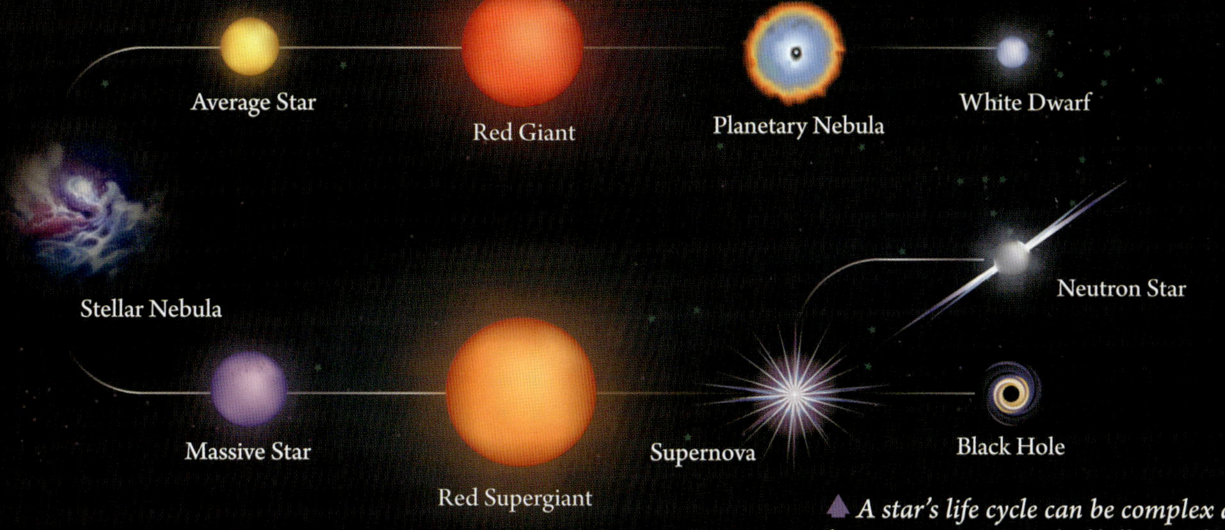

▲ *A star's life cycle can be complex and happen over a period of billions of years.*

The Sun is a yellow dwarf star. It generates energy by nuclear fusion, converting hydrogen into helium. The Sun's gravity keeps the hot gases within a confined space, thus enabling fusion to occur continuously. This process remains in equilibrium as long as it has enough fuel to burn and produce heat. This period is called the main sequence of the star.

The Sun is already about 4.5–5 billion years old. It is expected to continue to exist mostly unchanged for another 5 billion years before the hydrogen runs out. With the hydrogen supply exhausted, the star's main sequence comes to an end. It starts to cool down and collapse for about 100 million years. The energy released due to the collapse heats up the star even more and it expands in size, becoming a red giant.

Afterwards, the outer layers of the star explode away, leaving behind a small core, no bigger than the size of Earth. At this stage, the star is called a white dwarf. Its main constituents are carbon and oxygen. The white dwarfs lose their luminosity and fade away into space as black dwarfs. Most stars (up to 97 percent) face this fate in the Milky Way galaxy.

Large stars are hotter and brighter, but they do not exist for as long as a typical yellow dwarf. This is because large stars exhaust their fuel quickly. A star that is merely 20 times bigger than the sun will burn out its fuel 36,000 times faster than the sun and exist for a mere few million years.

◀ *A star becomes a white dwarf after losing its outer layers.*

Red Shift

Scientists have observed that the wavelength of light coming from distant galaxies increases. The more distant a galaxy is, the faster it is moving away. This phenomenon is known as red shift. It is proof for a rapidly expanding universe and also the Big Bang theory.

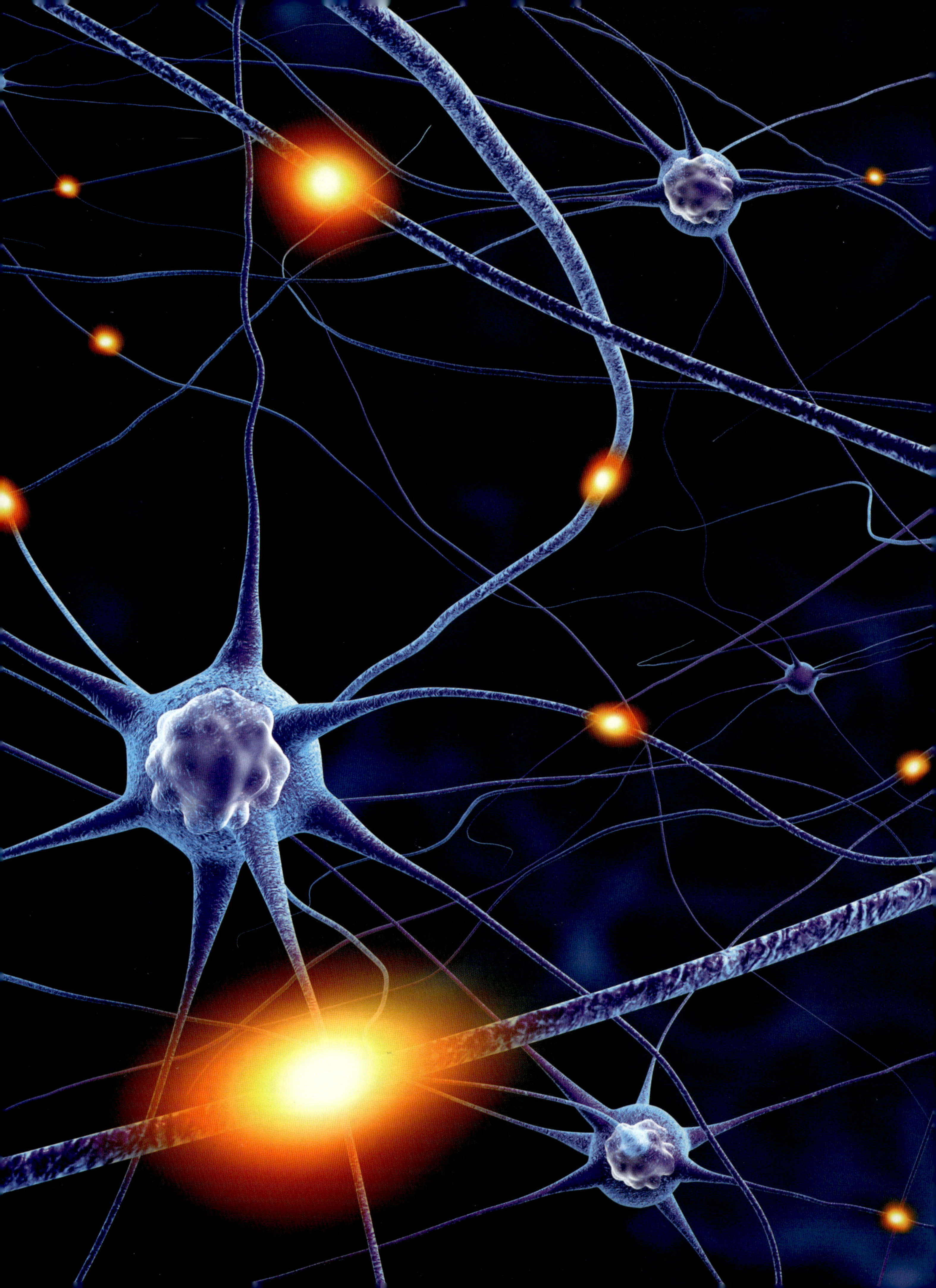